# Turn Up the Heat

# TURN UP THE HEAT

Jessica Conant-Park

& Susan Conant

BERKLEY PRIME CRIME, NEW YORK

**THE BERKLEY PUBLISHING GROUP**
**Published by the Penguin Group**
**Penguin Group (USA) Inc.**
**375 Hudson Street, New York, New York 10014, USA**
Penguin Group (Canada), 90 Eglinton Avenue East, Suite 700, Toronto, Ontario M4P 2Y3, Canada
(a division of Pearson Penguin Canada Inc.)
Penguin Books Ltd., 80 Strand, London WC2R 0RL, England
Penguin Group Ireland, 25 St. Stephen's Green, Dublin 2, Ireland (a division of Penguin Books Ltd.)
Penguin Group (Australia), 250 Camberwell Road, Camberwell, Victoria 3124, Australia
(a division of Pearson Australia Group Pty. Ltd.)
Penguin Books India Pvt. Ltd., 11 Community Centre, Panchsheel Park, New Delhi—110 017, India
Penguin Group (NZ), 67 Apollo Drive, Rosedale, North Shore 0632, New Zealand
(a division of Pearson New Zealand Ltd.)
Penguin Books (South Africa) (Pty.) Ltd., 24 Sturdee Avenue, Rosebank, Johannesburg 2196,
South Africa

Penguin Books Ltd., Registered Offices: 80 Strand, London WC2R 0RL, England

This book is an original publication of The Berkley Publishing Group.

First edition: March 2008

Library of Congress Cataloging-in-Publication Data

Conant-Park, Jessica.
   Turn up the heat / Jessica Conant-Park and Susan Conant.—1st ed.
      p.   cm.
   ISBN 978-0-425-21947-8
   1. Carter, Chloe (Fictitious character)—Fiction. 2. Restaurants—Fiction. 3. Waitresses—Crimes against—Fiction. 4. Boston (Mass.)—Fiction. I. Conant, Susan, 1946– II. Title.

   PS3603.O525T87   2007
   813'.6—dc22                                                                 2007043649

PRINTED IN THE UNITED STATES OF AMERICA

10   9   8   7   6   5   4   3   2   1

*For Alexa,*
*a loyal friend,*
*who survived college dining with Jessica*

# ACKNOWLEDGMENTS

For sharing amusing insight into the culinary world, narrating chef antics, contributing phenomenal recipes, and answering questions about fish trucks, we thank Jody Adams, Maria Angels and Julio Veliz, Michael Garrett, Justin Lyonnais, Bill Park, Mark Porcaro, and Michael Ricco.

For outstanding editing skills, we applaud David Grumblatt.

For assistance in testing recipes, we thank John and Meg Driscoll, Katrina Grumblatt, and Tony and Alexa Lewis.

For their unfailing help, we thank Natalee Rosenstein and Michelle Vega of Berkley, and our agent, Deborah Schneider.

# TURN UP THE HEAT

# ONE

EARLY May in Boston. There's nothing else like it. After almost six straight weeks of apocalyptic rain, the sky had suddenly turned an all-but-forgotten blue, the temperature had risen to the miraculously high sixties, and, best of all, the outdoor dining area at my boyfriend's restaurant was finally open. Josh Driscoll, love of my life, was the executive chef at the five-month-old Newbury Street restaurant, Simmer, and tonight, for the first time ever, Simmer's fortunate patrons would be able to savor the fruits of Josh's culinary genius while dining on the sidewalk patio. When Josh had called me earlier today, he'd practically been singing into the phone. "Chloe Carter, my lovely lady, you better get your ass down here to the patio tonight! It's going to be nice!"

Josh's spring fever was highly contagious: I was as excited as he was.

As Josh's girlfriend, I obviously had a major in at Simmer. Even so, my friends and I had had to wait forty-five minutes for an outdoor table that could accommodate all five of us, the five of us being me; my best friend, Adrianna; her fiancé, Owen; my social work school buddy and teaching assistant, Doug; and his new boyfriend, Terry.

Newbury Street restaurants were jammed tonight. The good weather seemed to have awakened everyone from hibernation, and all the outdoor eateries in this high-end area were packed with diners. Simmer was no exception. As we waited inside for a patio table, I looked around and, as I'd done before, felt amazed at how beautifully the place had turned out. I'd been around while Gavin Seymour, the owner, had been renovating the location, and I'd seen Simmer at its worst, with electrical wires dangling from the ceiling, holes in the walls, and floors made of crumbling concrete. Now, beautiful dark brown tiles covered the floor, modern light fixtures hung from the high ceilings, and wood moldings framed the textured walls. Gavin had wanted to create what he'd called a "worldly" feel to the restaurant; he'd been eager to have the decor and the ambiance announce that Simmer's menu wasn't limited to one style of cooking but was inspired by cuisines from around the globe. The room was filled with square tables and high-backed chairs. Because Josh had helped Gavin to pick out the china, the glassware, and the silver, I knew that all of it had been as expensive as it looked. Votive candles placed at each table gave the room a mellow glow and flattered everyone's complexion. I loathe eating at restaurants where the lighting casts a yellow tone or a weird shadow on my face; no matter how good the food is, it's hard to enjoy myself if I'm worried about resembling a ghoul.

And God forbid one not look sensational on Newbury Street, right? The problem with coming here to see Josh all the time was that I felt obliged to dress up. I mean, everyone in this sophisticated section of Boston was either independently loaded or living off someone else's money and, in either case, was a regular customer at Barney's. There was hardly an uncoiffed head of hair, a manicured hand not weighed down with Cartier jewelry, or a wallet not busting with platinum credit cards. I was torn between feeling totally nauseated by the disgusting display of wealth and pathetically eager to look as if I belonged. My deceased uncle Alan's monthly stipend kept me easily afloat, but I didn't have the money to go flinging bills around at Agnes B. and BCBG. I'd long ago run out of appropriate outfits to wear to Simmer and did my best to make my T.J. Maxx pants look like Chanel. Granted, there was a Gap on Newbury Street, but there were hardly streams of diners here in oversized hooded sweatshirts. It always took me at least an hour to get out of my apartment when I was going to Simmer. It never occurred to me to leave without pressing my wavy red hair between the burning blades of my flatiron; people on Newbury Street did not have frizz! And then I had to spend twenty minutes pretending that my L'Oreal makeup actually was from Paris, all the while slathering my blue eyes with brown liner and trying to color my pale cheeks a fresh-from-Barbados bronze. By the time I'd finished, I always felt passable on Newbury Street, but I remained basically disconnected from the obscene wealth that hit you at every snobby shop and from the stick-thin bodies that you passed on every corner. Not that there was anything horribly wrong with my body. But the average twenty-five-year-old around here weighed a hundred and ten pounds, and I was fifteen over that.

We'd just sat down at one of the ten tables that had been squeezed into a gated area on the sidewalk in front of Simmer when Josh appeared at our table. "Chloe, I just heard you guys were here. I'm sorry you had to wait so long." Josh leaned down and kissed me before brushing his arm across his sweaty forehead. He was dressed in his once-white chef's coat, now covered in permanent food stains from previous months plus fresh stains from today. His dirty-blond hair was damp at the hairline, and his eyes were heavy with exhaustion, but even the dark circles and puffy bags couldn't take away the sparkle of excitement. Business had been steady, and if tonight was any indication of how the spring and summer were going to go, Simmer was about to really take off.

Josh tossed a filthy dish towel over his shoulder and reached out to shake hands with Owen, Doug, and Terry, and then circled around the table to give Adrianna a kiss on the cheek. "How's it going, Mama?" he asked affectionately. Adrianna was almost five months pregnant but already looked about to go into labor before tonight's dessert.

She rolled her eyes. "Going great if you don't mind constant heartburn, fatigue, swollen hands, and having your ribs kicked from three to five in the morning."

"Owen kneeing you in his sleep again?" Josh grinned, and then rubbed her shoulder. "I'm sorry. I know you're having a hard time."

"Yeah, it's okay. I'm just grouchy. And starving." She looked up at him hopefully.

"*That* I can help with." Josh nodded assuredly. "I gotta run. I think Leandra is your waitress. Order whatever you want, and I'll comp it for you." One of the perks of being the executive chef at Simmer was that the owner, Gavin, let Josh sign off on orders so we didn't have to pay for anything except a tip. "I'll try to come out again later if I can." Josh made his way between tables to the front entrance. One couple seated near the door stopped him. Josh smiled as he accepted what I knew were compliments about his food.

Leandra appeared moments later. I'd met her a number of times before, because Josh's overwhelming work schedule meant that I was spending lots of time hanging around Simmer trying to catch glimpses of my boyfriend. In fact, I was beginning to look and feel like a barfly. Leandra was petite with very short white-blonde hair that somehow upped her femininity. (If I chopped off all my hair I'd look brutish!) She needed no makeup on her annoyingly symmetrical face, and Simmer's unisex staff T-shirt and pants left no doubt that Leandra was voluptuously female. I saw Adrianna, her usual supermodel body now rounded, scowl and toss her long blonde hair back over her shoulder. I involuntarily ran my hand down my own hair, checking for any dreaded frizz.

Leandra handed out menus. "Sorry. Hope you haven't been here too long. I can't believe how busy we are tonight, and they didn't schedule enough servers. Can I get you some drinks to start?"

"I'll take a Kirin," Doug said. "You want one, too?" he asked Terry.

Terry nodded and put his hand on Doug's knee. I still had a hard time grasping that Doug and Terry were a couple. Their homosexual relationship didn't bother me in the least; what alarmed me was Terry's style. He looked like a woman-obsessed rock star or maybe the host of a VH1 show on hair bands of the eighties. Every time he opened his mouth, part of me expected him to burst out singing, "Once Bitten, Twice Shy," "Unskinny Bop," or "Eighteen and Life." With thick, wavy, highlighted brown hair and rocker clothes, Terry was a total contrast to my social work school mentor, Doug. Doug was anything but conservative—on occasion, he wore neon—but it took most people, my parents excluded, about four seconds to figure out that he was gay.

Social work school was one thing, but I wasn't sure how Terry's image went over with his presumably more uptight professors and fellow students at MIT, where he was getting a PhD in physics. Studying at the Massachusetts Institute of Technology clearly put Terry in the category of über-intellectual. More importantly, he seemed genuinely to adore Doug.

Avoiding alcohol out of sympathy for Adrianna, Owen ordered lemonades for the two of them. I, on the other hand, felt the need to celebrate the arrival of spring with a crisp glass of Pinot Grigio.

Leandra reappeared a few minutes later with our drinks. As she set our glasses down, I wondered how she was going to get through the brutally hot and humid Boston summer in Simmer's required attire. Her heavy cotton short-sleeved black shirt looked like it didn't allow for much airflow, and the long black dress pants were stylishly tight with a slightly flared boot cut at the bottom. As if to assure a minimum of heat loss, all the servers and bartenders wore long black aprons with Simmer written across the top in white lettering.

"Okay, we need to toast," I said, raising my glass. "To the appearance of the sun, the end of school, and dinner with good friends," I proposed cheerily.

"Not so fast." Doug stopped me before I could take a sip of wine. "You still have finals to get through."

I sighed. "I haven't forgotten." Actually, I *had* forgotten about exams, at least momentarily, until Doug mentioned them. He took great pleasure in humorously reminding me that as a doctoral student, he was superior to me. Finals were going to be a nightmare. I had two long papers to finish writing and three two-hour in-class exams. It was at times like this that I regretted enrolling in social work school. Although I was finding more and more things to like about the experience, I still hid my ambivalence about school from my peers. Most of the other students were avidly devoted to their studies and their field placements (social work speak for internships), and I had enrolled only because of a clause in my uncle Alan's will that required me to accept an all-expenses-paid trip to the land of graduate school. In my late uncle's opinion, I needed a master's degree in *something*. Anything. Only then would I receive my inheritance. I'd been pretty resentful of this manipulative and controlling plan that came from the other side. When I'd originally chosen social work school, the choice had felt as if I'd drawn it out of a hat, but as the end of my first year approached, I was beginning to think that my choice hadn't been so random after all. The fit between me and the profession was better than I'd expected, and I was finding that social work skills actually applied to daily life. For instance, instead of just seeing Terry as a complete oddball, I was interested in the personality characteristics that pushed him to deviate from the norm. How did he manage to remain independent and unique? Why didn't he cave in to societal standards?

"Well, we're going to toast anyway, finals approaching or not." I raised my glass and clinked drinks with everyone.

I smiled across the table at Adrianna, who, despite feeling ghastly during her pregnancy, was as beautiful as ever. Maybe because she was feeling so terrible, she was making an extra effort to look as stunning as possible. Her hair and makeup were done to perfection, and she was wearing an adorable navy blue wraparound maternity top that hugged her round belly and her full chest. When my sister, Heather, had been pregnant with each of her children, she'd always worn voluminous tops that covered her body and hid her weight gain. Ade was doing the opposite: embracing her body's changes and accentuating her growing curves. But as much as she was displaying the pregnancy with her usual confidence, she was pretty tight-lipped about the entire concept of motherhood and had yet to express any feelings about being on the verge of becoming a parent. Children had never topped her favorites list; I'm not sure that she'd ever intended to become a parent, and I suspected she was more afraid than she was letting on. At least her fiancé, Owen, was enthusiastic, in fact, sometimes irritatingly so. But unlike Adrianna, he was practical. He had already started shopping for clothes, diapers, and baby equipment. Remarkably, Owen still had the sense to give Ade the emotional space she needed. As to physical space, I had no clue about how they expected to fit all that baby gear into their new apartment.

I did, however, feel sure that Adrianna and Owen would have a beautiful baby. In terms of looks, Owen was as attractive as Adrianna. His black hair, fair skin, and bright blue eyes, coupled with his charming personality, made him a dream. The hitch was his garish taste in clothing. The T-shirt he wore tonight had an arrow pointing to the left and the words, That's My Kid in There! To make sure that the ridiculous T-shirt would deliver its message with full impact, Owen had been careful to keep Adrianna on the correct side.

Although Adrianna and Owen had not planned on having a baby, the two of them were managing this enormous surprise fairly well. They were moving in together next week and had found a decent two-bedroom apartment around the corner from me in Brighton. To describe their new apartment as having two bedrooms was pushing it, since the second bedroom was actually a walk-in closet, but the tiny room did have a radiator and a small window, so it would work as a nursery, at least for a while. What's more, although Adrianna and Owen hadn't set a wedding date—they couldn't even decide whether to get married before or after the baby was born—they were nonetheless officially engaged. I was just happy that they were together at all, especially since Adrianna had freaked out when she'd found out she was pregnant and had foolishly made out with Josh's sous chef, Snacker, a number of times in some sort of rebellious denial. On the night the unsuspecting Owen was going to propose, in fact, just as he was about to propose, right here at Simmer, Adrianna had suddenly announced both her pregnancy and her recent history with Snacker. Owen had understandably flipped out, but fortunately, the two of them had quickly worked things out. Owen and Snacker, on the other hand, loathed each other but remained coldly polite, mostly for my sake.

"So what are we ordering?" asked the ever-hungry Adrianna. Despite complaining about heartburn all the time, the girl couldn't get enough to eat. "The cod with vegetables looks really good. This is a new menu, right?"

"Right. They've only been running it for a few days. It's got all the new spring items on it. Josh had to teach the kitchen staff all the recipes and how to plate the food. I think it looks awesome." I was bursting with pride at Josh's food.

I'd watched him sit at my kitchen table, pen in hand, while he brainstormed to come up with the perfect dishes for the menu. I'd also learned how he went about pricing them out. It was fairly appalling to learn how little it costs to make some plates and what restaurants charge for them. The basic rule was that you figured out what the protein portion of the dish would cost, like the steak or the tuna, then you'd estimate the cost of the other ingredients, add those together, multiply by three, and then add three dollars. So, a twenty-four-dollar entrée might only cost the restaurant seven dollars in actual food costs. Josh had explained to me that after following the basic rule, he would then adjust the price depending on how a dish sold. Pasta dishes were great because they sold really well, and the pasta was cheap to buy, so chefs could up the price on those menu items. It was also easy to up the prices for lobster and tuna dishes, which were obvious luxury foods and sold a ton. Chicken, on the other hand, often had to be on a menu to please the occasional customer who wanted it, but it generally didn't sell well, so a chicken entrée price would stay close to the formulated pricing cost.

Terry put his menu down on his plate. "I'm definitely getting the seared scallops with grilled pancetta, honey parsnip puree, and warm pear chutney. No question. Thank you for inviting us, Chloe. Doug has had such nice things to say about Simmer, and I've really been looking forward to coming here."

"I'm with you on the scallops," Owen agreed. "And the roasted pork quesadilla with apple salsa." It was very Josh to do something traditional like quesadillas but then serve it with an unconventional topping.

Leandra came to take our orders. "Everybody set?"

Despite having eaten at Simmer many times, I was still impressed that the servers didn't write anything down. Order pads were apparently beneath the upper-crust atmosphere of Newbury Street. If I'd been Leandra, I'd have had to run to the register, scramble to remember every order, and immediately enter it into the computer. She showed no signs of strain.

Just as Doug finished telling Leandra the entrée he wanted, Gavin Seymour appeared and welcomed us with the charm that's so useful to restaurant owners. Gavin was in his late thirties, very handsome, and dressed in his typically and somewhat misleadingly casual style. Tonight he had on soft khaki pants and a simple cotton shirt, but I knew from Josh that Gavin did most of his clothes shopping through his personal dresser and that his clothing all came from high-end shops. The plain shirt was probably from Brooks Brothers. If I ever have the luxury of having a personal dresser, I'm going to instruct my assistant not to waste my money on overpriced clothes that might as well come from Old Navy.

"Have you all ordered?" Gavin asked. We nodded. He took our menus then turned to Leandra. "Why don't you ask Josh to send out a few extra appetizers for this crowd? They all look especially hungry tonight."

"Of course, Gavin. I'll go put these orders right in." Leandra smiled directly at her boss and smoothly took the menus from his hand. I'd heard that she and Gavin were seeing each other. Gavin was another Simmer male known for his many romantic flings, but according to the wildly active restaurant rumor mill, Gavin and Leandra were having a full-blown relationship and not just making out in the backseat of Gavin's Jaguar after service. Although Josh said the two did their best to avoid public displays of affection, it was hard to ignore the glint in Gavin's eye as he watched her walk away from the table.

With all the love in the air, it really felt like spring. Doug and Terry, Adrianna and Owen, Gavin and Leandra, Snacker and whatever girl of the week, Josh and me. Things with Josh were great, but looking around the table at the happy couples, I found it hard not to miss him. Visiting him at the restaurant was the best chance I had of catching a glimpse of my chef—that or the late-night visits at my place. Not that I was complaining about that department. But I wanted him with me for dinners like this, too. Josh had repeatedly assured me that his crappy schedule would ease up over time. But Simmer had opened on New Year's Eve, and I was still waiting.

Best friends are good at reading thoughts. "I'm sure Josh will come out again when he can," said Adrianna in an effort to comfort me.

"I know, I know," I said. "I'm happy it's so busy tonight, but it also means Josh might have to stay late." *Again,* I thought.

Josh was working at least ten, if not twelve to fourteen, hours a day. He caught me one morning covertly trying to apply cold cucumber slices to his exhausted eyes while he slept. I hated Josh's schedule, but he wasn't the least bit surprised by the hours he was putting in. Josh felt strongly that

Simmer's success rested on him. Gavin might be the owner, but it was Josh who seemed to feel the most pressure to have the restaurant succeed. The majority of restaurants fail within the first six months, and Josh was determined that Simmer wouldn't be one of them. Now that he'd finally found the ideal place to showcase his culinary, artistic, and managerial talent, he was giving Simmer everything he had. The menu was all his, which didn't happen at every restaurant, and Josh had complete control over every dish that was served. Gavin had been really great to Josh, too, and promised him that the better the restaurant did, the better Josh would do in terms of both hours and pay. Right now Josh's salary was almost laughable, but Gavin just didn't have the money to pay him what he deserved. The start-up costs involved in opening any restaurant are astronomical. I wanted to believe Gavin's promises, even though it seemed odd that an executive chef working on Newbury Street didn't get a decent salary, never mind a fat paycheck. In spite of everything, though, I was thrilled for Josh and convinced that Simmer would be the place he'd really make a name for himself in the competitive world of Boston restaurants.

# TWO

LEANDRA arrived, followed by two young Hispanic busboys, all carrying plates of food. "Here we go," she said, delicately placing her plates on the table. "I'm sorry these took so long. We're having problems with this new computer system Gavin is trying out. All the orders have to be entered into this elaborate program, and then, theoretically, they're magically sent to the kitchen, but we keep having trouble. Anyhow, we got your orders through, and then Josh sent this out for you, too." Leandra set an oval platter in the center of the table. "Tempura lobster tails with a sweet chili sauce."

Oh, wow! Lobster was one of my absolute favorite foods. I took this additional dish as a sign of love from my chef.

"You know what I pay for these?" Owen said, reaching across the table to help himself to one of the golden servings. "And you know what I sell them for?"

"You probably pay nothing and sell them for a lot more," I guessed.

Owen had recently quit his position as a puppeteer's assistant to work as a seafood purveyor for a company called the Daily Catch. Before he'd found out that Ade was pregnant, he'd bounced from one quirky occupation to another. After hearing the news, he'd miraculously taken it upon himself to look for a somewhat traditional job.

"That's right, Owen." Doug jumped in with interest. "I haven't seen you since you started with the fish thing. What's that like?"

Looking proud of himself, Owen said, "I'm what's known in the business as a seafood *purveyor*. I work for a company called the Daily Catch. We sell seafood to restaurants. So I get up by six, check my cell phone for orders from chefs, write those down, and then write up a price list. See, every day I get faxes from the companies we buy the seafood from with their prices. We buy from them and then sell to the restaurants. I'm kind of the middleman, so I mark my prices up based on what we're going to have to pay. Then I take my delivery truck and drive down to the seafood district in South Boston's waterfront, where I put in my orders, load up the truck, and I'm off to deliver everything. I've only been with them for a few weeks, but I've already got a bunch of great accounts. And Josh even dropped his old company for me!" Owen beamed with satisfaction at having persuaded Josh to switch purveyors. Simmer had decent-sized orders for Owen almost every day, but Josh knew enough not to let Owen overcharge him. Josh had explained to Owen that he'd better be careful who he tried to screw over with prices, because when chefs caught on, they'd drop him. "I bet that's my cod right there!" Owen pointed his fork in the direction of a cod fillet that had been baked in foil with tomatoes, squash, zucchini, red peppers, scallions, fresh oregano, butter, wine, and garlic.

"So are you salaried? Or do you get paid on commission?" As soon as Doug asked the question, Terry held out a fork laiden with scallops for Doug to try. He chewed, swallowed, and smiled. "That pear chutney is to die for!"

"No, he's definitely not salaried." Adrianna shook her head. "And save some scallops for me. They look incredible."

"No, I'm not. I get a percentage of the profit made on the sales. It's basically like I have my own business through the Daily Catch. I run my accounts and set my daily prices based on whatever I've got to pay, and then the company gets part of the money I earn. Wait until you guys see my truck. It's just a regular pickup truck, but we added a refrigeration unit to the back, and I just got the company logo painted on. It's so cool. Want to come check it out quick? Josh let me park it in the back alley behind Simmer." Owen stood up as though we all might be itching to abandon our dinners to go out and admire his delivery truck.

"Owen, no one wants to tromp through the dirty alley right now, okay?" Ade grabbed his arm and pulled him back into his seat. "And, technically, it's not even *your* truck. It's your boss's."

"Well, yeah. But when I get enough money, I'm going to get my own from one of those car auctions and get the refrigeration unit installed on top. Or get a refrigerated van. That would mean better gas mileage. And with my own truck, I'd get a larger percentage of the profits. It's forty percent when you use a company truck and sixty percent when it's your own." The pork quesadilla was in the center of the table, and Owen took a section and scooped some apple salsa onto his plate. "Man, these are quesadillas gone wild!"

Ade spoke with her mouth full of cod and vegetables. "True, but it's nice that you get to use the company's one for now. And that monster will definitely get you through the Boston winters." She finished chewing and pointed at Owen with her fork. "He doesn't pay for anything except gas. His boss pays for all the maintenance, repairs, insurance, inspection fees, and all that. He's got to get the lock fixed on the back of the truck, and that won't cost him a thing. Not a bad deal. Oh, my God! That fish is so good. Is that fresh oregano? I love it."

"Oh, pass some over here." Terry reached for the plate of cod that was accompanied by plain couscous that soaked up all the delicious juices. "A broken lock, though? Aren't you worried someone is going to break into the truck?" asked Terry. "People probably think it's full of lobsters."

Owen shook his head. "Nah. I'm only at each restaurant for a few minutes while I'm delivering, and then the truck is empty the rest of the day and night. Someone could get into the back, but there's nothing there to take except plastic tubs full of ice or the dolly I use for larger deliveries. I'm getting the lock fixed in a few days anyhow. This has got to be the best job I've had! And best of all, I'm usually done for the day anytime between one and four in the afternoon. It'll be perfect when the little one arrives." Owen reached over and rubbed Ade's stomach. "Hear that? Daddy's gonna be making big bucks *and* is going to have plenty of time for you. Oh, did I tell you I got another account today? Big order for tomorrow already."

I was so happy for Owen. He was obviously doing well with this job, and his success was going to make life less stressful for him and for Ade. She was still working as an independent hair stylist, but because she'd been feeling so sick, she'd eased up her hours by keeping her highest-paying clients and slowly dropping off the less profitable ones.

We worked our way through the meal, savoring the delicious food and the good company. Doug excused himself to go to the men's room. When he returned, he scooted his chair close to the table and leaned in. "Hey, Chloe. Since you're a regular here, do you know what's going on with our waitress, Leandra, and that other girl back there?"

I peered in the direction Doug was pointing and saw Leandra almost nose to nose with Blythe. Or, rather, nose to boob, since Blythe was much taller than Leandra. Blythe's back was to me, but I could see Leandra's pretty face scrunched up in a snarl. "That's Blythe," I said with an unintentional sigh. "She's a hostess here, but sometimes she bartends or waitresses when they need her to. Why?"

"Just looking for some restaurant gossip. When I walked by them, they seemed to be having some sort of spat. I don't know what it was about, but I did hear Leandra say something to the other one about being flat-chested."

"Yeah, I'm not surprised. They don't really get along. Blythe can rub people the wrong way." Or at least rub women the wrong way. I had gone to college with Blythe, although I hadn't known her that well then. We were in some of the same circles, so I'd known her socially, but Blythe had taken icky classes like Introduction to Economics and Advanced Cell Biology, so we hadn't crossed paths too often. I'd run into Blythe again a few months ago, and with Adrianna out of commission for late-night partying, I'd ended up hanging out with her. I guess it sounds sort of pathetic, but I didn't have that many friends in Boston anymore. I'd met a few new people at social work school, most notably Doug, but a lot of my friends had moved across the country for school, jobs, or relationships. I was finding that after college, it was becoming much tougher to make new friends, so when I ran into Blythe, I just felt happy to see a familiar face. Blythe was taking a few classes at Suffolk University Law School, and I hooked her up with Simmer for some part-time work. I had sort of a love-hate relationship with her; one minute I loved her, and the next I wanted to claw her eyes out. And Ade just hated her.

Blythe's mother was Filipino, and her father was Irish. The combination had produced the intoxicating Blythe, who was infuriatingly attractive, although in a completely different way from Adrianna. While Ade had more of a model look, Blythe was less classically perfect. She had dark-brown hair that was cut in stylish angles that accentuated her cheekbones, shorter on one side than the other, gorgeous brown skin, and a tall body. She had one slightly lazy eye that somehow added to her looks. In fact, all of Blythe's supposed imperfections made her more attractive than she'd have been without them. As Leandra had evidently pointed out, Blythe was pretty flat-chested, but she always wore low-cut shirts that exposed her smooth skin. I always had the impression that Blythe wanted people to think that because she didn't have big boobs, her revealing shirts couldn't possibly attract the opposite sex, right? Even the permanent chips in her nail polish seemed deliberate, part of a calculated effort to convince people that she had a blasé attitude toward her appearance. Men often seem drawn to women who don't look as if they spend hours in front of the mirror loading on makeup and hair products. Blythe cultivated that kind of inadvertent-looking beauty. In combination with her sharp intellect, it dazzled almost everyone. Yet she rarely hooked up with guys. One thing I couldn't fault Blythe for was being slutty. And she was definitely entertaining to be around: charming, smart, and engaging. As if all of that weren't enough, she somehow managed to balance her law school studies with her work at Simmer; she was one of the busiest people I knew. Hormonal Adrianna was a lot fussier than I was about who she hung out with. Ade tolerated Blythe only for my sake and only after repeated assurances that Adrianna's place as my best friend was secure.

Josh returned to our table looking significantly more sweaty and food-stained than earlier this evening. He held a small notepad and pen in his hand. The top few buttons of his chef's coat were undone, a sign that he was finishing up for the night. I was surprised. It was only ten fifteen.

"Are you done?" I asked excitedly, hoping I'd actually get a little time with him tonight before he collapsed in an exhausted heap.

He pulled a chair over to the table and squeezed in next to me. "Yup. Just gotta write the prep list for tomorrow, and I'm good to go."

"What goes on to your prep list?" wondered Terry, flipping his hair behind his shoulder with a headshake. "Don't you guys have the same things to do every morning?"

"In some ways we do, but a lot can change from day to day depending on what business was like the day before. Like today I sold almost all our soup, so we'll have to make another one tomorrow. Sunday is usually our inventory day, so we've got to weigh all of our proteins, like the meats and cheeses, and then estimate amounts of our dry products, fill out paperwork on it all, and then put in any orders we need for restocking. Oh, yeah! We've got an eight top coming in for a lunch party, and they preordered everything, so that's got to get done." Josh started scribbling on his notepad as he talked. I loved some of the restaurant jargon Josh threw around. *Eight top* meant a party of eight. *Deuce* was a party of two. It was funny that even though I knew these terms now, I would never use them myself since I wasn't in the business. If I'd tried, it would've been like Justin Timberlake throwing around street slang, as if he'd grown up in the inner city instead of in Tennessee. Idiot. Anyhow, I wasn't going to humiliate myself by using lingo that wasn't really mine.

"Snacker is coming in before me tomorrow, so I'll leave this out for him and the other guys."

I noticed Owen flinch at the mention of Snacker's name, but he restrained himself from saying anything.

Josh continued. "I thought I'd have to stay late tonight, but the big dinner rush is over, and Santos and Javier can handle any orders that come in."

"I thought Santos was one of your dishwashers," I said.

"Well, yeah, he is. But he's also a line cook. He and Javier sort of do whatever I need them to do." The flexibility was typical of restaurant people. Everyone seemed to work double duty; a bartender might end up receiving food deliveries, a line cook might sweep the floor, and a server might help put away bar deliveries. "If you're me, you end up doing everybody's job half the time." Josh sighed, clearly beat. He'd been at work since seven this morning and had to be back here around ten tomorrow morning. Theoretically, Josh wasn't scheduled to arrive at Simmer until eleven, but eleven was right before lunch service began, and Josh still didn't trust everything to run smoothly without him.

"I seriously can't stay awake any longer." Adrianna looked even more tired than Josh. "Everyone kept telling me that after the first three months I wouldn't be so tired and I'd feel better, but I'm still waiting. Owen, can you drive me home in my car and then just take it back to your place?

Maybe Chloe would drive you back here tomorrow to get your truck?"

"Yeah, babe. Of course." Even though they were moving in together in a few days, Owen had been spending most nights at his apartment because he had to get his price lists, which were faxed over to his place every morning. "Chloe? Would you mind? If you can pick me up by six thirty, I can be down to the warehouse by seven."

"Yeah. No problem." I didn't relish the thought of waking up at six in the morning, but the need to give Owen a ride would get me up and moving. I had plenty of studying to do before finals came around as well as forty pages left to write in my papers. "Ade, you look blitzed. Can you sleep in tomorrow?"

Adrianna sat up tall in her chair, rubbed her lower back, and spoke through a yawn. "I don't have any appointments until ten, so I can sleep some. Are you sure you don't mind?"

"Absolutely. Go home and go to bed!"

Owen replied for her. "All right. Thanks so much. And now you'll be able to see my truck!" Owen sounded wildly excited. He dropped some cash on the table for a tip. I couldn't believe how great it was that Josh could comp this whole meal. What a privilege!

"Josh, as always, thank you for an excellent meal." Owen shook Josh's hand and then pulled Ade's chair out for her. The two said their good-byes. I blew Ade a kiss and promised to call her tomorrow to check in and see how she was feeling.

"We should take off, too, Doug." Terry wrapped his arm

around Doug's shoulder, pulled him in, and gave him a kiss on the cheek. As much as I couldn't stand the ostentatious wealth and fashion pressures of Newbury Street, at least the tolerance for homosexual displays of affection was high. Between the numerous salons, boutiques, clothing stores, and restaurants here, gay men made up half the population of staff and customers, and I was glad that Doug and Terry could feel comfortable. Doug gave me another stern warning about taking my finals seriously. Then he and Terry left hand in hand.

Leandra arrived, accompanied by Santos, to clear our table. "You heading out, Chef?" she asked, beginning to stack plates on the large tray that Santos held.

"Soon. I just have to finish my prep list, and then I'm going. Are you all set here?"

Leandra nodded. "Yeah, we're in good shape. Snacker just left, and the other guys are breaking down the kitchen now. I think there are only a few people left at the bar, but it's a mess back there, so Kevin will be busy later. Poor guy got shot down again by one of those barely twenty-one girls over there. I told him he could do better, but he keeps trying. So, what time do you come in tomorrow?"

"You don't want to know," Josh said with a smile. "I'll be here by eight or eight thirty, but Snacker and the others will be here before that, so leave a note if anything comes up while you're closing. I know, don't look at me like that." Leandra had crinkled her face into a questioning frown. "Don't ask me why we're having a full crew on first thing in the morning. I'm only following orders."

"Okay, but I might not be here that much longer. Wade and Kevin are locking up tonight, so I'll tell them. Nice to see you again, Chloe." Leandra flashed me a perky smile before piling the last of the dishes on Santos's tray, and then she turned to Owen. "So, when am I going to get a ride in that new truck of yours? I hear the fish business is booming." I couldn't tell if Leandra was being flirtatious or sarcastic, but either way, I didn't like it. And neither did Adrianna, who shot a death stare in Leandra's direction.

Owen was suddenly flustered and presumably uncomfortable. "Business is fine. Thank you for asking." I was glad he didn't mention Leandra's inappropriate request for a ride.

As Leandra walked away, she looked over her shoulder at us and gave Owen a wink. What the hell was that about? I shook it off and touched Josh's arm. "Josh, can we go say hi to Isabelle before we leave?" Isabelle had been working in the kitchen at Simmer since they opened, and I liked to check in with her once in a while because I'd gotten her this job. I'd met her in late December when I'd volunteered at Moving On, an agency in Cambridge that provided temporary housing for women in crisis. Isabelle had been kicked out of her house when she was sixteen, and until she had found help from Moving On, she'd been living mainly on the streets. I'd have thought someone with her background would be thick-skinned and street-smart, but Isabelle struck me as fragile and vulnerable. I adored her.

"Sure. I have to finish up this list and make sure the guys are all set back there."

I dropped more tip money for Leandra and followed Josh

through Simmer's heavy glass door into the main dining room. We made our way past a few lingering diners and bar customers to the back of the room. Josh pushed open the kitchen door. Cleanup was underway. Javier was busy using the industrial spray hose to clean oversized pots and sauté pans, and Santos was methodically scrubbing food and grease off the stainless-steel counters and cooking equipment. Josh still hadn't figured out exactly how the two workers were related (somebody's cousin had married somebody's half sister?), but they came off as father and son. Javier was in his midfifties, short, with a round belly that stretched his short-sleeved white kitchen shirt. His graying hair curled around his hairline. Santos was Javier's opposite, weighing half what his relative did and, at six feet, towering above him. While Javier was loud and garrulous, Santos was horribly shy and barely said a word unless spoken to.

"*Hola*, Chloe! *¿Cómo estás?*" Javier called above the din of rushing water.

"*Estoy bien, señor.*" I'd been trying to learn Spanish with the help of an online Spanish tutorial and had amassed a collection of travel phrases. "*Dónde está un buen restaurante?*" I asked with a smile. *Where is a good restaurant?*

"You are funny, señorita." Javier bellowed his wonderful laugh.

"All right, señorita." Josh smiled and shook his head at my Spanish. "I'll be back in a minute. Check the walk-in. Isabelle might be there."

I waved to Javier and Santos and went to look for Isabelle. After searching the walk-in refrigerator, where the perishable food was kept, I went to the dining room to see if I'd missed her there. Isabelle was near the bar, bagging table linens and aprons for the cleaners to pick up. I was happy to see her doing so well here, by which I don't just mean that she was competent at bagging linens. Josh said she was a good employee and that although she'd never worked in a kitchen before, she was becoming a good prep cook. Whatever Josh taught her, she picked up quickly. In some ways, Josh told me, he preferred working with people without kitchen experience because he could teach them to cook the way he liked and didn't have to break them of bad habits.

Isabelle smiled when she saw me. "I heard you were here tonight, Chloe. It's so good to see you. Guess what? Josh is going to teach me how to cut and debone fish tomorrow!" she said excitedly, her short black curls bouncing as she spoke. Like all new employees, Isabelle had been paying her dues in the kitchen by performing the most tedious of tasks, like peeling gallons of potatoes, so each time Josh taught her a new skill, it was a reward for her good performance.

"That's great. I'm so happy this job is working out for you. How is your apartment?" Isabelle had recently found a three-bedroom apartment that she shared with five other girls. In spite of the cramped quarters, she'd been totally giddy at the prospect of moving into a real place rather than living in social service housing in Cambridge.

"I love it! You wouldn't believe how cool my roommates are! One of them works at this TV station and . . ." Isabelle launched into details about the other girls. I listened to her happily describe her new life and new friends. The only time she paused for breath was when Simmer's owner, Gavin, passed by. I was pretty sure I detected a nervous blush color her cheeks. But who wouldn't have a crush on Gavin? He was young, handsome, wealthy, hardworking, and successful: the perfect catch. But Isabelle was only nineteen, whereas Gavin was in his midthirties, so I suspected that her crush would remain just that. Furthermore, Gavin already had Leandra. I talked with Isabelle for a bit while she finished with the laundry and then started to help clean the bar.

The general manager, Wade, nodded his appreciation to Isabelle. "Thanks for your help, Isabelle. We got killed tonight." His black T-shirt clung to his muscular chest and arms, and a simple silver chain peeked out from under his shirt. He had this weird Ryan Cabrera hair thing going on—lots of long gelled strands puffed out from his head—and he had his usual few days' growth of facial hair. I'd have put money on it that he spent more time in front of a mirror than I did.

"How was your dinner tonight, Chloe?" Wade asked as he began going through a mountain of receipts.

"Excellent, as always."

"Good. Josh made us all something to eat before the dinner rush. Did you have that new scallop entrée? God, that was good. Your boy has got talent. I can definitely say that."

"I did, and I agree. I loved it."

Kevin, one of the bartenders, began cleaning out the taps. I couldn't help but think what a crappy job it was to clean up at the end of the night. These guys had just spent hours serving wealthy customers and hobnobbing with

Boston's young and elite, and here they were dumping back-wash out of glasses and mopping liquor off the rubber mats that lined the floor behind the bar.

"Wade, could you grab me more tequila, rum, and triple sec? I'm low on everything." Kevin shook his head and started wiping off bottles. "I can't believe how much we went through tonight." Wade nodded and disappeared to restock the bar.

Since restaurants make most of their money from liquor sales, I was delighted to hear that Kevin was running low. With Josh's food and a little luck, Simmer could soon become a real moneymaker.

"Ready to go, babe?" Josh came up behind me and wrapped his arms around my waist.

"Yeah."

"Hey, Kevin? Do you need anything else before I go?" Josh asked.

"Nah. Thanks, though. Wade and I can handle this mess. See ya tomorrow." Kevin waved good night and continued polishing a bottle of Irish whiskey.

# THREE

W H Y the hell was my alarm clock going off this early? I reached over Josh to hit the snooze button and accidentally whacked my sleeping chef on the head. He was so overtired that he didn't flinch. I rolled over to go back to sleep and remembered my promise to Owen. I'd been on the verge of reentering a dream about Donatella Versace and Wentworth Miller, my *Prison Break* crush. Well, best to wake up from that, anyway.

I climbed over Josh and fumbled around in my closet to find something to wear. Owen and Ade had crashed at my place so often that Owen wouldn't expect me to look good at this hour, but I didn't want to run into any of Simmer's front-of-the-house staff, who'd all be groomed according to

Newbury Street standards, while I was in sweatpants and my hair was sticking out of a big clip. I took a quick shower but didn't dare wash my hair because I couldn't be bothered to spend an hour wrangling my curly strawberry blonde mane into smooth locks. My blow-dry from last night had done a good job of flattening itself while I'd slept, and I wasn't going to undo a good hair day. I tossed on jeans, a white camisole tank, and a cute, pink, fuzzy cropped sweater Ade had temporarily grown out of. My hair had been foiled to within an inch of its life, so I had enough blonde to pull off the pink without blinding anyone. Otherwise, Owen would've had to wear sunglasses on our drive over.

I started up my Saturn Ion, grabbed a couple of coffees at the Dunkin' Donuts in Cleveland Circle—practically the one Dunkin' in the entire world that didn't have a drive-through—and reached Owen's apartment at six forty-five. I beeped a few times, and Owen bounded down the steps. I immediately noticed his long-sleeved shirt that read, We'll Give You Crabs!

"Nice shirt, Owen." I rolled my eyes. "Does your boss know you're wearing that?"

"Course he does," he grinned. "He had 'em made for us! Hey, thanks for picking me up. Ade has been so tired with this pregnancy, and I'm sure she's still sound asleep. Oh, did I tell you? I'm going after work today to pick up a crib and a travel system that I ordered. Ade's going to love them!"

"Owen, where are you going to put all this stuff? Your new apartment isn't that big. Don't you think you should wait until closer to when the baby is going to be born?" I turned onto Beacon Street and headed for Kenmore Square. Even at this hour, Boston traffic sucked. I forced myself to stop at a yellow light and not block the intersection. My reward was a slew of horn honking from the cars behind me. "And what the hell is a 'travel system,' anyway? Where are you planning on going with this kid?"

"Well, the stuff was on sale, so I wanted to buy it now. And a travel system is this cool stroller that comes with an infant car seat you can plunk right into the stroller. It also has a base that you strap into the car, and then you can just pop the seat in and out without having to worry about the buckle. So when the baby falls asleep in the car, we can just keep it in the seat and plop it in the stroller. Cool, huh?"

"Very cool," I agreed, impressed with Owen's knowledge of baby paraphernalia.

When we neared Newbury Street, I asked Owen whether I could just pull onto one of the side streets near Simmer and leave him to walk down the alley to his truck. I wasn't crazy about weaving my relatively new car around Dumpsters and subjecting the tires to broken glass and crumbling pavement.

"I thought you wanted to see my truck," Owen said pathetically.

"Oh, right. Of course I do." I nodded with all the excitement I could muster at this hour.

Owen showed me where to turn to reach the back entrance to Simmer and the other Newbury Street businesses. Most of the buildings in this part of town were beautiful old brownstones and converted town houses, many with large bay windows that displayed high-end products. But behind the glamorous storefronts and equally glamorous stores, the alleys were the same trash-filled back streets you'd find in any other part of Boston. As I eased my car down the alley, I kept an eye out for anything that might puncture a tire.

I knew Simmer from the front, but the alley robbed me of my sense of direction. "Which one is Simmer's door?" I took my eyes off the pavement for a moment to glance around.

"Right there! Right there! See my truck?" Owen pointed excitedly at a white pickup truck. "Just pull over in front of me," he said, leaping out the door before I'd even shifted into park.

I got out and took a look at what was apparently the most thrilling truck of all time. It was just as Owen had described it last night: a white pickup with a white box unit the size of a small shed set in the bed of the truck.

"See? That's the refrigeration unit. Can you even imagine how much fish that could hold? I could make millions!"

The refrigeration box occupied the entire truck bed and rose above the cab of the pickup. "You're not going to fill that thing up on your deliveries, are you?"

"Well, no," Owen admitted. "Not yet. But I'm just saying . . ."

"It's very cool. You were right. I like the logo on the side there." *The Daily Catch* was scripted in red paint and surrounded by sea creatures done in black.

"I'm going to get it done on the box, too. Want to see the inside?"

"Um, sure."

Owen was about to open the back door to the truck when a raspy voice rang out. "Hey, guys! What's up?"

I turned around to see Snacker at the top of Simmer's back steps. He was propping open a heavy steel door. "Hi, Snack," I called. I could tell Snacker was as tired as Josh, but even severe fatigue couldn't change his olive skin, dreamy brown eyes, and chestnut hair: the perfect example of tall, dark, and handsome. On the one hand, I felt as though Snacker was the brother I'd never had. On the other hand, it was impossible not to drool a bit every time I saw him. I wiped my chin. "Owen left his truck here last night, so I drove him in to get it."

"Come on in. I'll make you some breakfast. And Owen? I've got an order for you, if you've got a minute."

"Yeah, no problem, man."

These two were forcing cordiality for my sake, and the result was totally unpleasant. The Adrianna incidents that had taken place in the winter still created plenty of tension between Owen and Snacker. The bad feeling was especially unfortunate because, if Snacker had never hooked up with Ade, these two might have been friends.

Owen followed me up the stairs. Snacker released his hold on the door as I passed through Simmer's back entrance. Since Snacker was trailing right behind me, Owen was forced to grab the heavy door himself. Owen muttered "Asshole" under his breath.

"You're here early, huh, Snack?" I asked. "I thought you chef types didn't have to come in until later?"

"Too much to do, too little time," Snacker said as we passed the doors to Simmer's storage rooms. "And we've got an early delivery today, so I wanted to be here. Our produce guy keeps trying to drop off rotten shit all the time, so Josh and I have been keeping an eye on him and going through everything before we sign for it. Last time, I refused the brown cabbage, and I had to run out myself to a super-market. But I don't mind opening, because I usually get a few minutes to myself before other people come in. Any-how, I'm glad you guys came around the back, because the front is locked, and we've got the music cranked."

Did they ever. We entered Simmer's main dining area, and Stevie Wonder's "Superstitious" echoed throughout the room. The doors to the kitchen were propped open, and even this early, delicious smells poured out. With all the lights on, the restaurant didn't have its usual atmospheric illumination. The floors showed their dirt. Stray napkins were piled on ta-bles, and half-filled glasses sat on the bar. I knew that Wade and Kevin had closed last night and wondered whether they had cut out early and whether they were going to catch some heat from Josh and Snacker for some of this mess.

"*Hola!*" A warm voice rang out, and a Hispanic woman in her sixties appeared with a vacuum in hand.

"*Hola*, Belita," said Snacker with a smile. "This is Chloe and Owen. Belita is one of our cleaning people. We couldn't open without her. Come give me a sweet kiss, señora." Snacker held his arms out and grinned.

"Oh, Jason. I always have kiss for you," Belita said happily. I always forgot that Snacker's real name was Jason. It seemed that half of Josh's friends went by names other than those on their birth certificates. Clearly not needing a second invitation, Belita wrapped her arms around Snacker and planted a big smooch on his cheek. "Okay. Now I work."

Snacker turned back to Owen and me. "You want that order now?" he asked Owen.

Owen nodded. "Yeah. I have to get going soon if I'm going to make all my deliveries on time."

"Come on back to the office with me. I've got it written down there."

I wasn't crazy about leaving Snacker and Owen alone together for even a second, but the coffee had run through me, and I needed to hit the bathroom. I left the two feuding boys on their own and went to the ladies' room. Simmer's restrooms had been totally remodeled when Gavin took over, and I wished that my own bathroom at home were half as luxurious as they were. The entire ladies' room was tiled with hand-painted ceramic squares in rich earth colors, and the three sinks were made of copper and had coordinating faucets and knobs.

Belita and a young Hispanic woman were busy cleaning up leftover lines of cocaine that had been neatly set up and then abandoned. When Belita looked at me, she seemed embarrassed. "Is Newbury Street sometimes." She shrugged.

I don't know which I was more surprised to see: cocaine or *leftover* cocaine.

When I returned to the kitchen, Owen and Snacker, to my relief, were not beating the crap out of each other. Each had, however, adopted a masculine-looking pose. Snacker was feigning casualness by leaning against a wall with both arms crossed, his chef's coat unbuttoned halfway, and a pen tucked behind one ear. Owen stood square in front of his rival, both hands on his hips, his chin raised a bit, and his expression falsely calm. Owen was one of the most unaggressive people I knew. He looked ridiculous.

"Have Josh call me when he gets in if you think of anything else you need," Owen said. "I'll probably leave the warehouse by nine, but I can always run back if you've forgotten something."

"Nope. We should be good with the list I gave you," Snacker responded. "Hey, Santos. Can you start the stock for me? And Javier, start cleaning the walk-in when you get a chance, please."

Owen shifted his weight to one leg. "Do you mind if I use your fax machine quickly? Mine was down this morning. I've got a few more price sheets to get out to my restaurants. Hopefully that will get me a few more orders in for today."

"Yeah. Help yourself," Snacker said without looking at Owen.

Owen refrained from snarling and went to the office.

A man's voice rang loudly through the kitchen. "Linens! Got your fresh linens! Any takers?" A round, middle-aged man clomped his heavy boots across the floor. He carried a tall stack of what I knew were aprons, napkins, kitchen shirts, and bar towels, all cleaned, pressed, and wrapped up in plastic. "Mornin'! Got your dirties for me?"

"Hello, my friend," Snacker said. "Just drop those in the front and help yourself to the bags. I think they're by the bar."

Once before, I'd been to Simmer early enough to see Josh open. He'd lured me there with the promise of a hot breakfast. Now, the thought of food made my stomach give an embarrassing growl. "Sorry."

Snacker laughed. "Hungry? I'll make you something to eat. How about an omelet?"

I wasn't about to protest, so I followed Snacker over to one of the flattop grills and happily watched him beat eggs and fill my omelet with goat cheese, diced red pear tomatoes, prosciutto, and julienne of fresh basil. I grabbed a seat on a stool and scooted out of the way so that Santos and Javier could move back and forth across the kitchen as they carried pots of liquid and sharp knives. I was struck with the amount of work that went into opening the restaurant each day. The cleaning, the scheduling, the food preparation and cooking, the need to take inventory . . . The work seemed endless!

Isabelle entered the kitchen, her dark curls pulled back from her face, her cheeks glowing with a hint of pink blush. "Good morning, Chef," she said softly. Isabelle had quickly learned to address both Josh and Snacker as *Chef*. In all other respects, the kitchen was informal; in that one, it definitely was not.

"Miss Izzy Belle! How are you, darling? Ready for a big

day? We've got that party later, so when you get settled, would you start the prep work on the salads?"

"Of course, Chef." She hung her bag on a hook by the office.

"But go get yourself a cup of coffee first if you'd like. Might as well enjoy the calm before the storm."

I was pleased to see that Snacker, as well as Josh, was taking good care of Isabelle. Chefs were notorious for their brash, demanding, and even manic personalities. Consequently, it was wonderful that Josh and Snacker hadn't yet scared off my young friend. Josh and Snacker were both devoted to the kitchen. They were demanding leaders and true perfectionists. Still, thank goodness, neither of them resembled *Hell's Kitchen*'s Gordon Ramsay!

My omelet was beginning to smell so delectable that I had to put my hand on my stomach to try to quiet the rumbling. I adjusted myself on the stool, looked around the room, and realized that the kitchen crew needed more room to work. Despite all the renovations that had been done before Simmer's opening last New Year's Eve, the kitchen was not especially spacious. Although all the appliances and work surfaces were new, Gavin hadn't expanded the original kitchen area, which occupied the same space as the kitchen of the restaurant that had previously been at this location. According to Josh, the kitchen was a tight fit when he had his entire staff working. There certainly wasn't any extra space on the stainless shelving units, all of which were filled with pots and pans and with a variety of small appliances, including some that I couldn't even identify. Even the walls were covered in papers and notices. I glanced up and discovered that pictures of food had been taped to the ceiling.

"Snack? What's up with the photos on the ceiling?" I asked.

"Oh, Christ. That's Gavin's stupid idea." He sighed and shook his head.

"You mean *another* stupid idea," added Santos, who deposited a tray of pork loin on a nearby counter and then headed off toward the walk-in refrigerator.

"Well, yeah," admitted Snacker as he served me my delicious-smelling omelet. I dug in and took a bite of the cheesy, overstuffed egg dish. "See, Gavin decided that not only should we have all the recipes for every dish up," he said, pointing to the papers affixed to the concrete walls, "but we needed pictures of how they should be plated, too. Josh and I tried to explain that with all the recipes, and the health and safety certificates, and the employee notices that have to be up, we didn't have room for more shit on the walls. Plus, Josh trains everyone to plate and serve the dishes, so it's needless to have pictures up as well."

*Odd. Extremely odd.* "So, Gavin expects you guys to be cooking and then periodically peer up at the ceiling to see a photograph of a dish? Good thing the ceilings aren't too high here!"

"It's pretty asinine, I agree. But it's his restaurant. We just work here, right?" He tossed his arms up in the air. Josh had never said anything to me about being unhappy with Gavin. Quite the opposite! Josh was thrilled to be able to control the menu, choose his staff, and run the kitchen as he chose. But pictures of food on the ceiling? Pretty weird.

"Snacker?" Owen called from the office. "Can I see you for a minute? I need to talk to you about your order for today."

"Sure thing."

While the feuding men talked, I finished my omelet and then decided to go check out Owen's truck on my own. I didn't feel like hanging around while Owen and Snacker talked about fish deliveries, and I especially didn't want to be present if Adrianna's name came up. Besides, I knew that Owen wouldn't rest until I'd admired his delivery truck. Mainly, I left on the grounds that if you can't take the heat, get out of the . . .

Anyway, once I was out in the alley, I was less interested in looking at Owen's truck than I was in finding out what it would be like to sit behind the wheel. Not that Owen's vehicle was some eighteen-wheeler, but I'd never driven anything bigger than a standard-size four-door sedan, and I was curious to discover what it would be like to sit behind the wheel of a big truck. So, hoping for a little thrill, I opened the driver's side door, took a tall step up, settled myself in the seat, and refrained from making revving noises as I placed my hands on the wheel. I didn't envy Owen having to drive this beast through little alleys like this one and, worse, having to fight with crazed, speeding Boston drivers, but I could see that it would be fun to be up so high. I hopped out and slammed the door, which was significantly heavier than the doors on my car. I walked around to the back and tried to compose glowing comments to make to

Owen about his beloved truck. With its square refrigeration unit, the truck had a funny shape that reminded me a bit of old-fashioned paddy wagons. Instead of having two doors that swung open to allow prisoners to move in and out, Owen's truck, however, had one garage-style door that slid up and down. A thin metal cord ran from top to bottom on each side of the door, and a heavy cloth strap hung from the bottom, both presumably parts of a pulley system to raise and lower the door. A rectangular metal handle with a key-hole stuck out.

I stared at the door and tried to think of some interesting comments I could make to Owen. I rubbed my nose in an attempt to wipe away the mild, but distinctly present, stench that emanated from the back of the truck. I'm a big fan of seafood, but the stink coming from Owen's delivery truck was more than unappetizing. What did I expect of a fish truck? Well, cleanliness, at least. Had Owen been foolish enough to leave fish to rot in the back of the truck overnight? Even I knew that the refrigeration unit ran only when the truck was on, so anything left inside was at the mercy of the weather. Maybe in the winter Owen could get away with this carelessness, but not in early spring! The smell wasn't even all that fishy. It was just plain gross. So far, my observations didn't exactly convey the enthusiasm that Owen was hoping for.

Eager to avoid disappointing Owen, I decided to check out the interior of the unit. For all I knew, the source of the foul odor was some large, rotting object—a rat?—on the pavement beneath the truck, whereas the refrigeration unit held gigantic lobsters kept fresh on ice or clever, attractive storage boxes or something else, in fact, anything at all, that would assure Owen that I loved the truck as much as he did. Owen had said last night that the lock was broken. Braving the stench, I grabbed the handle. To make the door budge, I had to use both hands. A high-pitched squeak suggested that the sliders could've used a shot of WD-40. Once I'd managed to raise the door halfway up its tracks, I climbed onto the step under the door, gave the door a good shove, and sent it fully up.

On the floor of the truck, surrounded by empty plastic crates, a metal dolly for moving heavy objects, shallow pools of water, and low piles of melting ice, lay the body of Leandra, our server from last night.

# FOUR

LEANDRA was on her back with her feet toward the door. She wore the same outfit I'd seen her in when she'd waited on our table. The white lettering on her trendy black Simmer apron almost shone in the daylight. Her dead eyes were open, and her skin was pale and slightly blue. Her head had rolled to the side. I could clearly see red marks on her neck. Staring at Leandra wouldn't bring her back to life. I jumped backward off the truck, bent over, gagged violently, and emptied my stomach.

"Chloe! What're you doing? I thought I was going to get to show you everything!" Owen's scolding voice came from the direction of Simmer. "What's wrong? Oh, my God, why are you throwing up? Snacker's cooking that bad?" He started to laugh and then looked at what must have been my ashen face. "Chloe?"

I pointed to the open door of his truck. "Owen, Leandra is in there. She's dead."

"What?" Owen paused. "Who's Leandra?" After another pause, he said, "You mean our waitress?" He rushed past me and flew up the step to the back of his delivery truck. He braced himself with one hand by gripping the side of the door frame. His other hand flew to his forehead. The gesture belonged in a silent movie. "Holy shit! Holy shit! This cannot have happened!" Owen dropped to the pavement. Then, repeatedly, almost compulsively, he ran both hands through his hair as he paced back and forth behind his truck. "This cannot be happening. I can't have her in my truck! Why is she there? What the hell is she doing there?" He stopped moving. "Chloe. You have to help me get her out of there. We have to move her onto the ground. Then we'll call nine one one, okay? She can't be in my truck! Do you know what kind of trouble I'm going to be in?"

I stared in horror at Owen. "Are you crazy? We can't move her!" Owen stepped back to his truck, and I managed to stand upright without fainting. Then I grabbed his arm tightly, as if I meant to squeeze some sense into him. "No, you are not moving her, Owen! She must have, I don't know, locked herself in there somehow and died from lack of oxygen, right? Don't do anything stupid. This must be some freak accident, and you'll only make things worse if you move her around."

"I've got deliveries to make. I've got this job now! I

can't . . ." Owen faltered. He looked at me in desperation. "What am I gonna do?"

I knew Owen felt like the whole world was crashing in on him, and I realized that he was more tightly strung than I'd thought. He had everything riding on this new job, but even for his sake, I wasn't about to help him move poor Leandra's body to a more convenient place. As an explanation to his boss and his clients of why he was failing to make his deliveries, the discovery of a dead body in his truck would be more than sufficient; it wasn't some dog-ate-my-homework excuse. "Owen, it's going to be all right." Turning to face Simmer's back door, I was happy to find it still propped open. I needed help from someone other than the panicked Owen. "Snacker! Snacker!" I screamed at the top of my lungs.

The cleaning woman, Belita, appeared. Instead of hollering that there was a dead body in the back of a truck, I tried to use my social work tact to convey the information in a calm and appropriate manner. "Belita, there's been an unfortunate accident. Someone has passed away. Could you get Snacker for me? And please call the authorities." *Unfortunate accident* was such a stupid phrase; *fortunate* accidents don't leave people dead. And why had I said *passed away* and *authorities*?

Belita shook her head at me, not understanding what I was saying. Tossing aside my incomprehensible social workese, I tried again. "Belita, Leandra is dead. Call the police. Get Snacker." If my online Spanish course had covered forensic terms, I'd forgotten them.

But plain English worked.

"*Dios mio!*" Belita vanished, I hoped, to go get Snacker.

"Owen, you'd better call nine one one, too."

Owen reluctantly pulled his cell from his pocket and punched in the emergency number.

Snacker, followed by Santos, Javier, Belita and her assistant, and Isabelle, flew out the kitchen door. "Chloe? What's going on? Belita said something about—" Snacker stopped speaking as I pointed to Owen's truck. He bounded down the stairs and rushed toward the truck.

"Snacker, don't go in!" I hollered.

He came to an abrupt halt in front of the open door. "Is that Leandra? Oh, my God!" He turned back to face me, his hand over his mouth, and walked away from the truck. "Did you call someone?"

I nodded. "Owen just did. I'm going to call Josh."

I went to retrieve my cell phone from my car while Snacker talked to Simmer's employees. Chefs have a show-must-go-on mentality; they believe that if food can be prepared and served, then it must be prepared and served. A typical chef, Snacker insisted on the need to continue prepping for lunch.

I called Josh repeatedly until he finally picked up his phone.

"I'm up, I'm up!" he grumbled into the receiver. "Is Snacker mad I'm not there?"

"No. There's a bigger problem." As I told Josh the little I knew about the unexpected appearance of Leandra's body in

Owen's truck, a police cruiser pulled into the alley. As it did, Santos and Javier vanished. I wondered, of course, about their immigration status. "Josh, police cars are starting to show up. I think you'd better get down here."

"Tell Snack I'll be right there. I'll call Gavin, too."

More official vehicles arrived, including a medical van and additional cruisers. Owen's truck was quickly swarming with EMTs and cops. Snacker gave up trying to get his group inside. When he approached a uniformed officer, I joined the two of them and said that I'd been the one who'd found the body.

"Ma'am, do you know who owns the truck?"

I glanced at the policeman's ID tag. Officer Trent looked about twelve years old. His teenage appearance made me resent being called *ma'am*.

"Um, the truck actually belongs to my friend Owen. He's right over there." I pointed to the distraught Owen. "Well, it really belongs to the Daily Catch. That's the seafood company Owen works for. But I can assure you he had nothing to do with this."

"Sir? Could you come over here, please?" Officer Trent called over to Owen.

Owen and I briefly described what had happened, and Owen confirmed what I'd said about the truck. "Look," he added, "I don't mean to be insensitive, but I really have to get to work. I haven't been at this job very long, and my boss is going to kill me if I'm much later. Sorry," he hung his head. "That was obviously a bad choice of words."

"You won't be getting to work anytime soon. We'll need to have everyone inside so we can get statements from each of you. Call your boss."

"Wait!" Owen looked up quickly. "I'm not in any trouble, am I? This is my truck, but—"

"We'll sort everything out inside," the officer said brusquely.

I waited in the hope that he'd somehow go on to say that Owen was off the hook. I waited in vain.

# FIVE

I don't understand why they're even in the restaurant,"
Snacker said with exasperation, "or why they're keeping us
here. Leandra was found *outside* the building. In *Owen's*
truck."

Owen glared at him. "Thank you for pointing that out.
Anything else helpful you'd like to add?"

Owen, Snacker, and I, together with the other employees,
were all in Simmer's main dining room, where Officer Trent
and his colleagues were keeping what felt like a close eye on
us, as if they expected one of us to make a run for it at any
minute. Santos and Javier hadn't bolted after all, but they
looked uncomfortable and stayed close to Snacker. The police
had sealed off the alley and all of the restaurant except the

area at the front of the dining room where all of us waited. Snacker had unlocked the front door so that other employees arriving for work could be quickly ushered into what had become a holding area.

"I don't know, Snack," I said. "And Owen, nobody thinks this is your fault. I wish Josh would get here, though."

Snacker looked irritated. "Did you hear that cop tell me that we can't even open today? Gavin and Josh are going to flip out. We had a party today for one of our best customers."

Snacker was extremely loyal to Josh and had been working just as hard as my boyfriend at making Simmer succeed against all restaurant odds. Snacker was an old friend of Josh's who had moved back to Boston for the opportunity to work with Josh at Simmer. The two of them and their friend Stein had an apartment in Jamaica Plain. I avoided the place, which was messy and smelled like boys because no one was ever home long enough to clean it. Periodically, Snacker would put in the effort to tidy the place up and make it presentable enough to bring women there. He was cute, there was no denying that, and since he'd been in Boston, he'd maintained a steady stream of smitten young ladies. Many a customer and waitress had been taken in by Snacker's dark hair, olive skin, and lean build, and he'd quickly become Simmer's resident heartbreaker. He had no interest in a long-term relationship unless it was between him and a restaurant, which was at least working out for Josh if not for the heartbroken stream of Boston women.

Josh entered through the front door, nodded to us, and was

greeted by one of the many uniformed people who had taken over the restaurant. After speaking for a few minutes with a severe-looking woman whose brown hair was knotted in a tight bun, he came over to us, wrapped his arms around me in a big bear hug, and said, "Jesus, Chloe. Are you okay? Tell me again what happened." He sat down.

As Owen and I recounted our story, Josh sat motionless with his chin in his hand. "I just don't believe this. God, poor Leandra."

"Chef?" Javier leaned in to Josh and began whispering quickly in Spanish. Santos stood nervously behind him.

Josh nodded repeatedly. "I know. I know. It'll be okay. I'll vouch for you, but I don't think they'll ask. Don't worry." Javier and Santos moved to another table, where they sat quietly. "There's Gavin," Josh said. "When I called him, I didn't tell him what happened, just that he needed to get down here fast. Chloe? Do you think you could tell him about Leandra? He's going to take it hard."

Snacker clapped his hand over his mouth then mumbled sheepishly, "I didn't even think of that. I feel like such an ass." Owen smiled triumphantly, as if Snacker had just proved himself to be what Owen thought he was, namely, a dirtbag.

The shock and confusion had somehow made me forget just how involved Gavin and Leandra had been. If Snacker was right, Gavin would be upset to hear that Simmer would be closed for the day. But Gavin's distress about the loss of business would be nothing by comparison with what he'd feel when he learned about Leandra's death.

"Oh, Josh, please. I don't know Gavin that well. Maybe it would better for him to hear it from you." Breaking the news would've been hard under any circumstances, but I especially didn't want to have to tell Gavin that Leandra's body had been discovered in such a smelly, undignified place.

"As the resident social work student, I think you're the one to handle this. Please?"

As usual, Josh was irresistible. I gave in. But I rose from my seat only to realize that the police were already telling Gavin about Leandra and that I was thus too late. When Gavin finished listening to the officer's devastating words, he walked toward us. Everything about him was somber: his expression, his posture, and his slow gait. "I assume you all know?" He wasn't crying, but his eyes were watery, and he avoided direct eye contact with any of us. As soon as we'd offered words of condolence, Josh, Snacker, and Owen suddenly made themselves scarce, leaving me to talk to Gavin.

I spoke softly. "This must be a terrible shock. Can I get you anything?"

He shook his head. "No. Thank you. I just . . . well, I just don't understand it. Everyone loved Leandra. Who would do this to her? Why would anyone want to kill her? She must have been killed after she left work. Some asshole probably mugged her for her tip money and then killed her. I've told all my employees not to walk to their cars or the T alone at night. What the hell was she doing? She's young and beautiful, and it was stupid of her to walk out of here with a wad of cash in her pocket. But my God!"

Gavin rubbed his eyes. When he removed his hands, I could see that the whites were even redder than they'd been before. "But this has nothing to do with Simmer. She is great . . . *was* great to work with, did her job well, and all that. No one here would've had any reason to hurt her. It was obviously an urban crime that's got no connection with us. With Simmer. So why are we all being held here for questioning?"

"I don't have an answer for you," I admitted. "But obviously the police need to gather as much information as they can right now if they're going to find out exactly what happened to Leandra. So we've just got to help them in any way that we can. At this point, that's the best thing we can do for her, right?"

Gavin shifted gears from bereaved boyfriend to restaurant owner. "You're right, Chloe. Okay, I have to talk to Josh and Snacker and figure out what's going on with our schedule."

So much for intensive grief counseling.

Gavin beckoned Josh and Snacker over. "We need to make plans about when we can open. What have the police told you?"

"We're definitely not opening today and maybe not tomorrow," Josh said. "They won't even let us in the kitchen to cook for everyone here. Can you believe that? I'll call everyone with reservations and see who I can reschedule. Maybe we can offer that party an extra course on the house to keep them happy. Snack, why don't you see if you can convince someone to let us in the kitchen."

I remembered Josh telling me that on September 11, 2001, the restaurant where he'd been working had stayed open. He and everyone else in the kitchen had spent the day cooking and talking to one another and to the few stray customers who'd drifted in. Preparing food and feeding people had helped him to get through that miserable day. When in crisis, chefs want to lose themselves in their work while simultaneously nurturing others. Now, Josh and Snacker wanted to take care of their employees by offering the solace of comfort food.

Gavin took a deep breath. "I've been told that I need to get all the other employees down here for questioning, too. Oh, here comes Blythe and Wade. Good. They can help with that."

Noticing that Owen was pacing back and forth, I rose and went to him in the hope of calming him down. "Owen, do you want me to call Adrianna?"

"What? God, no! Just . . . not now! Chloe, they're taking my truck away as evidence. I'm supposed to be picking up and delivering fish right now, not dealing with this."

"Owen, your truck is . . . it really is evidence. The police need it. They can't just remove Leandra's body and let you drive off, can they?"

Owen shrugged. "I guess not."

"Besides, the Daily Catch must have other company trucks, right? I'm sure your boss can let you use another one."

"I don't know." Owen paused, looked away, and muttered some very bad four-letter words. "Maybe. I'll go call my boss now and tell him what's going on and see if somebody else can make my deliveries for me. This sucks." I left him alone to make his calls.

Kevin, the head bartender, entered the restaurant, and then someone finally had the sense to get the coffeemaker at the bar going. Finally, with the apparent blessing of the police, all of us had coffee, if not food. I filled up a mug, added milk and a few teaspoonfuls of sugar, and joined Blythe, Wade, and Isabelle at one of the few tables we were permitted to use.

To me, Wade embodied everything obnoxious about Newbury Street. He was the essence of what's nastily called Eurotrash, except that he was merely a Eurotrash wannabe. Two things kept him from actually being Eurotrash. First, he was obviously American and had never come close to jet-setting around the world. Second, far from being a trust fund child (who am I to talk?), he actually had a job. But Wade liked to give the impression that money was falling out of his pockets, and although he'd grown up a few miles outside Boston, he spoke with a peculiar accent evidently intended to make him sound multilingual. When not at Simmer, Wade could be found at any one of the posh coffee shops and bars along this upscale street, where he'd hang around smelling of expensive, unadvertised cologne and receiving air kisses from anorexic, Valentino-attired young ladies who sported oversized sunglasses. But Josh liked him as a GM—general manager—and when Simmer's original GM had left after only two weeks, Wade had stepped in and done a great job.

"Dammit," Blythe complained, "I can't believe we're closed for the next two days. I was scheduled to work doubles as a server, and for once, I could've made some money. And finally someone actually scheduled me without six other servers working at the same time. I would've made serious tips." Leave it to Blythe to look stunning in the middle of a crime scene. My old friend was so naturally beautiful that even her poorly applied purple eyeliner didn't detract from her looks. She'd pushed her short hair back with a headband and, flat-chested or not, she managed to make Simmer's uniform look sexy and chic. Thank God I hadn't thrown on sweatpants this morning.

Instead of commenting on her coldhearted attitude, I said, "Snacker mentioned scheduling problems this morning. What's been going on?"

"You don't want to get us started." Wade laughed. "But everyone keeps losing money because Gavin is fanatical about plugging us all into his computer system and relying on whatever idiotic schedule it generates. And half the time we've got too many servers and bartenders working during the slow times, so nobody's making any money. And then when we're swamped with customers, we don't have enough people, so service isn't what it should be, and then tips are low."

It disturbed me to hear people focus on the business and not on the death of a fellow employee. Even Josh was wrapped up in trying not to lose customers. But I knew Josh, knew that he had a good heart, and understood that he was just trying to do what had to be done. Even so, I felt upset that the primary concern at Simmer was the restaurant's well-being and not Leandra's sudden and horrible loss of life. Evidently, the restaurant world did not stop for death.

# SIX

BLYTHE and Wade were both asked to give statements to the police. As I watched them move away, I wondered what they might know. How well had they even known Leandra? Realizing that everyone here was going to be questioned by the police triggered my sense of responsibility for Isabelle and prompted me to move in close to her. Of all the employees at Simmer, she was the one who seemed most alone. Yes, she now had roommates, but she was coming off years of fending for herself, years in which she'd had no family or no close friends. Now, just as she'd been settling into a job she loved and into a new life, a dreadful crime had occurred and, worse yet, had occurred in a place that she must have seen as the representation of her newfound safety and stability. "How are you holding up, Isabelle?"

"I'm fine. I mean, it's really sad and all about Leandra, but I didn't know her too well or anything. But you know what I can't help thinking? If Leandra had lived, Gavin might have married her, and she really wasn't such a nice person. I know I shouldn't speak ill of the dead, but it's true. Gavin deserves much better than what he got from her. He is really so nice, Chloe!" Her face colored, and she fidgeted with a paper napkin on the table. "I know there are a lot of complaints about Gavin, but he's doing the best he can. Really he is. He just wants Simmer to run as smoothly as possible, and it'll take a while to get everything going perfectly, right? I know everybody hates that restaurant management program on the computer, but eventually it'll even out and all the problems will be fixed. He has a plan." She spoke with confidence that went beyond optimism. What I heard in her voice was more than hope; it was absolute belief.

"I'm sure he does," I said with a reassuring smile. In fact, I felt far from reassured. I still wasn't used to hearing about staff discontent with Simmer's owner. Most of my knowledge of Simmer came from Josh, who'd painted a picture of harmony among the staff and grateful respect for Gavin.

A female voice called out, "Chloe Carter?" It was my turn to be interviewed by the police. A detective, Patricia Waters, had me sit with her at a table for two. Detective Waters tucked her shoulder-length auburn hair behind her ears and flipped a notebook open to a clean page. I provided basic information about who I was.

"And your boyfriend is the chef here? Josh Driscoll?" she asked, scanning her previous notes.

I nodded.

"Take me through everything you can remember from this morning, okay?"

I narrated the details of picking up Owen and talking with Snacker. The linens had been delivered, I said. Owen had used the office for faxing. Finally, I described the gruesome discovery of Leandra's body. I consciously opted to avoid mentioning the lines of cocaine I'd seen in the bathroom, and I said nothing of my suspicion that not all the employees here were legal residents of the U.S.

"Tell me why Owen's truck was parked here overnight. And did you know Leandra well? Were Owen and Leandra involved?"

I explained that Adrianna was pregnant and went on to say that because she'd been exhausted last night, she'd wanted Owen to drive her home. He'd done what Adrianna asked, and then he'd walked to his nearby apartment. In response to the question of whether I'd known Leandra well, I said no. I added that she'd been involved with Gavin Seymour, who'd seemed to be crazy about her. No, there was no relationship between Owen and Leandra. Owen was going to marry Adrianna. Just because Ade and Snacker had had a meaningless fling a while back didn't mean that my friends weren't perfect for each other! I stressed that no one should listen to anything Snacker had to say about Owen, because Snacker was not his biggest fan. As I didn't say aloud, I resented the implication that Owen had had anything to do with the murder. Instead of saying outright that Owen shouldn't be treated as a suspect, I emphasized his loyalty to Adrianna. I didn't say this aloud, either, but if Owen had been going to kill someone, it would've been Snacker! "Owen was the one who wanted me to see his truck," I said. "It's not like he was hiding it from me."

Detective Waters continued her questions. "Was Leandra involved with anyone before Gavin? While she was with Gavin?"

I shrugged. "I honestly don't know. I knew her from spending time here because of Josh, but we weren't close. Not by any means."

"Gavin is a handsome man, don't you think? There must have been other women who were interested in him."

"Probably," I said. Women who could've killed Leandra to get a shot at him? Obviously Isabelle's harmless crush didn't count, and I certainly didn't want to bring up her name. "I'm sure he's got tons of women all over him, but I don't know of anyone specific."

After another twenty-five minutes in which I described my observation of the linen deliveryman and gave a step-by-step description of finding the body and calling 911, I was done. I hoped I hadn't said anything to implicate Owen. Or Snacker. Had I given the impression that Snacker despised Owen so much he could have plopped a dead body in Owen's truck to frame him?

Josh and Snacker stood together, both increasingly irritated that they couldn't get into the kitchen. Owen stood with them but was uncharacteristically quiet.

"It's not like anyone got poisoned, right?" complained Snacker. "Everything probably happened in the alley and Owen's truck, not in the restaurant and certainly not in our kitchen." Snacker was taking every opportunity to point out Owen's connection to this crime.

"The thing is, we don't know how Leandra died. There were red marks on her neck, but there wasn't any blood, right? Did you see any?" I asked.

"No," Snacker admitted.

"Her death just couldn't have been natural. It's not like she suddenly felt ill, wandered into an unlocked fish truck, shut the door, and died." I paused. "At least that's not very likely."

"Maybe she killed herself," Josh suggested.

I rolled my eyes. *In a fish truck?*

Josh looked over my shoulder. "I'm up, I guess." He left to be grilled by Detective Waters. Owen finally decided to call Adrianna. Predictably, Snacker felt the urge to flirt with beautiful Blythe. And when Snacker felt an urge, he always succumbed to it.

Gavin sat alone. Ever the social work student, I decided that it was no time for him to be by himself. Consequently, I pulled out a chair, sat down, and adopted my best therapist posture, legs and arms uncrossed and relaxed, ready to receive what the client had to say.

Simmer's owner looked at me sadly, blew his nose, and reached for a glass he'd managed to sneak from the bar. I could smell the alcohol from my chair. "I really, really cared about Leandra. I'm not sure we were in love yet, but we were definitely heading there." He blew his nose again and wiped his sleeve across his eyes. "And to top it all off, this could really hurt Simmer. I've got great plans for all of us. I know we've got a few kinks to iron out, but the seminars I've been attending on restaurant management all say that the staff may take a while to be trained properly. I cannot stress enough how important it is to have exact methods for taking inventory and keeping track of everything. It might seem like petty stuff, but it's all about crunching numbers. There are so many ways to lose money that we've got to be on top of everything."

Gavin was talking more to himself than to me. He was, I thought, struggling to focus on anything but his girlfriend's murder. Denial. Typical defense mechanism. And a helpful one in getting him through this crisis. So I wasn't worried about Gavin's mental health. Simmer's finances didn't worry me, either. I assumed that the servers' hourly rate was pretty low—it always is—so Gavin himself wasn't losing a lot of money by overscheduling the front-of-the-house staff, whose principal source of income was tips. What really concerned me about Simmer was what Wade had described: namely, the effect of Gavin's number crunching and management efforts on the servers' tips and on the morale of everyone who worked at Simmer.

Gavin suddenly switched to speaking directly to me. "And you know what? Josh is the best chef around. Never mind what anyone says. What does a GM know about food or running a kitchen anyhow?"

Huh? I thought Wade really liked Josh. More often than

I could remember, I'd heard the GM gush about how delicious Josh's specials were, how hard Josh worked, and how great it was to have an executive chef of his caliber at Simmer. Now, come to find out, Wade had been bad-mouthing Josh to Gavin? The hypocrite! Instead of plastering his hair with all that gel, he should've used oily, greasy goo so he'd look like the slimeball he was.

Gavin took a large gulp from his glass. "We ought to be open today. Not only can we not afford to be closed, but Leandra knew how much this place meant to me. I know she'd want us to be open. What the hell happened, anyway? Leandra shouldn't have been alone. What was she doing? Where was everyone? It was Wade and Kevin who closed last night, I think. I think that's who it was."

"That's what I heard. Would it help you to talk to them?"

"I'd feel better knowing that they locked up and that nothing happened to Leandra in the restaurant. I'll never forgive myself if what put her in danger was a security issue here."

Gavin beckoned to his GM and his bartender, who came over to the table. Both wore tight black Simmer shirts. The too-tan, too-well-groomed, oh-so-Newbury Street look they shared was out of keeping with a murder scene as well as with the time of day. Both of them were, I thought, creatures of the night. Wade, with his perfectly gelled hair, at least looked ready to face the day.

Kevin had the same lean, muscular build Wade did, but Kevin was older than Wade—I guessed early thirties—with wide sideburns that ended in points midcheek and thick hair that had been slicked cleanly and firmly off his face. Kevin's pointy sideburns weren't meant for mornings, even for mornings in the artificial light of a restaurant, and his face was haggard. Kevin had some indefinable quality that made me feel a little embarrassed for him. He seemed to be getting too old to be shaping his sideburns and pouring drinks for Newbury Street's young, rich crowd. Most of Simmer's dining room customers were well over thirty, but the bar scene was always a young crowd. Maybe I was being unfair to Kevin; plenty of professional bartenders, servers, and hosts were out of their twenties. Perhaps he was trying too hard to fit in? Leandra said that Kevin had been shot down again the other night, and the thought of him hitting on barely legal women was embarrassing. Even Leandra had seemed to feel bad for him.

Wade leaned over and rested both hands on the table. "Everything was normal last night. Kevin and I were the last people here. We set the alarm, locked up, and left. Leandra left way before we did. We didn't see or hear anything weird. Like I said, everything was normal."

"Maybe I should have put video surveillance cameras outside. Do you think that would've helped?"

Kevin shook his head. "I don't think so. I mean, we don't even know what happened, really, but there's no reason to think this could have been prevented."

"Gavin, man," Wade said, "I know how hard this must be on you and on the restaurant. It's rough on Josh, too. I mean, he's so dedicated to you and Simmer. But it's not your fault. Just, you know, let us know if we can do anything for you."

Gavin looked down and spoke in an almost inaudible whisper. "Leandra. She had so many friends from having worked at so many restaurants around Boston. Kevin, you and Leandra worked together before, right?"

Kevin nodded.

"And everyone here knew what a great person she was and appreciated all her contributions to Simmer's success. She's really going to be missed by a lot of people."

Although Wade and Kevin again nodded, Gavin didn't get quite the passionate response he was seeking. Fortunately, he was too caught up in his grief to notice. From what I knew of Leandra, she'd been a far from congenial staff member. Not that she'd deserved to end up as she had. Still, I could see why her coworkers were having trouble voicing genuine sorrow.

I excused myself and went over to intrude on Snacker's flirting session with Blythe. What I walked in on turned out to be Blythe's description of a term paper she'd written in college about feminist perspectives on pornography. "So there's one school of feminist thought that decries all pornography as women selling their bodies as a commodity and sees pornography as totally degrading and belittling and all that. Another view is the one that supports a woman's right to choose what she does. That view doesn't necessarily approve of pornography but accepts a woman's prerogative to make decisions about what she does. And the third view actually argues that pornography can be beneficial and empowering to women."

"Uh-huh." Snacker was clinging to her every word. "That is really interesting."

*Interesting*, my ass. Snacker just ate up Blythe's talk about pornography. The little pseudolecture was vintage Blythe. She was managing to entice and even seduce Snacker by talking about sex and porn while still maintaining her academic air. I had to give her credit.

"Hi, guys. Hope I'm not disturbing you?" I winked at Blythe.

"Hi, Chloe." Blythe smiled warmly, but she had the decency to look a little embarrassed. "You're not disturbing us. Not at all. I can't believe what happened to Leandra." Jingling the silver bracelets on her wrist, she brushed her angled hair out of her eye. "I feel sort of bad that my last conversation with her was that tiff we had. She said that my breasts were so small that I looked like a guy. Granted, I'm no Pam Anderson, but she was really picking on me. The detectives seemed to really love that! Like I was so mad at her for what she said that I thought she deserved to die? But that's what she'd said. And I told them I couldn't have cared less what she thought about me. Did they give you a hard time, Snacker?"

Snacker was still so hung up on Blythe's having said the word *breasts* that I almost had to snap my fingers to pull him out of his fantasy. "Snacker!"

"Oh! No, not really. Just a lot of questions about Owen."

"I hope you didn't say anything stupid, Snack." I was worried that Snacker and Owen's feud was somehow going to make things even worse for Owen than they already were.

"I didn't!" he protested. "I just answered their questions."

"I'm sorry," I apologized. "I'm just a little stressed out for him."

"Of course," Blythe sympathized. "Listen, when all this cools down, we have to hang out again soon. I know you've got finals coming up, but we need a girls' night out again, okay?"

"You're on," I agreed happily. Girls' night out with Blythe was always fun. Because I had Josh, I didn't mind that Blythe got all the male attention when we were out together, and I enjoyed helping her filter out the losers who hit on her.

"Yeah, girls' night out." Snacker was almost drooling.

Blythe laughed. "Which does not include you!"

"It certainly does not," I agreed. "I'm going to see how Owen's holding up. Catch you guys later."

Owen looked almost as distraught as Gavin did, although for different reasons. Owen hadn't suffered the loss of someone he'd cared about, but it had been far from easy for Owen to find Leandra's body in his prized truck. It would've been awful enough to come upon a dead body anywhere at all, of course. But in a familiar and innocent place? A place he thought of as his own? Definitely not pleasant. Then there were the practical consequences. Owen was new at the Daily Catch and a new purveyor at the restaurants where he had accounts. His boss and his clients would understand what had happened, wouldn't they? All the same, they'd hardly be happy that he'd failed to make today's deliveries.

But I didn't get a chance to talk to Owen. Before I reached him, two uniformed officers approached him and led him off for what was certain to be a long, long interview.

# SEVEN

WHEN I finally got home, I was determined to shake off the emotional effects of the murder and get some studying done for my final exams. This was Wednesday, and my first final was on Tuesday. I needed to get kicking. My place was on the third floor of an old house in Brighton, a district of Boston, and the major selling point when I rented the condo from its owner had been the parking space out front that was included in the rent. Because the neighborhood was right near a lot of colleges and big universities, it was packed with students who were always fighting over the few legal parking spots on the street. I had a small living room, an even smaller kitchen, a tiny bathroom, and a decent-sized bedroom that doubled as my homework area.

I tossed my keys onto the coffee table in the living room and looked into the bedroom toward my desk, which had almost disappeared beneath mountains of papers and books. In my absence, a stack of articles about cultural influences on behavior disorders had toppled over and buried my keyboard. That course had been listed as *Cult. Influences on Beh. Disorders*, and I'd taken it to mean it was a class on cults. Still, cultural influences had turned out to be okay. Before finals, the one-bedroom condo had been small. Now it felt cramped and suffocating. I sighed and then went to the kitchen to throw on a pot of coffee. The caffeine I'd had this morning wouldn't get me through the studying, research, and paper writing that I had ahead of me. While the pot brewed, I filled up my cat Gato's bowl. While he ate, I stroked his silky black fur. In return, in typically cranky Gato fashion, he turned his head and bit my hand. Brat! I've heard that when cats bite, they're showing affection, but the people who make that claim about cats probably say the same thing about dogs. *Fido didn't mean to chomp off a chunk of your arm and send you to the hospital for three weeks! He was just trying to tell you how much he loves you.*

I heated milk in the microwave, stirred in some sugar, and filled my cup to the top with steaming coffee. Despite the horrors of the morning, I had to get focused on school. What I'd been learning in my classes told me that I was in a posttraumatic state, but I was actually more worried about Owen, Josh, and Snacker than I was about myself. What's more, I felt guilty about having left Gavin surrounded by employees who were probably failing to provide the support he needed. But I felt worst about poor Owen, who was probably still being questioned by the police. Leandra's body had been in his truck, so I could understand why the police were interested in him. Still, there was no other connection between Owen and Leandra. I reminded myself that I was the one who'd actually discovered her body and that, even so, the police hadn't locked me up. Consequently, Owen would probably be released after he'd made a formal statement. Or so I hoped.

Thinking of Owen reminded me that I needed to call Adrianna to see how she was handling the news about Leandra, Owen, and the truck. In fact, since we usually talk at least five times a day, I could hardly believe that I'd waited this long to call her. Yes, I was going to devote the entire day to studying, but a few minutes on the phone wasn't going to interfere. Certainly not.

Adrianna picked up after a few rings. "Hi, Chloe. How are you? God, I think I slept, like, eleven hours last night. My morning client canceled, and so now I don't have anything until four. I might go take a nap. I swear, I'm never going to wake up until this baby comes out."

"Well, you sound awake now," I said.

"Yeah, well, I had a cup of coffee, which I haven't done in months. My ob-gyn said it was okay to have a cup a day, but this is the first time I have, and I think it's hitting me pretty hard. So I'm exhausted and wired at the same time. How's the studying going?"

"I just got home, so I haven't started yet, but I wanted to see how you were doing." I assumed she wasn't thrilled to hear about her fiancé's body-in-the-truck problem.

"How I'm doing with what?" she asked, confused.

"Owen hasn't called you?" I couldn't believe it! What was Owen thinking? How could he possibly not have called Adrianna? He'd done nothing wrong; he was blameless. Why hadn't he told Ade?

Adrianna's tone changed. "No, he hasn't called me. What's he done now? Quit his job and become a trapeze artist or something?"

"No, he hasn't quit." I braced myself for her reaction. "Somebody died in his fish truck."

There was a very long pause followed by laughter so intense that Ade was in danger of pushing the baby out too early. "That's ridiculous!" she sputtered. "In his fish truck? That's impossible. How could anyone . . . Chloe, stop it. This is not funny."

"I'm not kidding!" I insisted. "It was Leandra. Our server at Simmer."

"What?" she said, gasping for breath. "Seriously? Leandra died in his truck? I thought you were joking. Did Owen find her there?"

I told her all about our morbid discovery and finished by saying that Owen was still at the restaurant talking to the detectives. "He said he was going to call you," I added.

"Well, he hasn't. I haven't heard from him all day." Now she sounded pissed.

"I think he was pretty worried about how you'd react." I refrained from mentioning her hormonal state, which made her burst into tears over the smallest thing, including any reference to her hormonal state. She and Owen had had a huge fight the previous week when he'd forgotten to pick up a Pino's cheese pizza on his way home. Well, they hadn't exactly had a fight. Rather, Adrianna had come close to throwing Owen out a window, and he'd calmly waited for her to cool down. Ade had felt neglected and forgotten and miserable, and she'd claimed that Owen didn't care about her at all. Owen, after offering profuse apologies, had run out to get the pizza. Returning home, he'd learned that his darling pregnant girlfriend had changed her mind and now wanted palaak paneer from the Indian restaurant on Beacon Street. The usually rational Adrianna had become unpredictable. Now that I thought about it, I couldn't really blame Owen for not calling her. Just wait until she learned that the police were interested in Owen! I didn't want to be around when she heard that.

"Look, it's not like Owen did anything," she said. "So why would I be mad? Like you told Owen, the seafood company will give him another truck to use until he gets his back from the police." Adrianna spoke with a mouthful of food. I actually encouraged her to eat as much as possible, and I did it for a selfish reason: the more she ate, the faster she outgrew her clothes, and the faster I got temporary hand-me-downs. That's an admission I could make about only one person in the world, and the one person is Ade, my best friend.

I said, "It's just that Owen is so concerned about making money right now. And preparing for the baby. He didn't want you to be disappointed in him."

"Of course I'm not disappointed in him! His business is

great." She happily listed a bunch of restaurants that were regular customers of Owen's. "The only problem he's been having is when his accounts don't pay up and he's got to go after them to collect money. But he hasn't been there long enough for his restaurants to rack up big overdue bills, so it's all right. Except, did you know that Simmer is COD? It isn't too surprising. I mean, since Josh's last paycheck bounced."

What? I had no idea that Josh's check had bounced. Nor did I know that Simmer had to pay cash for seafood deliveries. COD struck me as a bad sign. And if Simmer was on a COD basis with the Daily Catch, what kind of credit did the restaurant have with its other purveyors?

"Chloe?" Adrianna interrupted my thinking. "Oh, God. I'm sorry. You didn't know about Josh's check?"

"No, I didn't. I'm pretty surprised."

"Josh told Owen, who told me, so I assumed you knew."

"Well, it's probably just because Gavin overspent so much when he was renovating Simmer. Josh said that Gavin made the huge mistake of hiring people by the hour or the day instead of having a set price for the job, so he wasted a ton of money. But I'm sure it's just temporary. Simmer seems busy enough, so they've got to be recouping some of that loss. Gavin must owe tons of money, though, considering everything he had done there. That's just part of starting any new business, right?"

"Mmm . . . I suppose so," Ade mumbled through bites of food. "Anyhow, I'm sure Owen will call me later and tell me everything. If he was in any real trouble, he'd have called by now. Listen, I've got two garbage bags full of clothes for you, and I'd rather you take them now so I don't have to pack them up to move."

Yay! More clothes! "Cool. Can I pick them up tonight?"

"Yes, and you don't need to sound so happy about it. Don't take pleasure in my getting fat."

"Ade, there is a gigantic difference between gaining weight during pregnancy and just gaining weight. And I love you either way." Belatedly, I realized that *gigantic* had been a poor word choice. Fortunately, Adrianna didn't seem to notice.

"And don't ruin my stuff. I'm taking it back someday."

We hung up, and I finally started to do some work. During the study breaks I allotted myself, I tried to reach Josh, but he wasn't picking up his cell. Finally, a little after five o'clock, he called to say that he, Wade, Kevin, and some other staff from Simmer were going spend the evening with Gavin so that he wouldn't have to be alone.

"We'll be closed again tomorrow, so maybe I can see you?" Josh said. "Not how I like to get a day off, but I'll take it."

"Argh!" I groaned. "I've got a DSM review class tomorrow that Doug is leading, and I have to go to that." The DSM's official name was the *Diagnostic and Statistical Manual of Mental Disorders, Fourth Edition, Text Revision,* and it was intended for mental health professionals, a group that was evidently supposed to include me. Me! I just couldn't begin to picture myself actually categorizing someone according to the DSM's axes of mental disorders. I mean, my response to the DSM was that I'd much rather spend the day with my boyfriend. "But maybe tomorrow night?"

"Well, I was hoping to spend most of the day at home with you doing unspeakable things, but I can wait until tomorrow night to commit a handful of sins," he teased. "But first, maybe you'd want to come out with me and some of my fellow chefs for dinner? Digger called. He wants us to meet up with him and Lefty."

"Sure, that'd be fun. And *then* you'll do these unspeakable things to me?"

"Absolutely."

We hung up without my asking him about Simmer's apparent financial problems. I couldn't bring myself to mention the matter when the restaurant was about to stay closed for another day. Also, I figured that Josh had a reason for not telling me. The hours he worked put a strain on our relationship to begin with. Maybe he was concerned that I'd think that the financial problems were somehow his fault. I didn't think any such thing. On the contrary, as I probably needed to make clear to Josh, I had total confidence in his ability to do his job and do it exceptionally well.

With visions of dirty deeds dancing in my head, I still managed to work for another few hours before I gave up and drove to Adrianna's to collect my wardrobe. When I walked in, I wasn't surprised to see that her moving boxes were lined up neatly against the walls of her apartment. On each box was a large white label that stated, in purple block capitals, the contents of the box and the room in which it was to be deposited. Adrianna was the only person I knew who could maintain a high level of order and cleanliness while in the middle of a move. The last time I'd moved, I'd thrown the toaster in with my underwear and my books in with my hair dryer, and I'd wrapped my computer in a duvet. Nothing had been labeled.

"Could you possibly be more organized?" But I was laughing.

"I'm just trying to make the move as easy as possible. I'm sorting through stuff I never use and trying to get rid of extra junk. There's a box in my bedroom for you to go through. Take anything you want." Adrianna swooped her hair back into a ponytail and then adjusted the waistband of her pants.

"Clothes getting tight?" I smiled.

"A little."

"Oh, Ade, can you believe this? I still can't believe you guys are having a baby!" I couldn't stop myself from flinging my arms around her in a big hug. "I'm going to be an aunt! Sort of." Adrianna had always felt like a sister to me, and over the past few years, Owen had become the brother I'd never had. The hitch was that if Adrianna was my sister and Owen was my brother, then they were siblings, so their being together was pretty grotesque. Obviously, they weren't really siblings except in my mind. Owen, I decided, could be my brother-in-law. That felt better.

"Of course you're going to be an aunt. You're the designated aunt whether you like it or not." She started taping another box shut. "Oh, the clothes I told you about are right here. They're all yours for now." Ade pointed to an over-stuffed trash bag.

"So when do you think you guys might get married?" I

hoped that I wasn't nagging, but I wondered why Adrianna still didn't have a ring and why they hadn't set a date.

"I don't know. This baby thing makes things more complicated, I guess, in terms of planning a wedding. I'm just not up for anything else major right now. I suppose next year sometime. Owen thinks that the fall might be a nice time . . ."

Much to my surprise, Adrianna burst into tears, and I don't just mean soft crying, but huge, heaving sobs that left her in a state of near choking. Ade was not a crier. In all the years I'd known her, I'd seen her cry only a handful of times. One of those had been when she'd told me she was pregnant. Sure, the pregnancy had made her emotional, but she'd mainly taken her feelings out on Owen by being snippy and irritable. So far as I knew, she hadn't been falling to pieces.

Her weeping threw me. Worse, it alarmed me. "Honey, what's wrong?" I knelt down next to her on the floor, surrounded by boxes and items ready to be packed.

"I just . . . it's just . . . God, I don't know, Chloe! There's so much going on right now. This is not what I planned at all. And Owen is so freaking excited and happy, and I'm just . . ." She paused, clearly embarrassed. "And I'm not."

"You're not excited about the baby? Or is it about marrying Owen?" I asked softly as I rubbed her back.

She looked down. "About this baby." After more sobbing, she calmed down enough to speak again. "That sounds horrible, right? I'm an awful person for saying that, I know. But what the hell do I know about babies? Nothing, that's what

I know. I don't even like kids. You know that. And now I'm having one?"

Unfortunately, it was true that Adrianna didn't really like children. She certainly had no use for my niece, Lucy, and my nephew, Walker. Their noise, their messiness, and their crying irritated her, and she totally failed to see the cuteness I saw during Lucy's and Walker's moments of being adorable. I guess I'd assumed that she'd feel differently about her own child. Or child-to-be. When she'd discovered that she was pregnant, she'd been anything but enthusiastic. Owen's unfaltering exhilaration at the prospect of becoming a father, however, had overshadowed Adrianna's doubts, at least from my perspective. In fact, Owen had acted so wildly overjoyed that I now made a mental note to see whether his behavior fit the DSM's definition of a manic episode. Still, I had no excuse for failing to pick up on how freaked Adrianna was.

"You must be so scared right now, huh?" I said gently.

She nodded.

"That's okay. It's okay to be scared and question how you feel about having a baby. That doesn't make you a bad person, and it doesn't mean you're going to be a bad mother."

"Mother," she said. "I'm going to be someone's mother. That's just unimaginable to me. Look at my mother! Do you think I learned anything from her?" She shook her head and managed a laugh. "Definitely not." Ade grew up with a single mom who had tried to be her daughter's best friend rather than a real parent or even a parental figure. Her father was out of the picture.

"You can learn, Adrianna. You don't have to know everything about how to be a parent the second the baby is born. It'll take time, and you'll learn as you go along." I wished my sister, Heather, were around, but she and her husband, Ben, and their two kids were doing the whole nauseating Disney World vacation this week. Somehow my poor parents had been conned into going along. As much as my sister drove me crazy most of the time, she was an excellent, devoted mother who'd have words of wisdom for Ade. I did have some day care experience under my belt, but I had no children, and Ade, the mother-to-be, needed help from another mother. "Why don't you call Heather when she gets back from her trip? I know she'd love to talk to you. And as moms go, she's pretty great."

"See? 'As moms go.' How horrible is that? What that says is that most moms stink. And that's going to be me. A stinky mom!"

Oh, good Lord, she'd gotten hysterical again. "Have you read any books or anything about babies?"

"No," she whimpered. "I'm afraid they'll just make me feel even more incompetent. I don't even know how to change a diaper! And look what happened to Leandra!"

"I know that's terrible, but what does her death have to do with your having a baby?'

"Chloe! It just proves again what a sick world this is! How am I going to keep some tiny baby alive with the millions of dangers out there? Tell me that!"

"Owen is going to be there to help you," I reminded her. "This is something you guys will learn together."

"Yes, but I'm supposed to be the mom!"

"You *will* be the mom." I smiled. "And you'll do a great job. You and Owen. I know he spent the first few weeks acting like a caveman announcing, 'I am man! I make baby!' but you know what a great guy he is. You can talk to him, Ade."

My distraught friend fell apart again. "We're not even married! I mean, why should I care these days, right? But what if someone calls our baby a bastard? How awful would that be? You know, 'the bastard child across the street'!"

"Ade! No one is going to call your child a bastard! Sweetie, if it's that important to you to get married before the baby is born, Owen won't need much convincing. He was going to propose before he knew you were pregnant, so it's not like he feels trapped into a relationship with you. He adores you."

"I know he does. And I'm crazy about him, too. I'm just so overwhelmed right now, and I feel sick and disgusting all the time, and everything is mixed up and not what it's supposed to be. And I'm tired. Chloe, I'm so tired all the time."

I made Adrianna look at me. "Slow down, okay? You don't have to figure this all out right now. Let me help you pack some more. And then, why don't you call Owen? It sounds like you need to be with him now." I prayed that Owen wasn't locked up in some smelly prison cell downtown.

"Yeah," she nodded and wiped her eyes. "I do."

After we'd packed a few more boxes, I loaded my car with Ade's clothes and a few things I'd taken from her reject box: picture frames, a half-dead plant I was determined to revive, a hurricane candleholder from Pier 1, and a ceramic serving platter in the shape of a chicken.

She eyed the chicken. "Birthday gift from my crazy cousin. It's all yours," she said as I headed out the door.

"I'll talk to you tomorrow, okay?" I hugged her good-bye.

"Hey, Chloe?"

"Yeah?"

"Thank you. I don't know how I'd do this without you."

"Hey." I smiled at her. "You'd do the same for me. I love you." I waved and left for home.

# EIGHT

**W H Y** would anyone schedule a review class for *eight o'clock* in the morning? Was I never going to get any sleep? At 7:59 a.m. on Thursday, at least twenty-five other graduate students and I were crammed into a small meeting room on campus, all of us desperately clutching coffee cups that held our only hope of wakefulness. At least I wasn't the only one who'd been up late the night before. Doug, however, looked as if he'd slept enough for all of us. He was more bright-eyed than I'd ever want to be at this hour. I knew that he'd been up since five and had already jogged three miles.

"Everyone, let's get started. We have a lot to cover this morning if you want to pass your final exam in Mental Disorders and Diagnostic Skills. I've seen the test, and I want to suggest that you be overprepared. There are fifty multiple-choice questions, fifteen short-answer questions, and four essays. At least two of the essays are clinical descriptions of hypothetical clients. You will determine the appropriate diagnosis, back up your reasoning, and provide a treatment plan." He gave us his best stern teaching-assistant look. Oh, crap.

We reviewed paranoid, antisocial, and borderline personality disorders. Then we moved on to dissociative fugues, social phobias, posttraumatic stress disorder, conversion disorders, impulse-control disorders, and psychotic disorders; and to the complicated system we were supposed to use to categorize and label clients according to the rules of the DSM. At eleven thirty, we'd had only one fifteen-minute break, and my mind was wandering. I was going to see Josh tonight, and if I managed to stay awake after we'd gone out with his chef friends, I might actually get some quality alone time with him. The prospect of quality time occupied me for the next twenty minutes, at the end of which time I was beginning to think that I had a sexual compulsion: instead of memorizing the DSM categories, I was obsessing about getting naked and sweaty under the covers with my boyfriend.

Finally, Doug began to wrap things up. "Everyone, listen up!" he shouted over our restless chattering. "Something you may find helpful in remembering these diagnoses is to associate various disorders with specific clients you've worked with at your field placements, or even with characters from books and films. Do whatever you have to do to remember the symptoms, treatments, and prognoses for what we've talked about today." I briefly wondered whether the DSM could offer a way to identify a murderer, but I decided to ponder the question later. "Good luck. You'll all need it." Doug looked at me and winked.

We walked out together. "So, my friend, Doug. You've seen the test, have you?" I nudged him conspiratorially. "I'm sure you have some helpful advice to pass on to your favorite student, right?"

"Not a word," he grinned. "You'll do fine, though, I'm sure."

"Hey, I'm not asking for a copy of the exam, but you're going to tell me there are no benefits to having befriended a TA?" Actually, Doug was the one who'd befriended me, but I didn't say so, and neither did he.

"You've gained access to my charming sense of humor, my loyalty, my handsome face, my—"

I cut him off. "None of that is going to help me!" I pretended to pout. "I'll just have to lock myself at home and remain in isolation until next week."

"All right. One hint. Pay extra attention to anxiety disorders and personality disorders. And don't worry too much about the code numbers. There's only one question on that."

I looked around to make sure none of my fellow students were watching and then kissed him on the cheek. "Thank you! You're the best."

"Don't thank me yet. You still have a ton of work to do."

"Yes, sir!" I gave him a military salute. "Oh, Doug. I haven't told you what happened at Simmer." After I'd filled him in, we talked for a few minutes about Leandra and about the dangers of living in a big city like Boston.

Doug reminded me to be extra careful when I went to visit Josh at the restaurant. "Make sure you get someone to walk you to your car, okay? And call me if you need to talk about any of this."

"I promise. Do you need a ride?"

Doug shook his head. "Terry's picking me up and taking me to lunch. I've got another review class later this afternoon, but we'll have enough time to eat at a dark and romantic place he found in the North End."

"I'm jealous! Have fun."

When I got to Cleveland Circle, I double-parked and picked up a Pino's pizza. I was ravenous, and nothing except a thin-crust delicious lunch would get me through the afternoon. It wasn't what Josh served on Newbury Street, but a good pizza had a place in my heart. In fact, it seemed to me that Adrianna had almost been justified when she'd threatened to throttle Owen for forgetting a Pino's pizza when she'd been in the throes of a craving.

When I reached my condo, I balanced the pizza on one hand and opened my back door with the other. I could hear the phone ringing as I worked the old lock with my rusty key. Even with caller ID, I hated missing calls, and it drove me crazy to have caller ID display Unknown Caller or, worse, nothing but Incoming Call with no number. When caller ID let me down, I always felt convinced that I'd lost an opportunity to scream at some telemarketer about the National Do Not Call Registry! Missing a call with an actual phone number on caller ID meant that I'd spend twenty minutes Googling in an attempt to trace the call. Was I suffering from an anxiety disorder? Paranoia?

I snatched the phone off its base and practically screamed into the phone. "Hello!"

"Chloe, this is Gavin Seymour."

"Oh, Gavin. How are you doing?"

"Hanging in there. I'm actually calling to see if you'd do me a favor."

"Anything," I said honestly, although I couldn't imagine what I could do to help. Unless he wanted to tap into my half-trained clinical skills?

"I'm organizing a memorial service for Leandra. She was an orphan. Is that the word I want? She didn't have any family that I can locate. When her body is released, I'll arrange for cremation, but for now I'd like to have a gathering at Simmer on Monday. For her friends to share their memories. And grieve."

"Of course I'll be there. Do you want me to call people and let them know?"

"No, I can handle that. But I think it would be nice to have a memory book. Would you be able to put one together? I know it's already Thursday, but I'm sure that people from the restaurant would be more than willing to contribute to the book. Maybe the book is more for me than anyone else, but with no family around, I feel like I need to do something meaningful. Does that make sense to you?"

It did make sense to me. A memory book would give Gavin something tangible to hold on to. How I was going to have one ready for Monday was beyond me, but I obviously had to say yes. "Sure. And I can definitely do it. I think it's a lovely idea, Gavin."

"Thank you. I was thinking we'd all meet at the restaurant between lunch and dinner service, around three o'clock. Simmer is opening again tomorrow, so maybe you could stop by then or this weekend and have Leandra's friends make their contributions to the book? I really appreciate this, Chloe. Thanks again."

He sounded so grateful that I felt like a shrew for worrying about my exams and papers. But I hadn't known Leandra very well, and putting together a memory book seemed like a job for a close friend. Maybe she hadn't had any? I had the impression she'd been far from popular with her fellow employees at Simmer, but she must have had friends outside work. I had no idea who they'd been, and I had no time to find out.

After assuring Gavin that I'd have the memory book with me at Monday's gathering, I hung up, put all my DSM review materials on my coffee table, and dropped onto the couch. My eyes fell shut for a moment. God, I was tired. My lack of sleep and the stress of Leandra's murder were both taking a toll on me. I did discover her body, after all, and even though I didn't have a close emotional connection to her, it was still upsetting.

A scratching noise made me open my eyes. Ken, the hermit crab my nephew had given me for Christmas, was busy rubbing one of his claws against his glass cage in an effort to turn himself around. When Walker had presented me with this gift, I'd had a hard time even saying thanks, and that's putting it lightly. I'd had zero interest in keeping a pet that had ten legs and no fur. Ken had, however, grown on me during the past few months, and his cage was now full of water dishes, climbing structures, and cozy hiding places. Ken lacked a scintillating personality, but so far he hadn't bitten me, and that was more than I could say for Gato, who spent hours staring into Ken's cage, maybe because he liked Ken or maybe because he wanted to eat him. I couldn't tell which.

My stomach growled, and I reached for the pizza. After I'd inhaled two lukewarm slices, I decided to run down to the nearby CVS to pick up some supplies for this memory book I'd promised to do. The weather was great, and I didn't feel like fighting for a parking spot, so a quick walk seemed like a good idea, especially because it was impossible to walk and study at the same time. I grabbed my purse and another slice and started down the outside stairs, only to run into stupid Noah, my neighbor, who was in his usual half-naked state on a chaise longue on the grass. All Noah needed was for the weather to hit anything above fifty degrees, and his clothes flew off his body. Today he wore nothing but running shorts and sunglasses. A boom box was blaring Jimmy Buffett, and it took all the restraint I had not to start smashing Noah over the head with my purse to the beat of "Volcano."

I'd made the idiotic mistake of having a short fling with Noah just before I'd met Josh, and whenever I saw Noah, I was reminded of my bad judgment. Granted, Noah was dark, handsome, and muscular, but aside from his intoxicating looks, he was a prick—a womanizer, a playboy, a bachelor-at-large, however you want to say it. He'd been bed-hopping throughout our entire fling, and I was never going to live down the embarrassment of having looked out my window one morning to see a bleached blonde in a tank top exiting his place. To top it off, Noah felt no shame or guilt whatsoever about his behavior. Everything about him enraged me.

I'd just taken a rather large bite of my pizza and was busy sucking the cheese off the top when he saw me.

"Hello, Chloe." He pushed his sunglasses up onto his head and squinted at me in a sexy way.

I was doomed to have every encounter with Noah find me in some sort of humiliating circumstance. Now, melted cheese dangled out of my mouth, I had no napkins, my hair was mounded in an unflattering bun on top of my head, and I was wearing ragged capri sweatpants. My expensive Victoria's Secret padded bra pushed up and out what I had, but the effect didn't compensate for my overall look of pitiful dishevelment.

He laughed. "Enjoying your lunch, I take it?" Damn him for looking so good! I was the one who'd been dumped and humiliated. Consequently, I was the one who deserved to look spectacular when we saw each other.

Although my gut instinct was to slink silently away, I forced myself to remain calm. I finished chewing, swallowed the cheese, and did my best to wipe the grease off my face with the back of my hand. Then I cleared my throat. "Noah," I said coldly, "I see that you are taking advantage of the global warming crisis. Al Gore would be very disappointed in you. Go plant a tree or install energy-efficient lightbulbs."

"Oh, somebody's cranky today, huh? Do you need some cheering up?"

I exhaled loudly. "I'm cranky because I have final exams. I have work to do, which is evidently a foreign concept to you, since you devote all of *your* time to lolling around admiring yourself."

"I'm glad to hear you think I'm worth admiring." Noah beamed and pulled his sunglasses down.

Argh! I turned, marched off, and waited until I'd turned the corner to tug on a big underwear wedgie that I was sure Noah had noticed. He took every available opportunity to check out my, and everybody else's, ass.

My day so far had consisted of unpleasant events: the excruciating DSM review class, the unwelcome request from Gavin, and yet another maddening brush with Noah. At least I was going to see Josh tonight. The thought eased my mind, especially because Josh was the kind of boyfriend who didn't care whether I had food hanging out of my mouth or bunched-up underwear or ratty, unwashed hair. Even so, my appreciation for Josh made me want to dress up tonight. Not that I was planning on wearing a ball gown, but I did want to look good. What's more, meeting up with Josh's chef friends meant that we'd eat well. The prospect lifted my spirits.

I hit the CVS on Beacon Street and did my best to gather material for a memory book: construction paper, a photo album, and markers. After stocking up on a few household items, I walked down the aisle toward the register. Halfway there, I came upon a thirtysomething man wearing a muscle shirt that revealed arms covered in tattoos. He was clutching his cell phone and nervously scanning the aisles. "What do you mean, *wings*? Where are they flying to?"

I stifled a giggle and pointed out the feminine product he'd clearly been sent to buy. After I'd paid, I took a quick T ride to Coolidge Corner in Brookline and browsed at the Brookline Booksmith. I couldn't believe that Adrianna hadn't read anything about pregnancy or kids. No wonder she was such a wreck! What she needed was information. I put together a collection of what I thought were upbeat introductory books about pregnancy and babies. The superintroductory baby care book Ade actually needed would've had a title like *This Is a Baby* or *How to Avoid Dropping Your Infant on Its Head*, but I settled for a couple of Dr. Sears's books and a few humorous ones on the joys and perils of breast-feeding. I'd practically fallen over when Ade, who didn't like children, had said that she was going to breast-feed. I also upgraded my CVS photo album by buying an expensive scrapbook with a gorgeous fabric cover and rice paper pages. My hopes for the memories that would end up inside were anything but high, so it seemed smart to have an attractive, if deceptive, outer package.

By the time I got home, Noah's narcissistic sunbathing show was over; he was nowhere to be seen. His welcome absence made me think of Doug's advice about memorizing the DSM diagnoses by associating them with particular people: I wondered whether Noah counted as having a narcissistic personality disorder. I'd have to look up the full list of symptoms, but Noah certainly did display a "pervasive pattern of grandiosity" and a "need for admiration." Furthermore, he had the empathy of a rock. God, Josh would be rip-roaring mad if he knew that I was thinking about Noah. And Noah, the narcissist, would just love it.

At my computer, I printed out requests to Simmer's staff members to put their loving memories of Leandra in writing and to give the results to Josh or to me. At the top of the page I had a brief sentence encouraging the staff: *"Gavin hopes to fill a memory book with the staff's fond remembrances of Leandra. Please include any detailed feelings, anecdotes, or thoughts about Simmer's lost employee."* At the bottom of the page I wrote my phone number and e-mail address, and I even volunteered to write up the memories for anyone who wanted to call me. The easier I made the task, the more people who'd do it. Or so I hoped.

Josh called as the last page was printing.

"Hi, babe. You're still coming out with us tonight, right?"

"Of course. Where are we going?"

"Porcaro said to come see him at the Hub."

Josh always called Mark Porcaro by his last name. He was the executive chef at Top of the Hub, the restaurant at the top of the skyscraper known as the Pru, the Prudential building. Smack downtown, the restaurant offered fabulous views of Boston. Tall, wide windows wrapped around the dining and bar area. The Pru's Skywalk Observatory gave a three-hundred-sixty-degree panorama, and I was hoping that we'd get a chance to walk around. The city looked especially beautiful at night. But most importantly, the food at the Hub was awesome. I'd been there only once before, when Josh and I had had a few appetizers at the bar, but they'd been wonderful. Because we were friends of Mark's, I was sure he'd "take care of us," as Josh always said, meaning that delicious off-the-menu dishes would magically appear from the kitchen.

"Cool. Who else is coming?" I asked.

"Digger and Lefty are meeting us there, but they won't be free until ten. How 'bout I pick you up at quarter of?"

Digger and Lefty, whose real names I didn't even know, were both chefs. I was beginning to wonder whether the culinary industry had some peculiar regulation that required chefs to use pseudonyms. If so, Josh must have been granted a special exemption.

"Sounds good. That'll give me time to finish this stupid paper I have to write. And remind me to give you the flyers I have for you to pass out at Simmer."

"Flyers for what?" he wondered aloud.

"Nothing. Gotta run. I'll see you tonight!"

"Wait! I don't like the sound of this. What are these flyers about?" Josh laughed.

"You'll see." The less time I gave Josh to protest his assignment, the better.

# NINE

JOSH parked his Xterra in the underground garage at the Prudential. As we rode the elevator up what seemed like four hundred floors to Top of the Hub, I gazed at my boyfriend. I was unused to seeing him out of his chef's clothes. Well, I mean, I always enjoyed seeing him out of his chef's clothes, but tonight he actually had on *regular people* clothing. He was looking very handsome in his clean, stain-free ivory T-shirt and army green cargo pants. Josh was about as dressed up as he ever got.

"What are you smiling at?" Josh asked, wrapping his arm around me and kissing the top of my head.

The elevator doors opened. I didn't answer until we were waiting by the hostess stand near the bar. "I'm smiling at you. You look really good. And rested." Although he still had bags under his eyes, he looked better than he had in weeks. I could hardly believe that we were having a night out. I didn't even remember the last time we'd gone out anywhere together. I tried not to remember that our good luck was the result of Leandra's murder, which was the only reason that Simmer was closed tonight.

Josh nodded. "Well, I took a four-hour nap this afternoon, but I'm still missing weeks of sleep. You're not looking so bad yourself, kiddo."

I was glad that even in his exhausted state, he noticed my appearance. In getting ready to go out, I'd taken more time than usual. I had on a totally cute ivory baby doll dress with slight scrunching at the hems—another loan from Adrianna. I was pushing the arrival of warm weather, so I'd thrown on a cozy cashmere cardigan, also from Ade, to keep me from freezing.

The host seated us at a corner table and gave us menus. There was a Top of the Hub Tasting Menu and a Chef's Tasting Menu, both of which looked phenomenal and could be ordered with the recommended wines. I scanned through those and the regular menu, salivating at the descriptions. A bunch jumped out at me:

### Sautéed Foie Gras
*Peach Compote, Brioche Toast*

### Native Lobster and Avocado Citrus Salad
*Dill Oil, Fresh Tarragon Vinaigrette*

### Crispy Calamari
*Asian Slaw and Roasted Pineapple Dressing*

### Jonah and Lump Crabmeat Cake
*Avocado Cream, Crispy Plantains, Corn Salad*

### Pan-Seared Scallops
*Orange Fennel Salad, Potato Galette, Chorizo Emulsion*

### Hazelnut Crusted Salmon
*Apple Celery Root Salad, Sweet Potato Puree, Apple Gastrique*

### Adobo Rubbed Grilled Center Cut Pork Chop
*Creamy Masa, Tomatillo Cream*

*Apple gastrique?* Whatever it was, it sounded delicious.

"Chloe? Are you still with me?" Josh sat across from me and was nudging my menu with his.

I had spaced out while studying the menu. "What? Oh, yeah. I'm here. It's just that the food looks so incredible."

Josh cleared his throat. "Okay, I'm feeling a little jealous here. Now, Porcaro's a good chef and all, but don't forget about me," he said teasingly. Then he hid behind the menu.

"I don't love you just for your food, you know." I looked at him seriously. "Although it helps."

Josh peeked out at me from behind the menu. "I'm going to have Porcaro send out hot dogs if you don't watch yourself."

"You have nothing to worry about, and you know it. Oh,

Digger and Lefty are here." I pointed to his friends, who were walking toward us. The three chefs had worked together a few years earlier at a now-defunct restaurant. They'd stayed in touch mainly by leaving one another voice mails. It was a rare occasion when their schedules let them get together in person.

Digger was the executive chef at a small but fabulous one-year-old tapas restaurant in the South End, where Lefty was his sous chef. Both of them looked as tired as Josh, but they were clearly happy to see their old friend. Digger was in his late thirties but already had lots of gray showing in his wavy locks, which he wore pulled back and fastened with an elastic. His dark, leathery skin made me think he'd spent too many long days in the sun while growing up in Hawaii, but he was ruggedly handsome. He was still wearing kitchen clogs, and when he leaned in to hug me hello, I enjoyed the familiar kitchen smells. Josh always carried that same scent after work. In fact, the kitchen odors permeated his chef pants and coats so thoroughly that even after I'd taken all of Josh's work clothes and laundered them myself, they'd still smelled fresh out of the kitchen. I'd given up and told him to keep using his laundry service.

Lefty greeted me in his usual formal style. "Hello, ma'am," he said as he nodded politely and shook my hand. In spite of all the times I'd hung out with Lefty, he still insisted on calling me ma'am and treating me with old-fashioned courtesy, even though he was only a few years older than I was.

"When are you going to start using my name?" I asked him.

"I can't do that, ma'am."

I smiled at him. Lefty's formality suggested that he had grown up in the South or had been in the military, but he was from Lynn, Massachusetts, and spent his working life as a civilian in Boston. He was charming and incredibly sweet.

Digger sat next to Josh, and Lefty next to me.

"S'up, Dig? Good to finally see you!" Josh gave him a manly clap on the back. "How's the restaurant going? Lefty giving you problems as usual?"

"Yeah, you know him. That pain in the ass is full of back talk and can't cook his way out of a hole. Right, dude?"

"That is correct, Chef." Lefty cracked a smile.

"Nah, it's all good there. The usual shit, but it's good. I've still got that moron Pete working for me, but mostly I've got a solid staff." Digger downed his entire glassful of water. "God, I'm thirsty. We were hustling tonight at work."

"Which one is Pete again?" Josh asked.

"Pete's that guy who talked his way into the cook job. He's Lefty's backup. Anyway, he talked a good game, and, like an asshole, I hired him. When it came time to put on the coat, it turns out he can't boil water without screwing something up. No matter how many times I show him how to do something, he always screws it up. Last week he sent out seven rare cods in a row. I mean, Jesus, who wants to eat uncooked cod, right? I just walked out of service. I said, 'I'm done. Nobody call me. The rest of you can deal with this.' And so I left. But Pete hasn't undercooked the cod since. His latest problem is that he keeps sending out the tuna without the balsamic reduction. He's unbelievable."

"So how are you going to fix that problem?" I wondered aloud. Digger presumably couldn't keep walking out of dinner service.

"Easy. I told Pete that every time he sends the tuna out without the sauce, I'm gonna kick him in the shins."

My mouth dropped open. "You are *not* going to do that, are you?"

"I already have. I don't knock him to the floor or anything, but yeah, I kick him in the shins. He's doing much better."

I looked at Josh, expecting him to be at least somewhat startled, but he nodded in understanding. "You gotta do what you gotta do, man. There are always idiots in a kitchen. Speaking of raw food, remember the chicken story?" Josh and Digger started laughing.

"What's the chicken story?" I asked.

"You tell it, Josh," said Digger, grinning. "I can't. I'll get too pissed off again."

"Chloe doesn't want to hear that story," Lefty said.

"Yes, I do. Tell it!" I demanded, always eager for insider kitchen tales.

Josh leaned back in his chair. "Digger and I were working together at this family-style place, and the owner had booked a rehearsal dinner party. Now, the bride was the daughter of the bank manager from the bank that had the note on the restaurant, so obviously we were supposed to do a bang-up job, right? Digger and I were basically running the show, but we weren't doing much of the actual cooking that night, although we'd done all the prep the day before. Everything was fine until the entrées were served, and all of sudden the kitchen door goes flying open, and the bank manager comes in practically breathing fire and screaming that we've ruined his daughter's wedding. Turns out all the chicken is perfectly browned on the outside and still clucking on the inside. The guy in charge of cooking the chicken had the temperature too hot and browned the birds off too fast."

"Oh, God. That is really disgusting. The bank guy must've been furious," I said.

"He was good and mad, and we were shaking in our clogs because the owner was going to know about this, too. So this guy doesn't hit us or anything, which was lucky, and he ends up just saying, 'We are done for the night.' And the whole party left."

"Did you guys get fired for that? Or your cook?"

Digger shook his head. "No, no one got fired. We blamed the cook, but obviously it was our fault, too. We had to accept some of the responsibility, right?"

"What happened to the cook?" I asked, giggling. "Sounds like it was really all his fault."

Josh looked at Lefty. "He's sitting right next to you."

I turned to Lefty, embarrassed for him. "I'm sorry I laughed at you."

"Ma'am, it was my fault. There was no excuse."

Digger reached across the table to mess up Lefty's neat hair. "Yeah, but I took him with me when I left anyhow, right, dude? You know when someone deserves a second chance. And he hasn't undercooked a chicken since. It's just Pete I gotta worry about now. Who knows what he's doing tonight? But at least we'd stopped serving when Lefty and I came to meet you guys."

"What're you losers doing here?" Chef Mark Porcaro appeared at our table. "Chloe excluded from that, of course." He smiled at me and then shook hands all around.

Mark had the same rough, nearly fireproof, hands that Josh did. Josh called them *asbestos hands*. Chefs could dunk their fingers into simmering sauces, test the heat on griddles, or pick up hot-from-the-oven food with their bare hands. It never failed to make me cringe when Josh dipped a finger into a boiling pot.

"Did you guys order yet?" Porcaro asked. Many restaurants stopped serving dinner at ten or offered only limited menus in the late evening. Because Top of the Hub offered a full menu until one in the morning, it was the perfect meeting spot for chefs when they got off work at their own restaurants.

"Not yet. What should we get?" Josh asked. "I think Chloe might want one of everything you got."

I held up my hand to stop him. "Very funny. That might be a little much, even for me. Although I have to try the crispy calamari dish."

"You want me to just send out whatever?" *That's* exactly what you want to hear from a chef like Mark Porcaro.

"Anything you want. Thanks, man." Josh shook Mark's hand again and let him go back into the kitchen to work on whatever treats he was going to create for us.

Our server arrived to take our drink orders. We got Heinekens all around.

"Josh, how's Simmer doing? Do you guys have steady business yet?" Lefty asked.

"It's coming along. Still unpredictable. One night we're swamped, the next we're empty. But I think the warm weather is really going to help us, especially with the patio area we have."

"Yeah, if those Newbury Street shoppers can put down their Gucci bags long enough to eat anything." Digger snorted. "I'm just kidding. But I'd think you've got an interesting crowd coming in there, to say the least."

"You're not kidding," Josh agreed. "Chloe, I don't know if I told you this one, but last week these two couples come in late. At like nine thirty, right, when we're basically starting to break down. Two business-type men with their wives—all dolled up. So they get liquored up and make it through their apps fine. And the problems start. So one of the men had ordered the swordfish, and I had one piece of it left. Would have been fine except that I wasn't paying attention, and I burned it. Seriously burned it beyond recognition. Their server went out and explained that, in fact, there wasn't any swordfish. And this guy just flips out and demands to see me. So I go out covered in grease, I'm all sweaty and smelly, to talk to this group of dressed-up tight-asses. I said to the guy, 'Look, I'm sorry, but I lost your swordfish. What else can I get for you?' and he completely doesn't get what I'm saying because he's had too much top-shelf liquor. He starts yelling at me because he truly believes that I literally lost his damn fish. 'You don't just *lose* a piece of swordfish! It must be there! How can you not find it? I can't believe you call yourself a chef. The appetizers were shit anyway!' This guy was a piece of work."

"So what happened?" I had no idea that customers ever behaved that way.

"Well, then he takes the wine bottle that had been chilling in a marble cooler on their table, and he smashes the bottle on the cooler and continues screaming at me, and there I am, having just worked fourteen hours, and I've got to deal with this punk. Wade and Kevin came and threw him out before he got it together to do anything with the broken bottle."

"Dude, that sucks!" Digger clapped his hands together. "Everybody is entitled to be unhappy with their food, right? But that is out of control. I've never had anything that bad happen. Usually it's just someone saying nasty stuff like I need to learn how to cook, or the plate doesn't match the description on the menu. Your food must blow to have made that guy so mad!" Digger leaned to the side before Josh could whack his arm.

Porcaro returned with two servers, all carrying plates of beautiful food. One tray held an absolutely delectable-looking assortment of sashimi and maki complete with splays of finely cut vegetables, wasabi paste, and thinly sliced pickled ginger. What else? Swordfish with a mango salad and coconut jasmine rice; smoked duck confit with a goat cheese tart, golden raisin sauce, and fig syrup; pan-seared halibut with roasted tomato, baby artichoke, a potato truffle hash, and vegetable bouillon. Also, the foie gras, the scallops, and the salmon that I'd noticed on the menu. Wow! Oh, and the crispy calamari with the Asian slaw and roasted pineapple dressing!

"I'll see if I can pop back out in a few minutes, okay? Enjoy! And I hope everything is all right," Porcaro said with completely false modesty. He knew he was good.

Lefty, of course, gestured for me to help myself first. I didn't protest. But I did have to fight my way around Josh and Digger. I bit into a ring of chewy calamari and moaned with delight. The calamari had been tossed into the slaw with the sweet pineapple dressing to become the ultimate spring salad. Phenomenal.

"Mmm . . . Hey, did you guys hear about Leandra?" Josh asked as he noshed on a piece of fresh yellowtail that he'd piled with wasabi and ginger.

"We were just talking about that on the way over." Lefty nodded. "That is awful. Wait! She worked for you, didn't she?"

Josh's mouth was too full to answer, so I spoke for him. "Yes. She was a server there. Actually, I was one of the people who found her. Did you know her?"

"Lefty and I have both worked with Leandra before, only at different restaurants. She's worked all over the place, so the odds are we would've run into her at some point. Pretty nasty story. Do they know what happened yet?"

I shook my head. "No, although it seems pretty clear she didn't die from natural causes." Those marks on her neck? I still had no idea what had caused them. "And, well, since you two knew her, maybe you could help me with something." I popped a piece of duck into my mouth. "I don't know if you knew that Gavin and Leandra were dating, but he asked me to try to gather some stories, memories, thoughts, that kind of thing, to put together into a book. Maybe you guys have something I could put in?" I was pleading.

"I'm not sure most of the memories I have of her are going to work for your book," Lefty informed me politely.

"Why wouldn't they work?"

"Leandra had her moments. She could be a little difficult." Lefty looked at Digger for help.

"She was a bitch," said Digger.

"How do you mean? Did a lot of people hate her?" If Digger or Lefty could point out anyone who might have hated Leandra enough to kill her, it might take the heat off of poor Owen.

"It's not like I wished her dead or anything," Digger began. "But she was nasty and rude a lot of the time. She was one of those people that would kiss the customers' asses and then treat the kitchen staff like shit. She'd flirt with the front-of-the-house guys and then make fun of them behind their back. Act like she was too good for them."

Lefty agreed. "Leandra hurt a lot of feelings everywhere she worked. She was pretty good at her job, but she could be a monster to work with. Restaurant people like to have fun. Plain and simple. And Leandra did her best to ruin that. For instance, we always play practical jokes on the new staff, okay? Nothing too awful, and it's all in fun. So when Dig and I worked with her, we made a batch of cayenne cookies one time. Chefs cook for the staff a lot as a way to say thank you for their work and all that, but this time we baked up a bunch of nasty cookies. Spicy. Everyone else who ate them got mad at us, sure, but they eventually laughed and didn't hold a grudge. Leandra threw a hissy fit and started telling us what a bunch of juvenile assholes we all were, and then she told the owner. Pardon my language, ma'am. Not that he was going to fire us or anything, but still. Then the weird thing was, the next time a new girl was hired, Leandra got her a soda and laced the straw with Tabasco sauce. Leandra laughed so hard she almost choked. That's the kind of person she was." Lefty bit into a scallop and took a swig of his beer.

Digger jumped in. "She might have been good at her job, but she was the first person to point a finger at someone else. Like, at a restaurant, the chef's food cost gets blown to shit from things like bad servers who take forever with their tables or let food sit out so long that we can't serve it anymore. People make mistakes with orders, and food has to get thrown out. Stuff like that. Leandra didn't do that, but she had no problem shouting about who fouled what up. You just don't do that. Maybe you bitch about it with a few other people, but Leandra was the one who was always ratting people out to the GM or the owner. Again, not that she deserved to die for that, but she wasn't liked much. Damn, this swordfish is kickin'!" Digger licked mango salsa off his lips. "Oh, sorry, Josh. Maybe I shouldn't mention swordfish. Don't want to give you flashbacks."

"Thanks for the sensitivity. I think I'll be okay," Josh assured him.

"Josh, was Leandra like that at Simmer?" I asked him.

"Yes and no. I mean, she and Blythe hated each other, but I think that was because they are so similar in some ways. They both get a lot of attention from the guys and all that and they're both pretty outspoken. Were, I guess. Were. But, yeah, Leandra was good at pushing people's buttons. Just a general snottiness and bitchiness. But once she and Gavin started dating, she calmed down a little."

"He must have seen something in her, though," I said. "Leandra must've had some good qualities. Otherwise, Gavin would've dumped her right away. He seems like a normal enough guy. I can't imagine he'd put up with constant awful behavior."

Or, I wondered, had Gavin discovered that Leandra wasn't the woman he'd thought she was?

"I don't think Gavin knew about everything she did," Josh said. "Like, Leandra called Isabelle 'rat girl' all the time because she used to live on the streets, but I don't think she said that in front of her boyfriend and boss."

Now I was pissed. It was one thing to call Blythe flat-chested but quite another thing to call Isabelle "rat girl." Leandra *was* a bitch! Poor Isabelle! It ticked me off to think that I'd found her a job in Josh's kitchen only to have her subjected to name-calling. "Didn't you do anything?" I demanded.

"There wasn't much to do except tell her to lay off, which I did. But Isabelle has to learn to fight her own battles. And it's not like we have an HR department."

That was true. Was it ever! Very few workplaces of any kind would have tolerated the kind of behavior that the chefs had just described. I couldn't imagine that employees at Goldman Sachs, for instance, would be allowed to kick each other in the shins or lace straws with Tabasco in between managing assets. I'd spent the past year interning at the Boston Organization Against Sexual and Other Harassment in the Workplace. Although I was in the habit of referring to it as the BO, I'd actually learned a lot about handling inappropriate workplace conduct. In the world of restaurants, however, conduct that would have been outrageous elsewhere was considered normal. There was an unspoken rule about paying dues: You had to put up with abuse to prove yourself worthy of your position and to move up in the ranks. If you complained about how you were treated, you faced a serious uphill battle that you'd fight with little or no support. Restaurants run by big corporations didn't allow that kind of hazing, but it flourished in small independent establishments, which, sadly enough, were often the places that served the best food. The macho quality of the initiation rites wasn't surprising, since most professional chefs were men. There were exceptions: Julia Child, Jody Adams, and Lydia Shire came to mind, as did the female chefs featured on the Food Network. Even so, and in spite of the stereotype of home cooking as women's work, the culinary world was dominated by men. Why? That's exactly what I asked the table.

"You're right," Digger agreed. "It's dominated by men, and it probably comes from a couple things. The kitchen can have a pretty nasty caveman attitude. Culinary school is brutal, and I think a lot of women drop out of the profession then. Like, when I was there, I had this crazy old Swiss chef as one of my instructors. Real bastard, that guy. And one day I went to go change the oil in the Frialator. So the oil is kept in this big vat in a stainless steel cabinet right next to the Frialator. Well, someone had rigged it so that when I opened the door, the whole goddamn thing fell out and spilled dirty oil all over this twenty-by-ten area. Okay, obviously not my fault, but this Swiss chef made me clean the whole frickin' thing up by myself. You can imagine how much fun that was." Digger snorted at the memory. "Then he made me spend the next two days doing nothing but peeling vegetables. Not fair, right, since I didn't monkey with the oil vat?"

I nodded.

Digger continued. "Now, how many women would put up with that?"

"Most women probably have more common sense than to tolerate obnoxious, juvenile behavior," I agreed.

"I went to the CIA," continued Digger, referring to the Culinary Institute of America, "and I'd say the ratio of men to women was four to one. By the second year, there were even fewer women. The kitchen is a vulgar, intense, foul-mouthed place to be. Guys are always grabbing each others' asses, there's tons of sexual jokes being told, and all that crap. And women don't want to put up with it."

As I saw the problem, there was no need for women to learn to suck it up; on the contrary, that kind of bullshit shouldn't be allowed in the first place. I hated to consider what my beloved Josh might be like. I knew, however, that Josh went out of his way to make his female employees comfortable—the few he had, that is.

Josh jumped in. "The other reality is that the hours you have to work as a chef aren't family friendly. Most women who want children don't want to be gone from their kids twelve hours a day and really don't want to work until past midnight. Right or wrong, men are more willing to do that. They're more willing to put in the hours, claw their way to the top, and tough it out. But," Josh continued, seeing my feminist side beginning to boil over, "let me say that I've worked with a couple excellent women chefs before, and I *do* wish there were more women in this field. But it's a chauvinistic field. There's no denying that."

"You've only worked with a *couple* of women chefs?"

"Yeah," Josh admitted. "But I'm not even thirty yet, so give me some time." He smiled in the hope of lightening my declining mood.

"How come Isabelle is the only female in your kitchen now?" I was irritated.

"Because when I was hiring, I didn't have any women come in to interview. I have no problem hiring women, but if they don't apply, I can't hire them."

"Okay, well, that's not your fault, I guess," I conceded.

"Same here," volunteered Digger. "I've worked for more than two women, but still only a few, and I'm well *over* thirty, and I've worked at a lot of places. Some of the women chefs have been crap, and a few have been great. Actually, one of my biggest influences was the first chef I worked for, who was a woman. She was the most awesome chef. She used great flavors. She went through hell with us and gave us just as much crap as we dished out. I think most women in the kitchen have this tendency to be real timid, you know? You gotta pay your dues and peel fifty pounds of potatoes when you start out, no matter who you are or who you know. Women take that to mean that they're being ignored or treated unfairly. And in this profession, a woman has to stand out and grow some balls. You can't hide out or be squeamish. When you get out of school, it's easy to disappear into a hotel job and shape cantaloupes to make a pretty fruit plate. Women give up and don't always want to play the game."

"So a woman has to act like a man? Like an imbecile?" I crossed my arms and glared at Digger. "Do you think any of this has to do with the whole idea that women in positions of authority are labeled bitchy and men are labeled confident?"

Lefty braved the conversation. "Unfortunately, yes, ma'am. That is very likely. Like they were saying, this is not a perfect profession. There are still very outdated attitudes in the culinary world, and we're all guilty of allowing that to happen."

I settled for saying, "Yes, you are. It's not the nineteen forties."

Lefty got points for acknowledging men's contribution. I probably lost points for finding it cute that he called me ma'am. My one year of social work hadn't granted me the

magical power to remedy female oppression or even to eradicate sexism from my own attitudes. But maybe the vivid
picture that Digger, in particular, had portrayed of the macho environment in restaurant kitchens could give me some
insight into Leandra's murder. I hoped, and strongly suspected, that the atmosphere in Josh's kitchen fell toward the
lower end of the machismo continuum. Furthermore, it
sounded as if Leandra, far from resenting idiotic antics, had
willingly participated in them. Still, it was possible that
one of Simmer's employees had taken a joke too far. Could
Leandra have been accidentally killed in a kitchen prank? If
so, Josh, Snacker, Isabelle, Javier, or Santos might have had
something to do with her death. But Leandra hadn't actually worked in the kitchen. Were Simmer's front-of-the-
house employees, people like Wade, Kevin, Blythe, and the
other servers, also guilty of fraternity-style behavior? And
what kind of prank gone wrong could have resulted in Leandra's death?

Even Top of the Hub's out-of-this-world dessert menu
didn't make me feel better. And I still had nothing to put in
Leandra's memory book except one unflattering word: *bitch*.

# TEN

JOSH slept over. Cranky though I was about the dinner conversation, I trusted Josh to treat people fairly. I pushed aside my annoyance at the culinary field's rampant unfairness to women and let Josh compensate me for it. Plus, this was one of the few nights I had with him when we were both awake, and I wasn't about to pass up such a pleasurable opportunity.

My overworked chef left for Simmer before eight the next morning. I got out of bed sometime after nine. The only positive spin I could put on my Leandra memory book assignment was that I'd get to see Josh again today. To get material for the memory book, I was obviously going to have to march down to the restaurant and physically extract positive remarks from the employees. The possibility of inventing loving remembrances crossed my mind. In fact, it appealed to me. The hitch was that the entire Simmer staff would attend the memorial service on Monday, and it would be a little awkward to present a memory book filled with quotations that sang Leandra's praises attributed to people who had disliked her. So, using my imagination was a last resort. I was sure that if I approached the Simmer staff in person, everyone would be hard-pressed to say anything but nice things about their deceased coworker. That was the plan.

Before leaving for Simmer, I opened all the windows to my condo to let fresh spring air into my little space. Even with the windows closed and locked, it would've been easy enough to break in. If a burglar showed up in my absence, at least there wouldn't be any damage to the doors or windows. Or so I rationalized.

When I reached Simmer, I stood outside the front door on Newbury Street and phoned Josh, who left the kitchen to let me in. I'd had zero interest in revisiting the back alley and had driven around side streets for twenty minutes until I'd found a parking spot. The weather forecast called for blue skies, bright sunshine, and temperatures in the mid-sixties, so I was sure that the patio would be packed for lunch today. Consequently, a lot of the staff would probably be scheduled to work, and I'd have an excellent chance of cornering Leandra's colleagues and squeezing quotable remarks from them.

Josh swung open the front door. "Hi, babe. How you

doing? You still mad at me?" He pulled me in close and kissed my neck softly.

"I wasn't mad at you."

"I knew you weren't that mad since people who are really mad wouldn't have let me do what I did last night. Right?" he teased.

"Get that look off your face." But I couldn't help smiling. "I really wasn't mad at you. I was just disappointed to hear what you guys had to say last night. But everything that was said just goes to point out what rational beings women are. And frankly, Digger's comments, especially, reflect badly on the male species. I just think it would be responsible of you to do your part to change the culinary world's attitude toward women, at least in your kitchen. Be a role model."

"Chloe, seriously. Right now, I am doing everything I can just to keep this place running!"

His tone of voice told me that I'd chosen a bad time to enjoin him to stand up for women's rights. My face fell.

"God, I'm sorry. Come here," he wrapped his arms around me. "You're right. You are. I'm swamped right now. That's all. Snacker just got here, and Javier doesn't come in until this afternoon, and I really need those extra hands today. That's no excuse, but I've got so much going through my head all the time. I'm going to work on it, though, I promise. It's important."

I hugged him back. "It's okay. And thank you."

"I love you."

"I love you, too."

Josh kissed the top of my head. "Let's go in. Be prepared.

It's going to be a madhouse back there soon, so I don't know how much you'll get out of these people."

We stepped into the kitchen. Santos was sweating over the stove, where he was stirring steaming vats of a highly seasoned broth. Isabelle was at one of the stainless counters working on vegetables. Snacker was on the phone rolling his eyes and looking exasperated. Wade, Kevin, Blythe, and several servers I didn't know were rushing in and out of the kitchen.

"Why are things so nuts today?" I asked Josh.

"This is what happens when you reopen. Everything has to be prepped again, and we're still getting more orders in. Belita and her assistants just showed up. Don't ask me why they're late. The waitstaff is here early because that party that we canceled the day Leandra died is now coming in to-night, and that has to be perfect, so they're making sure everything is in shape. And the patio should be booming for lunch and—"

"Breathe!" I interrupted him. "Why isn't Javier here yet?"

"What? Yeah, I don't have time to breathe today. And Javier isn't scheduled to work until later in the day because I'll catch hell from Gavin for my labor cost, and he's already pissed at me over my food cost. Anyhow, good luck with your memory book."

"Perhaps you'd like to be the first to give me something for the book?" I said wistfully.

Josh sighed. "Sure. Give me the paper."

I handed over a page, and Josh snapped it into his clipboard. I remained silent for a moment, desperately hoping no one would need him for sixty seconds.

"There you go," he said, returning his page.

"That's it?"

Josh had written all of four words: *"Leandra will be missed."*

"I'm sure *someone* will miss her," he insisted. "I'm not going to lie on a memorial page! I'm sorry she was murdered, really I am, but I can't honestly say that I'm going to miss her. Here, I'll add more." Josh grabbed his page back.

*"She was a hard worker who interacted energetically with her fellow employees."*

"That sounds like she was doing calisthenics with everyone!" I complained.

"Take it or leave it, kiddo." Josh shrugged his shoulders.

I growled. "I'm going to find someone who has something nice to say about this poor girl."

"I love you for your optimism. I have to talk to Isabelle."

"She better not be peeling carrots or sculpting cantaloupes all day!" I warned him as he walked over to her station.

Josh's written comments did not bode well for my assignment.

Aha! Belita, the cleaning woman I'd spoken with the other day, crossed the kitchen and went into the dining area. She might be able to give me something about Leandra. With luck, it would be something positive. Belita, after all, hadn't worked directly with Leandra.

Waving my papers above my head, I scurried into the dining room. "Belita! Belita!"

She turned to me and put down her bucket and mop. "Oh, *hola*, Chloe." She smiled warmly and then brushed some straggly hair from her face.

"*Por favor,* could I talk to you?"

"*Sí*, okay," she said, nodding. "I so honest, you know? Not like some of these others here!" She gestured to the bathroom. "I obey laws, okay? Who else, with this drugs everywhere? I do nothing wrong."

Did Belita think that I was here to ask her about Leandra's murder? "I just wondered if you had any happy memories of Leandra that I could write down here." I showed her my memory pages. "Maybe you could ask your friends if they have anything to say about her?"

"Leandra?" Belita blew air from her lips. "She like the others, you know? Nobody sees me here except nice Jason and Josh. And that Gavin, he pay me in cash, which I like very much. But that girl never see me!"

*Leandra regularly ignored the cleaning crew.* I couldn't write that! "Would anyone else you know want to say something?"

"That Kevin! He takes bottles. All the time, he is taking bottles. Javier tell me this. That poor Gavin! He nice, nice man to me!"

We had hit a communication breakdown. Among other things, I didn't know enough Spanish to discuss memory books. And what did Belita mean about Kevin? He was taking bottles? Her accent, however, made *Kevin* and *Gavin* sound similar. Maybe I had misunderstood. Or maybe not.

Both Kevin and Gavin picked up and moved bottles. Kevin was, after all, a bartender, and Gavin owned Simmer.

"So Kevin took bottles?" I tried to clarify.

"*Sí,* Kevin take Gavin's bottles to him! All the time! That Leandra know, and she no care!"

I still wasn't following, and I didn't have time to try to decipher what she was telling me. I wished that I'd taken Spanish in high school and felt embarrassed that I couldn't understand Belita. She knew a hundred times more English than I knew Spanish. "Belita, did you like Leandra at all?" I was willing to take anything, even some neutral comment.

"Leandra was bitch!" Belita declared as she spat into a bucket.

I sensed a common theme.

"Okay. Well, thanks anyway."

"You? You is nice girl. You, I like." Belita patted my cheek and left to do her work.

Isabelle was one of the sweetest people I knew. I could certainly count on her to give me something appropriate for Monday's celebration of Leandra's life. I again braved the kitchen, where I now found Isabelle slicing beef tenderloin—and not, I was pleased to note, carving fruit displays.

"Hi, Isabelle," I greeted her.

"Hey, Chloe! Look, Josh is letting me slice the beef for the party today. Isn't that cool? Josh said I've been doing such a good job with everything else he's taught me that he's going to let me take on more responsibilities. I'm even helping him plate the dishes for that party!" She must have been the happiest beef slicer in the entire world. I silently thanked Josh for supporting her.

"I'm so glad that you're enjoying your job. Josh must be impressed with you if he's giving you more responsibility. He makes everyone pay dues and earn his respect, so you must have been doing something right." In case she felt unfairly treated in Josh's kitchen, I passed along some of my feminist insights from the previous night's dinner.

Isabelle's only response was to say, "Josh is great! I love it here!" She smiled as she continued working.

I explained about the memory book and asked whether she had anything to contribute.

Isabelle's face hardened. "Leandra didn't like me very much. Did you know she called me 'rat girl'? She used to tease me about having grown up the way I did, and she said Josh only gave me this job because he felt sorry for me. Do you think that's true?" She clapped the knife down onto the cutting board.

"No. Josh didn't pity you, Isabelle. Josh talked to you before he offered you this job, right?"

She nodded.

"Well, he must have seen something in you that gave him a good feeling about hiring you. Nobody made Josh hire you. You got this job on your own, and you're keeping it on your own."

Leandra was lucky to be dead. If she'd been alive, I'd have murdered her myself! Well, I'd have felt like it. In reality, I'd have delivered a nasty talking-to that included words like *ignorant* and *insensitive*, and I'd have engaged in lots of dramatic finger-pointing.

"Leandra was terrible," Isabelle said. "She fooled Gavin into going out with her. He is nothing but wonderful, and I don't know how she tricked him into liking her, but she did. So, no. I don't have anything to give you for this memory book!" The usually soft-spoken Isabelle had raised her voice enough to make Josh and Santos look over.

I didn't like the way Isabelle was acting. I understood it, but I didn't like it. She clearly had a big crush on Gavin. Could she have been so distraught about his relationship with Leandra that she'd murdered her? The truth was, I didn't know Isabelle very well. I'd met her when I'd volunteered at the agency that had been helping her to get off the streets and create a better life for herself. She'd seemed sweet and eager to work hard, but I hadn't known and still didn't know much else about her. Josh said she was a quick learner who was devoted to his kitchen. She could still have a dark side, couldn't she? It was unthinkable to me that Isabelle was involved in Leandra's death. Almost unthinkable.

My thoughts returned to Belita's statement that Kevin was taking bottles. Could Belita have meant that Kevin was *stealing* bottles of liquor? Would a Simmer employee do such a horrible thing? What kind of person would undercut Gavin's and Josh's efforts to make Simmer a success? The same kind of person who would commit murder? If Leandra had found out about the stealing, she might have confronted Kevin and threatened to tell Gavin. I knew all too well how hard Josh was working to make Simmer profitable and how deeply Gavin cared about his restaurant. Meanwhile, their main bartender, Kevin, was stealing from the restaurant? What a terrible thing to do! Restaurants, I knew, made most of their money from alcohol sales. I'd been a little horrified to learn just how high the markups on alcohol were. The funny thing about restaurant alcohol sales, Josh had explained to me, was that cheaper bottles of wine were the ones that were marked up most, whereas the expensive, high-quality wines were marked up least. If someone—Kevin?—stole a bottle of wine that had cost Simmer ten dollars and would have sold for twenty-eight dollars, the restaurant's loss would be greater than the original cost of the wine. But any thievery would cost the restaurant *something,* and if Leandra had discovered that someone was pilfering, she might have been outraged enough to confront the culprit. Perhaps Gavin's girlfriend had paid dearly for protecting Simmer? Or, more true to her character, she was somehow protecting herself? My impulse was to present the idea to Josh and Gavin, but I was far from sure that I'd understood Belita correctly. She might not have meant that Kevin had been stealing.

I returned to the task of gathering material for the memory book. I hoped that the front-of-the-house staff, who'd worked closely with Leandra, would have fond recollections of her. At this point, I'd have been overjoyed to hear even a few neutral statements about Leandra: she'd liked roses, her favorite food had been raspberry sorbet, she'd preferred bourbon to scotch, and she'd been crazy about dancing to zydeco. Anything!

Snacker had slipped past me while I'd been speaking to Belita. He was now schmoozing Blythe while she set up tables. Forget it! I loved Snacker, but I wasn't up for watching him salivate all over Blythe today. I'd try again tomorrow. I popped my head into the kitchen and quickly waved goodbye to Josh, who was on the phone and scribbling on a notepad. He looked so stressed out that I didn't want to disrupt him. He covered the phone with his hands and blew me a kiss.

When I passed Wade, who was on the patio wiping down tables, I held out my stack of pages for the memory book. "Hi, Wade. Would you do me a favor and hand these out to the staff? My e-mail and phone numbers are on here, so people can get in touch with me."

"Sure thing. I'll make sure to have people give you something. It's really nice of you to do this." I hoped Wade thought it was *so nice* that he'd force loving memories out of everyone at Simmer.

I was driving home when my cell rang. Adrianna.

"Hi, honey. What's up?"

"Oh, Chloe! Where are you? Can you stop by?" She sounded distressed.

"Of course. I'm on my way back from Simmer. I'll be there in a few minutes." The books I'd bought for her were in the car. This would be a good chance to drop them off.

Ade pulled open the door before I had time to knock. She looked anything but happy. "The police are still pestering Owen! Can you believe that this is happening right now?" At least she wasn't crying this time. But, boy, was she mad.

"What do they want from him?" I stepped into her living

room—or what was left of it. Boxes took up most of the space, including space previously occupied by air.

"They made him go down to headquarters to give another statement. And he asked me to say that I'd spent Tuesday night with him. I can't do that! Chloe, it's not true. I told him he doesn't have anything to hide, and he said it would just make things a lot easier if I gave him an alibi for this Leandra mess. I know he's right about that. But I can't lie to the police." Adrianna paced the floor.

"Does he have his truck back yet?" I asked. "Has he been making his deliveries at least?"

"They still have the truck, but like we thought, his boss let him use another one, and Owen seems overly pissy about it, if you ask me. I mean, who cares what truck you use to drive fish around Boston? But he has lots of accounts and big orders, so he should get paid pretty well this week. At least there is that. Are you hungry? I made these seven-layer bars that I can't stop eating."

I was always hungry. "Yeah, those sound good." They weren't exactly lunch food, but I wasn't complaining.

"Oh," I managed between mouthfuls, "I got you something."

"You did?"

I handed over the bag with the books on pregnancy and baby care. "I thought these might make you feel better. I know how upset about stuff you've been recently, and I thought it might be helpful for you to read what people who've actually had babies have to say. I didn't really know what to pick for you. You can return them if you like."

"You're the best!" When Ade flung her arms around me and squeezed me, I felt her belly push into mine. "I'm totally going to read them! You're right. I've just been hiding out trying not to think about being pregnant, and it's not working out for me. I've got to take charge here and be more in control. Knowledge is power, as they say, right?"

"I'm so glad you like them."

"And I'm going to call your sister, too."

I gave Ade another hug. "She'd love to hear from you. And this mess with Owen will get straightened out. I promise."

I was going to make sure of that.

# ELEVEN

BACK at home, I devoted the rest of Friday, including the evening, to conquering the DSM. I made piles of flash cards with symptoms and descriptions on one side, and diagnoses on the other. I did my best to follow Doug's suggestion to associate the diagnoses with people I knew. So, had Kevin succumbed to kleptomania? Or to something more sinister? What about Snacker? For the purposes of the exam, I categorized him as suffering from hyperactive sexual desire disorder, a diagnosis I based on his need to flirt shamelessly with every woman in sight. I then decided that Gavin was having a major depressive episode consequent to Leandra's death. Josh's diagnosis was acute stress disorder—in response to pressure at the restaurant—and Belita's was obsessive-compulsive disorder. Her need to clean? Yeah, I was stretching the categories more than was acceptable, but I was determined to do well on the test, no matter who got stuck with which diagnosis. My only regret was that I didn't know people with the interesting or peculiar symptoms required to help me remember agoraphobia (with or without history of panic disorder) and dissociative amnesia. At this rate, I'd succumb to trichotillomania: the irresistible urge to yank all my hair out.

I called Doug to see whether he had any brilliant advice for a struggling social work student.

"He's not telling you what's on the test," Terry said as soon as he picked up the phone. Stupid caller ID.

"I wasn't calling for that," I lied. Doug must have warned his boyfriend to screen my calls. *"Beware of students seeking classified information!"*

"I'm sure you weren't." He laughed. "Doug isn't here, anyway. Do you want to leave a message?"

"No. No message. Just called to check in." Another lie.

"I heard about our waitress from dinner the other night. Doug told me. What a traumatic experience you've been through! How are you handling it?" Doug's attitude had evidently rubbed off. Or maybe Terry was good at interpersonal relations on his own.

We talked for a few minutes about Leandra. Then I told Terry about my dinner with the chefs and about the archaic attitude toward women prevalent in the professional culinary world. "Listening to Digger made me want to scream!"

"So what are you going to do about it?" he asked calmly.

"What can I do about it? Change an entire profession? Yes. Find a job that consists solely of yelling at idiots about stupid behavior and forcing them to behave properly! That's what I'm going to do about it." There. Problem solved.

"Chloe, let's back up and rethink matters. After all, you're basing your view on the words of a few chefs. Their stories and experiences are not the final word on what it's like for a woman in that profession. Some of what they said may be valid, but some of it may not. Don't get carried away before you have a lot more information."

I was silent for a moment. "Okay, that's true," I finally admitted.

"And what about everything you've learned in this internship you've had this year? It's a program that educates people about workplace harassment, right?"

"Yes, and it's a 'field placement.' Hasn't Doug taught you that?" I laughed. Terry seemed as able as Doug would've been to talk down a fired-up social work student. I smiled, imagining Terry counseling me while shirtless and clad only in leather pants and hideous jewelry, his long hair teased high. "And I should figure out a way to educate both women and men in this crazy restaurant business and to teach tolerance and empowerment and equal rights and lots of other catchphrasey things!"

As I spoke the words, the realization hit me that I *was* fired up! And about something related to school! I *did* want to be a social worker—and not because Uncle Alan had forced me into graduate school, but because I passionately wanted to tackle the injustices of the culinary world. I felt so much like the Grinch discovering the joy of Christmas that I wondered whether a cartoon heart was growing inside me.

"There you go. I'll tell Doug you called hoping to get cheat notes. Bye, Chloe."

I hung up. I was stunned. After a year of whining and complaining my way through school, I finally understood why I'd picked social work, which had not, after all, been a random choice. Far from it! All along, lurking deep inside some hidden part of me, there had been this drive to save the world! Well, maybe just to *improve* the world. Okay, just the *culinary* world. But at least I was now on the right track. I laughed at what Josh would think when I began preaching the nonsexist, nondiscriminatory gospel of social work to Boston's restaurant employees. I'd give seminars about supporting one another and appreciating diversity. Ha! Or maybe I'd teach women chefs and kitchen employees how to handle moronic men in their industry. While I was at it, I'd encourage egalitarian male chefs to train their less-than-perfect peers to behave like normal human beings! Naomi, my field placement supervisor, was a die-hard social worker who'd love my plan. She was dating the owner of a Newbury Street art gallery, Eliot, so maybe I could meet up with her in town one day soon. Feeling revitalized, I spent Friday night enthusiastically studying and writing.

After a few hours of work, I did take one break to check my e-mail in the hope that someone had responded to my plea for memories of Leandra. My only message, however, was from my friend Elise, who lived outside Los Angeles.

While not working as a lawyer, Elise spent most of her time fruitlessly trying to spot celebrities. Her e-mail announced that her husband, Brandon, while picking up take-out Japanese food, had found himself next to Jeremy Piven. (Jeremy Piven and Elise, by the way, both enjoy vegetable tempura.) Brandon's encounter wasn't the brush with fame that Elise was hoping for, but she regarded it as a start.

Her e-mail went on to say that her husband, after getting two traffic tickets for minor violations, had received a guilt-inducing letter of admonishment from the state of California. According to the letter, the state understood that although Brandon *believed* himself to be a safe driver, his driving record indicated that he was, in fact, a *much worse driver* than most other Californians. The letter then switched to a tone of encouragement. The state of California, Brandon was assured, believed that he had it in him to change: to become a safe driver and to cease endangering the lives of others with his reckless behavior. While California hoped that he would change, the choice was his.

I loved it! The state of California had studied social work! Taking this positive approach was much better than simply handing out fines and appointing court dates. Yes, social work was the route for me! I might even begin to apply California's method immediately in my efforts to elicit positive memories of Leandra: *You may think that you have nothing nice to say, but you could choose to put aside your residual hatred for the deceased and be a better person by digging deep and remembering Leandra's better qualities. The choice is yours.*

I slept well that night in spite of a convoluted dream in

which I was carrying a monstrous picket sign outside Simmer while simultaneously chanting, "Hell no, we won't go!" and stuffing my face full of foie gras. In the morning, I took a steaming shower, blew my hair straight, flatironed it until I smelled burning hair, and slugged down a cup of coffee. Then I checked my e-mail, my phone, and my cell for contributions to the memory book. Nothing. I hoped that if I ever had the misfortune to turn up dead in a fish truck, there'd be more material in my memory book than what I had for Leandra's. Here it was, Saturday, with the memorial service only two days away, and the only memory I had so far was Josh's forgettable one, and two uses of the word *bitch*. I resolved that I'd make one last pleading attempt to elicit memories from Simmer's staff. If the effort failed, I'd just have to invent recollections and sign them Anonymous. I couldn't bear to think of Gavin opening the memory book only to see blank pages or, worse, pages filled with stories of Leandra's horrible behavior.

Later that morning, determined to complete the memory book to my own and Gavin's satisfaction, I showed up at Simmer. When I was still in the dining area, even before I swung open the door to the kitchen, I could hear Josh yelling. I entered his domain just in time to see him dump a container of stainless whisks and ladles on to the floor, thus creating a metallic clatter that echoed off the walls. "Why don't you take these, too? Go ahead!" He was screaming at nobody in particular. "Take whatever the hell you want! It's not my restaurant, right?" Josh tossed his hands up in the air and looked around the room at his staff. Isabelle, Santos, and

Javier were visibly shaken, but Snacker was trying to hold back a smile.

Josh caught my eye and dropped his hands. "I'm taking a break outside." He went into Simmer's back alley to cool off.

I'd heard many rumors about Josh's temper but had rarely witnessed it myself. From what I'd heard, he'd calmed down quite a bit in the past few years. Before that, he'd been prone to explosions. Josh attributed his outbursts to a passion for his work and a desire for perfection in the kitchen. I appreciated and respected his dedication, but I still didn't buy it as an excuse for throwing utensils.

I asked Isabelle what was going on. "I guess that some pieces of expensive cooking equipment are missing. Josh is upset. Obviously."

"What's missing? Does he think someone stole them?"

"A mandoline slicer and a really nice eight-inch chinois, which is like a strainer that we use for filtering stocks and sauces." In spite of my anger that the equipment had been stolen, I loved hearing Isabelle show off what she'd learned. "Also, a stick blender and Josh's favorite knife, a Wüsthof chef's knife. At least that's what he's noticed so far. He knew about the blender and the mandoline a few days ago, but he just noticed the other things, and he's freaking out. And yes, he definitely thinks someone stole them. And I'm afraid he probably thinks it's me because of my past."

I tried to reassure her. "I'm sure he doesn't think it's you. He's just really upset right now. He was generally yelling at the world, not at you."

"I didn't take anything, but I know who did, Chloe," Isabelle practically whispered.

"You do? Who?"

Isabelle leaned in close to me. "Blythe."

"What? Why on earth would Blythe be stealing this random stuff? What does she need a chinois for?"

"It's awful, but she's selling the stuff on eBay. Stuff that she's stealing from Gavin! After everything he put up with from Leandra, now he's got people stealing kitchen equipment!"

"How do you know she's selling all these things on eBay?"

"Josh lets me use the computer in his office sometimes to check my e-mail. I don't have a computer of my own, but when I started here, he offered to let me use his if I wanted. I'd never had e-mail before or anything like that, so I was really grateful. He taught me how to set up an account and everything." I was once again reminded of how wonderful my chef could be.

"Okay, so . . . ?" I prompted her to continue.

"Oh, well, the other day when I was taking my break, I went to the office to make a phone call, and Blythe was in there on the computer. As soon as I walked in, she clicked the mouse a few times and then left. I didn't think anything of it, but when I got off the phone, I thought I'd see if I had any e-mail. The browser was already open, just shrunk down on the side of the screen. And when I clicked it, her eBay page opened up with her listed as a seller, and it showed all the items she was auctioning off, including a couple of Simmer's things."

Holy crap!

"Poor Gavin, right? It's so unfair to him!" she complained.

Isabelle really had to get over this Gavin thing. And if Blythe was stealing from the kitchen, Josh was the one who'd catch heat from Gavin. Everything that happened in the kitchen was Josh's responsibility.

"Have you told Josh or Gavin about what Blythe is doing?"

"No! And you have to promise me you won't, either! I don't want to be the one ratting out my coworkers. I love this job, and I don't want to screw it up. Please don't say anything," she begged me. The taboo on ratting out struck me as a legacy from Isabelle's life on the streets.

I was facing my first real ethical dilemma as a social worker. If Isabelle was in any way my client, then I had to respect her confidentiality. And I did feel that she was my client. I had met her through a social service agency, and I had helped to set up an interview with Josh. I'd taught her how to go about finding a safe, affordable apartment. I regularly checked in with her and followed up on what we'd talked about. She trusted me to be professional. I couldn't betray that trust. According to the social work code of ethics, I was to break confidentiality only if a client was a danger to herself or others, or if I had the client's permission. The larceny at Simmer was unethical, but it wasn't causing serious harm to anyone. Damn ethics.

Josh's foul mood made this a bad time to talk to him about the problem, anyhow. He'd have to calm down before I'd even want to be around him. In any case, I needed to check eBay myself. As a novice computer user, Isabelle might have misinterpreted what she'd seen. Maybe Blythe had been searching eBay because she wanted to replace the missing items. And there was no point in bothering Gavin, who was in enough distress already about Leandra's death and didn't need to be confronted with a comparatively minor problem. Anyway, I had to respect Isabelle's wish to be kept out of it. But if I stumbled on Blythe's eBay merchandise myself, would the code of ethics allow me to tell Josh?

Isabelle interrupted my thoughts. "Oh, Chloe, did you hear? The police told Gavin how Leandra died. Everyone here just found out. She was strangled with the ties of one of Simmer's aprons. There was evidence found on her body that matched the aprons. Isn't that gross?" She wrinkled up her pale face in disgust.

A Simmer apron? Then Leandra hadn't been killed by some random passerby in the alley. When I'd found her in Owen's truck, she'd still been wearing a Simmer apron, so her own almost certainly hadn't been the murder weapon. Who had access to the linens? Which employees? Probably all of them. Customers? Probably not. For some reason, I wondered about Belita. Belita hadn't liked Leandra, but she was only one of a great many people.

"But she wasn't raped or anything, thank God." Isabelle looked embarrassed. "I mean, I know she was strangled, which is terrible, but I guess it's good that something else bad didn't happen to her before that. You know what I mean?"

"I do. I know what you mean." I found myself disturbed

and distracted by the news that something as innocuous as an apron had been turned into a murder weapon and that the murderer had been in Simmer. In *Josh's* restaurant.

"I hate to bother you again with this, Isabelle," I said, "but I really need some things to put in this memory book I'm doing. It will really mean a lot to Gavin." As much as I didn't want to encourage her crush on Gavin, I was desperate.

And the tactic worked. Isabelle said, "I guess so. You can write that she worked hard to make Gavin happy. That's probably true enough."

Finally! I had something!

"Thank you. I'm going to talk to Snacker now."

"But you promise? You won't throw me under the bus, right?"

I promised her that I wouldn't say anything about Blythe. Again, it was funny to hear Isabelle use the language of the kitchen. Restaurant people always seemed to be talking about being "thrown under the bus" to refer to backstabbing, a phenomenon all too common in the restaurant world. Since knives suitable for stabbing were all over the place in kitchens, whereas buses were, of course, absent, I'd never understood the preference. Anyway, Isabelle now spoke like an insider. I silently wished her luck.

Snacker had hung up the phone. I grabbed him before he could evade me by burying himself in kitchen preparations. "Snacker? Please?" I did my best to look pitiful. "I swear, if you give me a quote, I'll leave you alone!"

"Chloe, I just don't have anything to say."

"You could *choose* to remember something positive about Leandra, like she was . . ." I said, filled with the spirit of California's registry of motor vehicles.

"She was hot. Will that do?" Snacker shrugged. "I have to run. Good luck."

At least the comment was positive. It was also easy to translate: *Leandra was a beautiful woman with much to offer the world.*

I found Kevin the bartender up front removing bottles from a cardboard box and affixing those funny little pouring spouts to the top. "Hi, Kevin."

He looked up from his work. "Hey, Chloe. How are you doing today?"

Kevin's sideburns were even more pointy than usual. It always amused me to see men experiment with their facial hair. But I refused to be distracted from my cause, even when I noticed Kevin's tight black Simmer T-shirt clinging to his muscular body as he lifted another box up onto the counter. "Did you get the form I had Wade pass out? I'm trying to gather some happy memories of Leandra for the memorial on Monday."

"I did get it. I just haven't had a chance to write anything," he said apologetically.

Sensing that Kevin might be the lone soul who'd give me a good recollection or remark, I offered to do the writing for him.

He said, "Leandra and I worked together before at another restaurant, and she was a great waitress and a nice person. I'll probably miss having her around."

I wrote: *"I worked with Leandra for years and found her to be highly skilled at her job. She was an exceedingly compassionate and warm person whose presence will be greatly missed."*

"That's great. Thanks, Kevin."

"No problem."

I came close to telling him that it had been a gigantic problem for almost everyone else.

# TWELVE

BACK at home, I settled in at the computer to see whether I could find some of the items stolen from Simmer on eBay. Although I'd bought a few things from the online auction service, I was by no means an expert eBay shopper, and I'd never sold anything there at all. When I opened the cheery, welcoming home page, with its primary colors and its wealth of shopping categories, I immediately remembered that I loved everything about eBay. As much as I wanted to browse through antique linens, DVD collections, and discount designer clothing, I reminded myself that my purpose was to search for the stolen goods. Well, I did take the time to log in. On eBay, you never know what you'll come across, and if I happened to stumble on something irresistible, I'd better be all set to bid, right? I entered my online ID and password. The first time I'd gone on eBay, I'd had no idea what to expect and was beyond intimidated by the entire process of setting up an account, bidding, and figuring out how to pay. It turned out to be very simple: just like regular online shopping except cheaper. Well, usually cheaper. A few sellers set unreasonable starting bids or charged outrageous shipping fees, but there were plenty of good deals, too.

Individuals or companies listed items for auction, and people like me entered our highest bids, the most we were willing to pay. There were pictures of almost all items, together with descriptions and, sometimes, a disclaimer about the item's condition and a statement about flaws. Almost any search terms produced results because nearly everything imaginable was on eBay: half-used bottles of shampoo, brand-new ovens, antique bird feeders, sterling silver flatware, women's dress shoes scuffed down at the stiletto heels, almost anything at all. Most auctions lasted for about a week. If you won an item, a congratulatory message showed up in your e-mail.

But my purpose wasn't to win. Rather, if the stolen kitchen equipment actually was on eBay, I was hoping to find one seller who listed all of the items. Sellers used eBay IDs, not their real names, to identify themselves. In theory, the entire process of selling and buying was fairly anonymous, except that if you actually bought something, you had to give the seller your name and address, of course. I had no idea whether it was possible to identify sellers' real names. If I found the items from Simmer, could I trace

them to Blythe? I didn't know. But I had to start somewhere.

I began by looking for an eight-inch chinois, which
seemed to be the most distinctive item missing. It took me
a couple of tries to remember to check the little box marked
"Search title and description." When I did, I got nine results. In a store, I'd have expected to pay at least a hundred
dollars for a chinois. The bidding was about to close on the
first item in my list of results. The high bid was just over
fifty dollars, plus shipping, of course. I clicked on that first
result and got the item's page, which gave the details, including the place from which it would be shipped. This first
chinois was coming from Ohio. I returned to the list and
tried again. The fourth try pulled up a chinois from Boston.
Yes! I clicked a link to see the seller's other items.

Yes, dammit! Along with the chinois, this seller was auctioning off a handheld stick blender, a mandoline, and not
one, but two, Wüstof chefs' knives. Also, a very cute "gently worn" green peacoat, a desk lamp, a king-size Calvin
Klein duvet cover, and a "vintage" Santa Claus statue that
looked more tacky than vintage to me. But what were the
odds that somebody not affiliated with Simmer would be
selling all the items missing from the restaurant? If this was
Blythe, as Isabelle thought, why was she ripping off her
place of employment? Maybe Isabelle had been mistaken;
maybe the thief was someone else. Who was likely to steal
from Gavin? If Blythe wasn't the culprit, why had Isabelle
said that she was? What could Isabelle have against Blythe?
And did the stealing have anything to do with Leandra's

murder? Could Leandra have discovered that Blythe was stealing and then threatened to tell Gavin? Leandra could have done what I was doing; she could have searched on eBay for proof that Blythe was a thief. If Leandra had confronted Blythe, I couldn't imagine that her response would've been to grab a Simmer apron and use its ties to strangle Leandra to death. Still, as I'd just reminded myself, I had to start somewhere.

The only way to find out whether the eBay seller was, in fact, Blythe was to win an auction. Payment might be sent electronically to an e-mail address, but the seller would provide a return name and address on the package, or so I assumed. There was one minor hitch: If I bought something from Blythe, she would obviously recognize my name. The seller wanted payment by check or PayPal. Either method would provide my name; there was no way to use an alias. But I didn't have to be the buyer. Blythe knew who Adrianna was but probably didn't know her last name. Consequently, I decided to enlist Ade and to bid from her computer. There was probably no way to trace me if I used my own computer, but I felt a tad paranoid and didn't want to risk it. Besides, Adrianna would look great in that peacoat.

I called Ade, who said that her computer was still hooked up. "Why do you need my computer? What are you . . . ?"

"See ya in a minute."

I drove to Adrianna's apartment. When she opened the door, she had a leery look on her face. "What's going on, Chloe?" Her thick blonde hair was in a simple ponytail, and she wore a fitted scoop-neck top and cargo pants. She was the most adorable pregnant lady I'd ever seen.

"How would you like to become the proud owner of a green peacoat? Or a stick blender? Or perhaps a desk lamp for your new apartment?"

"Not particularly."

"Too bad. You are." I explained what I was doing and promised to reimburse her for whatever she ended up spending. I said nothing about the possible connection between Leandra's murder and the eBay items that had been filched from Simmer. Ade was already upset that Owen was being questioned by the police. I didn't want to raise false hope about getting him off the hook. "Consider it a pregnancy gift!"

"I'm not in the mood to argue with you, but I don't see why you don't just go talk to Gavin or Josh about this."

"I promised Isabelle. Oh!" I clapped my hand over my mouth. I'd just completely broken my promise by blabbing everything to Adrianna! The Office of Ethics and Professional Review of the National Association of Social Workers would be furious! "Pretend you don't know anything!"

"Chloe, I'm pregnant and tired, and I have the worst indigestion of my life, and I don't even have an eBay account, so I don't know anything, and that's close to the truth. Just go be me on the computer. My credit card is in my wallet. And you better pay me back!"

I squeezed between a few boxes, sat down in front of the computer, went to eBay, and started setting up a new account for Adrianna. "What do you want your user ID to be?"

"Do I seem like I give a shit today?" she hollered from the kitchen.

I dubbed her *grouchymama* and filled in all the correct boxes. "You're all set!" I called out happily.

"I still don't give a shit!"

"How can you not give a shit? This is shopping!"

I repeated my chinois search until I again found the seller offering the suspect items. Only one of this mystery seller's auctions was ending soon. Actually, it was ending at midnight tonight. And I'd lucked out. Yes, I had the perfect excuse to bid on the adorable peacoat! The current bid was only twenty-one dollars, but eBay bids always rose toward the very end of an auction, so I entered a maximum bid of eighty dollars, in other words, an awful lot of money for a used peacoat and more, I hoped, than any ordinary eBay shopper would be willing to offer. I really didn't want to have to buy Ade an eighty-dollar coat right now, but anything in the name of justice! I would look very cute in it, too, so until Ade lost her pregnancy weight, I could wear it through next fall . . .

"Chloe? Are you done yet? Come in here and eat with me."

Adrianna had put together a plate of marinated artichoke hearts and mushrooms, the special Italian salami called sopressatta, sliced Fontina cheese, Brie, ripe plum tomatoes, fresh basil leaves, olive oil, and French bread. No wonder she had bad indigestion!

"Who has this much food in the house a few days before moving?" I asked.

"Pregnant people who don't want to cook anything. Want some water?"

I nodded, and Ade pulled out two bottles of Poland Spring.

"I could drink about thirty of these a day. I've never been so thirsty in my life. I figure that I pee all the time anyway, so what's the difference? So, what's going on with you? How are you and Josh?"

"Good. Except that I hardly ever see him because he works all the time. I knew it would be like this when the restaurant first opened, but it's been since New Year's. Shouldn't things ease up soon? Seriously, Ade, he is so tired he can barely stand half the time, and he's a little snippy and cranky because he's beyond exhausted." I piled a bread slice high with Fontina, tomato, and basil, drizzled some high-end olive oil on top, and took a bite.

"The restaurant is still very young, though. To you, it might seem like it's been ages, but four or five months is a short time in that business. Chloe, you know how many restaurants close in the first six months. So, they have to do everything they can to stay open this first year." She swilled more water and then popped a mushroom in her mouth. "Gavin dug himself a big hole by the time he opened Simmer. That's one of the reasons they have to pay Owen COD. It'll take a while for them to start making money. Or just to start breaking even."

"So what do I do until then? Until Josh's schedule eases up?"

"Nothing. You enjoy the time that you do get with him.

You're just about done with school for the year, summer is coming, and you'll have some free time to go hang out down at the restaurant with Josh when he gets a break. You two just have to make the most of the time you do have together."

"You're right. I wouldn't trade him for anyone else in the world. I just hope we can get through this okay." I cut off a thick slice of the gooey Brie, smeared it on the bread, and topped it with a marinated artichoke heart. Perfect.

"Are you two having problems?" She looked concerned.

"No, no. Not at all." Our slight tiff about women in the culinary profession didn't really count as a relationship problem. At least I hoped not. "We're great. I just miss him." Was I tearing up? I hadn't realized how hard it had been to have Josh working so much.

"Sweetie, it's going to even out, I promise. Josh is crazy about you." Ade sounded unusually soft and loving. Maybe her hormones were preparing her to soothe a teething baby.

I wiped the tears from my eyes. "What about you and Owen? Any thoughts on getting married?"

"Lately, I've probably seen him as much as you've been seeing Josh. Not that bad really, but we're both so busy trying to fit in work and packing right now that we haven't had too much time together."

I realized that I had not seen Owen since the day Leandra appeared in his truck. "I miss Owen, too. It seems like he always used to be around, and now he's not. I'm not used to it. Aren't we pathetic, sitting here complaining about our men?"

Ade stood up. "You know what we need? Cheesecake

with tart cherries! I happen to have just that in the fridge."

Two slices later, I was overstuffed. After that, I enlisted Adrianna's help with Leandra's memory book. We talked over the situation and agreed that the only reasonable solution was to concoct the kinds of happy recollections and flattering descriptions of Leandra that Gavin wanted.

I scribbled notes on a legal pad while Adrianna brainstormed. "Okay," she said, "let's have somebody say, 'She was the first one to volunteer when we needed someone to work late, and she never once complained about putting in that extra effort.'"

I nodded. "That's good. Keep 'em coming."

"'Leandra was loved by all her coworkers. I will especially miss the sound of her laugh echoing through the dining room.'" I couldn't imagine who at Simmer would have said such a thing, but I wrote it down anyway. The time was too short for truth.

"Oh, here's a good one," Adrianna said excitedly. "'Leandra was a bright soul in a dark world.'"

"Nobody talks like that," I protested with a laugh.

"I don't see you coming up with anything better!"

True enough. I wrote it down and prayed that I wouldn't be punished for the sin of lying. "What about something that a customer might say?"

"'It was always a delight to have Leandra as a server. She made a delicious dinner even more enjoyable with her loving spirit.' Do you like how I threw in the compliment to Josh there?"

Ade and I kept going for another ten minutes or so before we called it quits. Then we worked out a plan to camouflage the fabricated memories. I would type out all the recollections, genuine and fake, and intersperse them throughout the book. Separately, I'd list the names of everyone who had reportedly contributed. There would thus be no direct link between the material and the names.

"Do you want to watch a movie or something tonight?" I asked Ade. "I'm sick of studying."

"Actually, Owen is coming over tonight. He should be done with his deliveries by late afternoon, and then he's taking me out to dinner at Rialto, if you can believe it. I told you he was doing well with this job!"

I was so jealous. Rialto was in the Charles Hotel in Cambridge, and the executive chef was Jody Adams, who did absolutely spectacular food. Yes, a famous female chef! Even by Josh's tough standards, Jody Adams was a real chef. She not only created the menu but worked the line, too; on many nights, she was actually in the kitchen cooking. Josh had no use for the kind of chef whose name graced the menu but who stayed tucked away in a corporate office and left the real work to the sous chefs and line cooks. My parents had taken me to Rialto a bunch of times. One night, I'd had Jody's phenomenal truffled egg creation served in a hollowed-out baked potato. As I wouldn't say to Josh, it was one of the best dishes I've ever eaten. But cheap, Rialto wasn't, so I was impressed that Owen was taking Adrianna there.

I went home and set to work on Leandra's book. After keyboarding the material, real and fictional, that I'd gathered, I printed it all out. How pathetic was it that basically no one had anything positive to say about this dead girl? Very, that's how. Consequently, I was glad that Adrianna and I had remedied matters. I took the printed pages, a pair of scissors, and a glue stick to the living room, where I sat in front of the televison, cut out strips of paper with the supposed recollections on them, and glued the strips on to the pages of the album I'd bought. I tried to make a little go a long way by leaving lots of space on each page. That arrangement, I hoped, made it look as if Leandra had had lots of friends. Any friends. Any at all.

I wrapped myself in a light cotton blanket and lay down on the couch to watch *The Office* DVDs that I had borrowed from Owen a few weeks ago. I spent the rest of the afternoon and all evening alone. At one point, I called Josh on his cell, but when he picked up, all he did was yell that he was up to his knees. Or maybe that he was in the weeds? Either way, he couldn't talk. He shouted a cute, "I love you," and then hung up before I could say anything. At least he sounded as if he'd recovered from his pan-throwing mood. Still, alone on a Saturday night, I felt like a chef's widow. I didn't even have any good food in the house. During Simmer's first few months, Josh used to bring home dinners for me, neatly packed in to-go containers from the restaurant, but since business had picked up, I rarely got treats like that. In one way, I didn't mind; Josh was so tired at the end of the work-day that I didn't want him to bother making anything for me. But I missed those days of off-the-menu chef's specials that he'd brought over late at night just for me.

I spent twenty minutes throwing cat treats across the room and watching Gato chase them. The activity left him purring, and, for once, he came over and snuggled with me. *Small pleasures,* I thought to myself. At ten thirty, after watching salesman Jim confess his love to secretary Pam, I dragged myself off the couch, to my bedroom, and into bed, where I evidently fell into a coma that lasted until the next morning. What roused me was the phone, which had slid so far under the bed that it took me a few moments of fumbling to find it.

The caller was Josh, whose voice carried not a hint of the previous morning's pan-hurling rage or the evening's work stress. "Good morning, lovely! How'd you like to see your long-lost boyfriend again tonight?"

"Really? How did you manage that?" I lay back down and shut my eyes.

"Snacker asked Blythe to have dinner at our apartment, so obviously you and I need to be there to supervise and keep him in line. Stein is working late, so he won't be there."

"Who's going to be at Simmer? Is Gavin going to be mad?" I yawned.

"Snacker has the day off, the bastard, but if I leave at six, Santos, Javier, and Isabelle can hold the fort down for the rest of the night. Sunday nights aren't usually too busy anyhow. They're going to have to handle it, because I don't give a shit right now. Apparently, unless someone is murdered, I work all the time, so I'm going to take the night off. Gavin will have to deal. So how does tonight sound? Snacker is going to be making tamales all day today, so that'll be dinner."

"Dinner sounds very good," I murmured. "I can't believe Snacker has the day off from cooking and is spending it making tamales. You chefs are crazy. I'll see you tonight." A Sunday tamale dinner sounded perfect! I was willing to brave any giant dust bunnies that were sure to roll across the apartment like tumbleweeds.

The phone rang again the second after I hung up. Adrianna, who seemed to have pulled herself together yesterday, had fallen to pieces again. Not only did she feel even sicker than usual, but she was really upset about Owen. I could hear her voice breaking over the phone.

"There is something going on with him, Chloe! He was questioned by the police *again*! They are calling him a 'person of interest.' He looks worried all the time, and he is weirdly quiet. Kind of withdrawn. He's even wearing normal clothes in normal colors! When we went to dinner last night, I expected him to pick me up wearing one of his crazy neon suits or something, but he just had on plain pants and a plain shirt!"

That *was* alarming. And a "person of interest" didn't mean an interesting person. "Maybe Owen thought you'd like him to look more regular for once. After all, he was taking you out for a very nice meal at a place that presumably has some sort of dress code, right? How did he act during dinner?"

"He just wasn't himself. You know how chatty and fun Owen always is. Now he seems beaten down or depressed or something. I don't know what it is. But he couldn't possibly have murdered Leandra! You know he's not that kind of a person. But the police don't know that. What are we going to do? We can't afford a lawyer!"

I tucked the phone under my chin and rubbed more sleep out of my eyes. "Oh, my God! Do you think he needs one?" Worried though I'd been, I hadn't realized that Owen's situation was this serious.

I heard Adrianna blow her nose. "I don't know if he needs a lawyer. I don't know anything about this kind of stuff. He's just been trying to cooperate with them as best he can so that they'll see he has nothing to hide. But he won't tell me any details about what they're badgering him about. Chloe, Owen hasn't done anything wrong!"

"I know he hasn't. Just tell him to hold on, and everything will be okay." My words sounded inadequate even to me.

"Before I forget to tell you, I got an e-mail from the eBay seller. I won that stupid coat. You won it. We did. I did. But guess what? It's Blythe. She signed the e-mail with her real name. She didn't seem to be hiding anything about herself, so I guess she didn't recognize my name. Maybe she's just eager to pawn off everything she's stolen."

Yes! In spite of the bad news about Owen, I was elated. I could hardly wait for tonight's dinner, when I'd have the chance to look for signs that Blythe had had something to do with Leandra's murder. Blythe didn't strike me as a killer, but how many times had I heard news reports in which monstrous criminals were described as "wonderful neighbors" and "model citizens"? Maybe tonight I could get a better feel for Blythe. I'd have to be careful, of course, to avoid mentioning Adrianna's name. I must do nothing to suggest any knowledge of Blythe's eBay activities. I'd have to be on guard and exceptionally observant. At the same time, of course, I'd have to act normal. This dinner could be more than a little awkward. As a budding social worker, I should be good at playing amateur sleuth while also interacting with my peers in my usual role of being Josh's girlfriend. But then again, I wasn't enrolled at the Nancy Drew School of Social Work. More's the pity.

# THIRTEEN

I knocked loudly on Josh and Snacker's door and eventually heard Snacker yell, "Come in!"

Experience had taught me to enter cautiously. Stepping into the living room, I expected to find the usual dirt piles. The apartment was, however, cleaner than I'd ever seen it before. The unprecedented state of tidiness could have only one explanation: Snacker had gone on a cleaning spree to impress Blythe. Josh had had no time and no motivation to spruce the place up—I already knew how he lived and loved him anyway—and the third chef roommate, Stein, was at work. Sharing the three-bedroom apartment was advantageous to all three chefs. Each paid less rent than he'd have done alone, even for a little studio or a cramped one-bedroom unit, and everyone gained square footage. The living room was spacious, especially with the clutter now put away, or at least hidden, and each roommate had his own decent-sized bedroom.

"Hi, babe." Josh greeted me with two Coronas held in one hand. "Beer?" he asked as he leaned in for a good, long kiss.

"Mmm, you bet." I handed him a large wooden salad bowl I'd brought that contained red leaf lettuce and a jar of spicy garlic and lemon vinaigrette. I was hoping some serious garlic breath might keep Snacker and Blythe apart. I took a beer and followed him through the living room to the kitchen.

"Blythe is already here, and we're just about to start assembling the tamales. Snacker has enough food to feed an army."

Blythe was seated at the square kitchen table. Snacker stood behind her chair with his arms wrapped around her as he demonstrated the proper way to roll a tamale. "Okay, now you've got your filling in here, and we've left enough room around the sides to fold the banana leaf over when we're ready to roll it. Add some chicken, red pepper strips, a green olive, and a few capers. Then we'll top it with the sauce . . . Now start rolling! Don't let that sauce spill out!" Snacker put his hands over Blythe's.

I looked at Josh as if to ask, *Is he serious?* Josh rolled his eyes in agreement.

"Oh, hi, Chloe." Blythe looked up from her tamale lesson and smiled warmly. "I'm so glad we're all getting together tonight. Miracle everyone is free, huh?" Blythe looked irritatingly perfect. Her loose-fitting sleeveless peach shirt showed off her beautiful skin tone. As usual, her maroon nail polish was almost totally chipped off, and as usual, she somehow managed to pull off the bizarre fashion faux pas without looking ragged.

"I know," I said. "I'm psyched to learn how to make tamales. What a cool idea!"

"Yeah, I thought it would be fun," Snacker said happily. "I got the recipe from this guy I used to work with a few years ago. Once in a while I make a huge batch like this and stick them in the freezer or give them out to friends. I've got enough here to make at least a hundred of them."

"Yeah, I can see that." On the counter was a massive metal bowl overflowing with chicken thighs. A large pot of red sauce sat on the stove. I peered at the ingredients on the table. "What are you wrapping them in? I thought tamales were rolled in corn husks."

"A lot are, but these are Guatemalan tamales, so they're wrapped in banana leaves. You can buy frozen banana leaves at some supermarkets, but I got these from this awesome Spanish store around here. Also, this recipe calls for chicken thighs on the bone. Lots of tamales are made with boneless chicken or pork, but the bone gives them much better flavor. My friend got this recipe from his mother, and the original calls for a whole bunch of lard. Who cooks with lard anymore? So my friend changed the lard to olive oil and added the onions and garlic to the sauce. Want to roll one?"

I nodded and took a seat next to Blythe. As I filled and

wrapped, I peeked at her out of the corner of my eye in search of any sign that she was guilty of murder. I found none. What was I hoping for? That in between wrapping tamales, she'd suddenly confess to a grisly crime she'd happened to commit earlier in the week? That she'd rise from her seat and try to strangle one of us with a banana leaf?

Snacker, Blythe, and I continued wrapping tamales. Meanwhile, Josh took our finished ones and began to set them in a large Dutch oven on top of the stove that was lined with yet more banana leaves. The chefs were, of course, used to industrial kitchen equipment. Here at home, they were stuck with a decrepit electric stove with coils that unexpectedly popped out. It seemed to me that cooking here must drive them crazy!

"How do you cook these exactly?" I looked into the pot. "Do you steam them?"

"Basically," Snacker said. "We pack the tamales on top of the banana leaves, fill the pot about a quarter full of water, cover it, and then boil it for a couple of hours. That's why we wrap them all really tightly in the leaves and then again in foil, so we have perfectly sealed packets. We don't want any water getting into the ones on the bottom."

When the pot was tightly packed, Snacker placed another heavy pot on the stove for another batch of tamales. "We have to cook all of them tonight," he explained. "Then we'll just stick what we don't eat into the freezer, and they'll taste perfectly fresh when we reheat them. I've already got a bunch done, and we should be able to finish making the rest pretty fast."

When I grabbed another Corona from the fridge, I saw that it held enough beer for tonight, plus fresh meat and enough produce to last for the next few weeks. Because Josh usually stayed with me, I hadn't been here in a while, but it seemed to me that they were better stocked than on my last visit. I shut the fridge and looked around the kitchen. Open shelves were filled with bottles, storage containers, oversized plastic spice jars, and bags of flour and rice. I took a second look at the bottles, many of which were bigger than the standard-size ones I bought for myself at the supermarket.

"Did you guys get these at one of those wholesale stores or something? This is the biggest bottle of sesame oil I've ever seen." There were also many expensive olive oils and vinegars that I strongly suspected were too pricey for Snacker, Stein, and Josh's budget. "Wait a minute! This is the same oil you have at Simmer." I held up a very tall, slender bottle of Spanish olive oil. Its label had elaborate script and was covered with distinctive pictures of stone statues.

Silence fell. Then Blythe giggled.

The truth hit me. "Did you guys steal this stuff from Simmer?"

"I don't really think of it as stealing," Snacker answered unabashedly. "It's more of a way to collect what we deserve. Bonuses, I guess. Where do you think I got all this chicken we're using?"

I stared at Josh, who, I assumed, would be horrified to learn what Snacker had been doing. Josh, however, looked not at all surprised. "You, too, Josh?" I felt like Julius Caesar: *Et tu, Brute?*

Josh just shrugged and kept wrapping foil around a tamale. "Snack's right. Once in a while we have to take a little something."

"Doesn't this kill your food cost and everything? I thought you were worried about that all the time! And you're stealing all this stuff? Oh, you guys took that beer in the fridge, too!" I didn't know whether to laugh or cry. I could understand why overworked and underpaid chefs might feel entitled to everything they could get their hands on. But the social worker in me was alarmed at the blatant thievery. And, of course, I was worried about Josh's job. What if he got caught?

Josh stood up and poured water into the pots of tamales that were ready for cooking. He covered them, turned up the heat, and grabbed Coronas for himself and Snacker. "Yeah, it can take a toll on the food cost, so you have to be careful about it. But, look, Chloe. Everyone steals from restaurants. Just the nature of the beast, I guess. But not everything in this kitchen is stolen. Gavin lets us buy a lot of stuff from the purveyors for our own use, so we get it cheap. When it comes to stealing at a restaurant, you don't always see it, but you know it happens."

"It's not just these criminal chefs," Blythe said lightly, teasing Josh and Snacker. *Yeah,* I thought, *tell me something I didn't know.* She stood up and went to the sink to wash her hands. "The bartenders always have their own cups behind the bar, drinking the restaurant's liquor. And the waitstaff will take stuff like silverware and napkins." The pot calling the kettle black! A restaurant cliché if there ever was one! When Belita had said that Kevin was taking bottles, she really had meant that he was stealing—just like everyone else at Simmer. And Blythe? Was she one more ordinary restaurant thief? Or something worse?

"It happens at every restaurant," Snacker agreed. "But it's the customers who are the worst. Christ, they'll take the salt and pepper shakers right off the table, steal their napkins, candleholders, small vases, all that kind of stuff. Women just drop stuff into their purses."

"Nobody really gets caught," Josh said. "It's just part of restaurant life. The only time it pisses me off is if someone steals a whole eighty-dollar tenderloin that I could've sold for three hundred and fifty dollars in plated dishes, and it blows my food cost to hell. Or when someone does something really stupid, like steal obvious appliances. That's just dumb. But the worst is when someone takes something from my toolbox. Like my knives. That's my money they're taking, and I'm sick of having to lock up and bolt down everything I own in my kitchen." Josh practically shuddered. "Don't even get me started on what's been taken from me."

Blythe didn't flinch. Maybe she was a great actress. Maybe she truly believed that she'd had the right to steal from Josh's kitchen and that her pilfering would have no impact on my underpaid chef. "There are two things that always hold true in this business," she said. "Everyone steals, and everyone sleeps with each other."

Snacker sat up straight at that statement.

"Oh, speaking of which," she continued, "I found out that one of my friends from law school, Katie, slept with our Kevin. She picked him up at a bar!"

"Well, hey! All right, Kevin!" Snacker clapped his hands together. "Come on, guys. Let's go sit in the living room while the tamales cook. Should be about another hour and a half."

I downed my Corona and took another from the fridge of stolen food. I stared at the assortment of vegetables and meats resting comfortably in Josh and Snacker's kitchen and shook my head. Then I shut the refrigerator door and headed for the living room.

Snacker cranked up some Black Crowes and held Blythe closely while he spun her around the room and belted out a raspy "No Speak No Slave." Blythe laughed and kept her arms wrapped around his neck. She did seem to like Snacker, but I wasn't entirely thrilled with the prospect of the two of them as a couple. In fact, I wouldn't know what to think of Blythe or how to feel about her until I'd sorted out her role in stealing from Simmer. Or, of course, in murdering Leandra.

Josh was on the couch looking at me. God, I just loved him. No amount of fatigue could wipe away how gorgeous he was in my eyes. I sidestepped the dancing pair and sat on Josh's lap. I ran my hands through his dirty-blond hair and kissed him softly on the lips. "I love you," I whispered in his ear.

"I love you, too, babe. I'm glad you're here," he whispered back.

By the time the tamales were finally done, the four of us had gone through a good portion of the pilfered beer. The apartment lacked a dining room, so we sat at the kitchen table.

"Who's hungry?" Snacker asked loudly as he placed a platter of steaming tamales in the center of the table.

I reached behind me and lifted my garlicky salad bowl up and onto the table. I nudged it toward Blythe.

"Here's to Simmer!" Josh toasted, raising his bottle high in the air. Blythe, Snacker, and I all clumsily clinked our bottles against his.

"Okay, now open them neatly!" Snacker demanded as we reached for delicious-smelling bundles. "We have to show a little respect for the tamale! Fold your foil back and tuck it under the packet, and then gently peel back the banana leaves to reveal the contents! And don't go dumping it out in a big mess, either!" Snacker was shouting excitedly. "Oh, yeah! Look at that baby!" Steam was rising up from his plate.

Fact: to a person in a beer-induced haze, there is no better food in the world than fresh, hot tamales. "Good God, these are perfect," I said with a groan.

"Yeah, my friend really hooked me up with this recipe, huh?" Snacker looked very pleased with his dish. "You ladies will have to take some home with you."

"Yeah, if there are any left," Josh said with a laugh.

We worked our way through the salad and an obscene number of tamales without making much of a dent in the hundred or so that we'd cooked. The ones I'd take with me would be perfect for the nights I ate at home alone, the nights when Josh was working. And there'd be many nights like that. I sat back in my chair and faintly regretted that last tamale. I was stuffed. "Snacker, you have to give me this recipe. I bet these would be great to give as holiday gifts to friends."

"Oh, definitely. I usually do exactly that. And you're in luck because I've already got a bunch of photocopies of the recipe. Here," Snacker said as he reached behind him and grabbed some sheets off the counter.

I gasped as I skimmed through the ingredients. "Fifty chicken thighs! Forty tomatoes!"

"I know it sounds crazy, but if you're going to go to the trouble of making tamales, you might as well make one giant batch," Snacker explained.

"I guess that's true. It's pretty labor-intensive, huh?"

"True, but totally worth the time," Josh added as he licked his fingers.

"Hey, Snacker," Blythe began. She pointed to his hand. "How did you get that big scar on your finger?"

"Battle scar from a few years ago," he explained. "Not a big deal. Everyone done here?"

Josh started laughing. "Not a big deal, is that right? You're not going to tell them?"

"Come on, dude! Don't do that to me! I'm trying to make a good impression here." He winked flirtatiously at Blythe.

"If she still likes you after this, then you're safe!" Josh spoke way too gleefully. He stretched back in his chair. "So this was back in the days," Josh started in his best storytelling voice. "Back in the days of mayhem, when we were known to get a little wild. Not like now, of course, because we are very serious and professional at all times."

"Yeah, whatever." I laughed. "Go ahead."

"Snacker and I were working at this awful little restaurant together, where we were both line cooks. All we served was crappy frozen appetizers that we had to fry up for service and stuff like that. But the place was always packed, and the so-called chef was hardly ever around, so it was always me and Snacker frying up mozzarella sticks and wings. So one night," Josh said as he took a swig of his beer, "Snacker and I were getting slammed at the restaurant, and he cut his finger pretty badly on a meat slicer. I tried to get him to go to the ER, but he said he wanted to wait until after service, since it was only the two of us and a dishwasher there. So we wrapped his finger up in a pile of bandages and taped it good and tight, so he had this big old sausage on his hand."

Snacker continued. "It was still bleeding a lot, though. So after a while, I went to change the bandage. When I pulled it off, all this blood started spurting out, and I guess I passed out."

Josh started giggling uncontrollably as he spoke. "So obviously I had to take him to the hospital. When we got there, I kept telling them that Snacker had been throwing up and that he felt really sick and all that."

"Why is this so funny?" Blythe asked. "This is a horrible story!"

Snacker slammed his beer down with a smile. "Because Josh was trying to convince them that I couldn't take any medication orally, and the only way to get any medicine into me was to stick it up my—"

"No!" Blythe gasped.

I leaned over and playfully pushed Josh. "Some friend you are!"

"And that's how I got this lovely scar." Snacker held his hand up in the air, and we all clinked bottles again in honor of his kitchen wound.

"On a serious note," Blythe said once we'd stopped laughing at Snacker's misfortune, "what do you guys think about Leandra? Can you believe that she was killed with an apron from Simmer?" Blythe's speech was starting to slur.

"Pretty freaky," said Josh.

"Who has keys and the alarm code and could have gone in and out of Simmer after hours?" I wondered aloud.

"All of us do." Snacker gestured to Josh, Blythe, and himself. "And obviously Gavin. Wade and Kevin. And Leandra. What we don't know is if she was killed inside and moved outside to the truck, or whether she was killed in Owen's truck. Either way, it seems the killer ditched the apron with our laundry, because I don't think the police found anything in the Dumpster in the alley."

"I can't believe we have this memorial thing tomorrow. What a joke. But if you ask me, it was probably Wade who killed her," Blythe offered up. "He is such a backstabber, I wouldn't put it past him." Snacker and Josh nodded in agreement.

"Well, I don't know if he killed her, but he *is* an asshole," Josh said.

"What's wrong with Wade?" I asked everyone. The only thing I could remember to Wade's discredit was Gavin's having said that Wade was putting down Josh. Now, I had the feeling that there'd been more than that isolated incident.

Josh put his arms on the table and leaned in. "Oh, he does shit like act like my best friend and then go and bad-mouth me to Gavin. For instance, one time, we had a small party for dinner, and I misread one of the orders, so things were about ten minutes late. Not a big deal, right? And the customers didn't complain. But Wade took it upon himself to tell Gavin about it and say that I couldn't keep up. Another time, I asked him to run to the store for me and pick up a gallon of scallops because we were low. Wade acted like it was no problem, that he'd be happy to help. Later I found out that he told Gavin that I was too lazy to do it myself, that I'd screwed up our ordering, and on and on. One minute he's your best friend, and the next he's shitting all over you. What're you gonna do?"

"Yeah, and I'm so sick of him kissing Gavin's ass all the time," Blythe said with a burp. "Wade talks crap about Gavin like we all do, but he's Gavin's faithful lackey. And meanwhile Gavin is running Simmer like it's a chain restaurant or something, with his stupid management software."

Snacker said, "Gavin doesn't know what's going on at the restaurant most of the time. Josh, and even Wade, probably know three times more than Gavin does." He nodded in Josh's direction.

I started carrying plates to the sink. "But mostly you guys like Gavin, right?"

"A lot of time, he's fine," agreed Josh. "But then you've got the times he says stuff to me like, 'I'd outcook you any day,' or 'How ignorant can you be?' and 'Can't you get it through your thick skull?' Yeah, he's a dream. He thinks he can outcook me, and meanwhile he's trying to have me pre-cook and then freeze fish when it's getting old. But the best is when he tries to jump on the line!"

Snacker started laughing. "Yeah, any time Gavin tries to work with us, he gets all flustered and irritated because he can't keep up, can't deal with the chaos, and can't keep from burning everything. Plus, he loses orders and just tries to cook whatever he feels like off random order slips!"

"Yeah, Gavin's a *great* chef," Josh said with plenty of sarcasm. "Oh, and then there's that time he blew up at me in the office, screaming that my food cost had gone up ten thousand dollars in one week."

"What? How the hell did that happen?" I felt sick. Could Josh have messed up that badly?

"Oh, my food cost was fine. It had gone up by a *hundred* dollars, which is nothing, but Gavin didn't figure that out for another few days! He'd entered something in the wrong column of his goddamn spreadsheet. Do you think I got an apology?" Josh shook his head and tossed his hands up in the air. "But it's his restaurant, right? He can do whatever he wants."

"Did he really do that?" Blythe sounded genuinely surprised. "I had no idea he was that bad to you. I know what I've heard him say to the servers, but I didn't know he treated you like that, too."

"Gavin doesn't give Josh credit for much." Snacker patted Josh's back. "One time, one time," he held his finger up in the air, "he told Josh he was the 'heart and soul' of the restaurant. But the few times he's been interviewed for articles or reviews on Simmer, do you think he sings Josh's praises? No way. All he tells reporters and reviewers is how Simmer was *his* dream, *his* vision, and he takes all the credit. That's why you never see Josh's name in the paper. Gavin doesn't want to share any of the credit."

I was embarrassed to admit that I hadn't noticed the omission. There had been only a few reviews of Simmer since it had opened. The first review, a memorable one, *had* mentioned Josh. For some reason, it hadn't dawned on me that the subsequent reviews had been about Gavin Seymour's new restaurant and not about Simmer's brilliant chef. The reviews and articles had described and praised the decor, the atmosphere, and the food, but Josh's name had not appeared. Josh must have noticed. I felt guilty that I had not.

"Snacker, that's how it works. You know that." Josh tried to wave off his friend's words. "Gavin's attitude is that he put me in a position to do what I want to do, but he gets to reap all the glory. He's not going to allow anyone to write an article about Simmer that doesn't feature himself. Who cares about me, right? He wants the credit for how good the food is. Like he had something to do with it."

I felt terrible about how underappreciated Josh was. "Does Gavin ever pull you out of the kitchen to meet customers?"

"Oh, sure. When it's larger parties, or he wants me to explain the specials. If it will make him look good to diners, then he'll bring me out and say wonderful things about me in front of people. But mostly he pushes the fact that Simmer is *his* restaurant. Which it is, right? It's his money, his power, he's the boss, right? I'm just a cook." Josh spat out the word *cook* as if it meant that his talents extended only to frying eggs and slinging hash.

I didn't know whether the beer was causing or simply revealing such bitterness, but I suspected that hidden truths were creeping out. I was slowly learning that Josh had been protecting me from how tough things were for him, and I guessed that he had been working overtime to maintain my impression that life at Simmer was great. Not that I blamed Josh for resenting Gavin's brushing aside his significant contribution to Simmer's success. But I had had no idea how difficult Gavin was behind the scenes. Josh worked himself to chronic exhaustion for a penny-pinching salary with no benefits, while Gavin paid himself generously, took all the credit, and saw to it that he got all the recognition. The overall picture was nasty. The stories about sexism in the culinary world had been bad, but I now saw them as depicting only one part of a pervasively ugly scene. I'd intended to ask everyone here why the dishwashers and the cleaners were the only Hispanic employees at Simmer, but I decided to tackle that issue another day.

I threw my hands up. "Why do you guys do this to yourselves? Why don't you get out of the business?" Stupid question. I knew what the answer would be.

Josh softened a bit, and I saw some of the twinkle return to his eyes. "I'm a chef. It's who I am, and it's what I do. I don't know anything else. And I'll put up with what I have to until I can get my own place."

It was what Josh wanted more than anything else: a restaurant of his own that he could run *his* way. But I couldn't imagine how he'd ever get the money together, especially with the salary he was earning now. A bank loan would be a gigantic risk. Would Josh take that risk? Probably. And would a bank even give him a loan?

The four of us spent a few more hours talking together and listening to music before Josh and I decided to call it a night. We crashed in his room and left Snacker and Blythe on the couch in the living room. I still didn't know what to think about Blythe's auctioning off stolen goods on eBay, and didn't know whether the thievery connected her to a greater crime. But I fervently hoped that Snacker wasn't literally in bed with the enemy.

# FOURTEEN

**M**Y cell phone shrilled loudly and woke me early on Monday morning. Man, did I have a raging headache! Must have been all those tamales . . .

I rolled over in bed and fished my phone out of my purse. Shit. It was Naomi Campbell, my field placement supervisor. The sight of her name on the cell phone always made me feel slightly anxious; no matter how often I reminded myself that my Naomi Campbell merely shared a name with the phone-hurling model, I could never completely shake the expectation of bizarre abnormality. I suddenly remembered that I was supposed to meet Naomi at the office for my final student evaluation.

"Hello," I murmured into the phone. My voice was almost inaudible, but faintness was all I could muster.

"Good morning, Chloe! Are you ready for your performance evaluation this morning? Can you come in at ten instead of noon?"

I did my best to silence the enormous belch that erupted from my stomach. "No problem. See you soon."

I'd totally forgotten about this evaluation. The absolute last thing I felt like doing was hauling myself out of bed to hear Naomi tell me what a failure I'd been in my field placement. Naomi was deeply, even spiritually, devoted to the Boston Organization Against Sexual and Other Harassment in the Workplace, and I was sure that she had spent the past year in constant disappointment that she had ended up with an intern far less devout than she was. Unfortunately for Naomi, I was the only intern she had. In fact, since Naomi and I were the only people who worked at her so-called organization, the term itself was somewhat misleading. Anyway, as Naomi's intern, I'd done my best. Okay, maybe not my *very* best or even my ordinary best. But I had definitely improved during the year, hadn't I? Well, I'd improved, although probably less definitely than Naomi had hoped I would.

My major task at the BO, an acronym I never used in front of Naomi, had been to respond to hotline calls. When Naomi had first referred to the hotline, I'd envisioned a red phone with flashing lights that would ring nonstop with calls from women in need of help. Despite our efforts to "get the word out," as Naomi always said, I was lucky to get one call a day from a woman experiencing harassment at her job. I enjoyed the few calls that came in, and I learned to handle them pretty well, but I'd filled my two days a week at the BO largely with attempts to look busy: I'd tossed papers around the office and pretended to do research on the Internet. I could imagine all too well Naomi's evaluation of my performance.

I looked at the clock. Eight thirty. Josh was long gone, and Snacker probably was, too. I had to get moving. Stumbling to the bathroom, I could barely tolerate the sense that my brains were bashing against my skull. On the sink, I found a large bottle of aspirin—probably stolen from somewhere, too—and swallowed two while I gulped water from the faucet. I took a steaming shower and sulked about the hangover from hell, the impending meeting with Naomi, and Leandra's memorial service, which I'd have to attend later today at Simmer. I wrapped myself in what I hoped was a semiclean towel and opened the bathroom door.

"Hi, Chloe." In front of me stood Blythe, who looked as bad as I felt.

"Oh! Hi. I didn't know you were still here." I pulled my towel up a bit.

"I had way too much to drink to drive home, so I really had to sleep here," she said sheepishly.

"Uh-huh . . . and . . . ?" Something must have happened between Blythe and Snacker. I did my best to pretend that I was hearing wonderful news. In fact, if Blythe was the thieving eBay seller I thought she was, then the news that she and Snacker had spent the night together was thoroughly bad.

Blythe shook her head. "No, nothing like that. Well, okay, a little maybe," she admitted with a small smile. So much for my garlic vinaigrette warding off Snacker. "But nothing serious. I like Snacker, but he's probably too much of a playboy for me. Anyhow, can I use the bathroom? I have a class that I'm going to be late for."

I stepped into the hall. "Yeah, sure. Sorry. I have to get going, too, so I'll see you at the memorial thing this afternoon?"

"Oh, God. That's right," Blythe said with a sigh. "I'll be there."

I filled a plastic bag with tamales, sped home, breaking a lot of traffic laws on the way, and, in an attempt to look professional, threw on good pants and a blazer. With no time to dry my still-wet hair, I slicked it back into a tight ponytail, grabbed the term paper that I had to drop off at school later, and fought my way through traffic to make the ten o'clock meeting with Naomi.

"Your last day!" Naomi's voice bounced off the concrete office walls. She spun around in her chair and looked at me with a mix of what appeared to be pride and sadness.

This *was* my last day. The reality hadn't hit me before. Now it did: I wouldn't be coming to this gloomy, windowless cell anymore. I wouldn't be staring at the phone waiting for it to ring, or taking lunch breaks that were too long, or fretting over how to transfer calls from my phone to Naomi's. Maybe I would miss these two cramped rooms, the cafeteria tables that served as desks, the smell of Naomi's patchouli incense. Probably not.

But I would miss Naomi. Although we were polar opposites, I had grown to like her. Her die-hard social worker style had initially put me off, but I'd learned to appreciate how great she was at this job and how many women she rescued from horrendous harassment.

"I can't believe it's over. I'm going to miss you," I said to Naomi. God, she did look weird today, though. Her long hair was, as always, done up in clumps of braids that hung down her back. She wore her favorite Birkenstock sandals and a bizarre peasant dress patterned with purple and orange swirls. Her chunky wooden-bead necklace was such an unfortunate fashion choice that I had to restrain myself from reaching out and yanking it off her neck.

"And I am going to miss my favorite intern! Come sit down. Let's get this evaluation over before I fall apart!" Naomi's eyes glistened slightly.

I took a seat on a dining room chair that Naomi had bought for three whole dollars at a yard sale. My supervisor opened a thick binder and leafed through page after page of irrelevant letters, flyers, notes, and articles before she eventually found my evaluation form.

"I have to say, Chloe, that I was a little skeptical when you first started here last fall. But I'm happy to say that I have seen such growth in you! I feel that you are really on your way to becoming an exceptional social worker." Naomi beamed at me.

Was she kidding?

"You and I have very different work styles, but that doesn't mean that you aren't able to do anything you want in this field. It's taken you some time, but I can see that you are really beginning to define yourself in this profession. I've given you very good marks in most areas." When she held out the evaluation form, I could see that she had, in fact, scored me high. "We don't have to go over all of this. I think we have spent enough time each week discussing your performance in our staff meetings."

Another thing I wouldn't miss: staff meetings! With only two of us working at the BO, we could hardly have avoided meeting, but Naomi nonetheless insisted that we hold regular staff meetings to discuss the organization.

"Thank you so much for everything you've done for me, Naomi. You have really been great, and I've learned a lot from working with you, and—"

Before I could finish my sentence, Naomi threw her arms around me and started rocking me back and forth. Luckily, my hangover was subsiding. Otherwise, I might have hurled all over the horrid industrial carpet. I should have known there was no way I'd escape one of Naomi's hugs. In her view, this stressful line of work demanded that we offer support and express our solidarity by reaching out to each other. In other words, she was incessantly engulfing me in hugs and insisting on holding hands. I vaguely wondered whether I'd spent the year being harassed at an antiharassment agency, but I hugged her back, nonetheless.

"Now, before you leave, you must tell me what's going on with you. How are you handling finals? Are you reaching out for support from your fellow students? And from your friends and family?"

"Finals are looking okay. I think I'm ready, but we'll see when I actually get into the room to take those tests." I considered telling her about my goal of correcting sexism in the culinary industry, but I couldn't face the hyperenthusiastic response I'd be doomed to endure. Naomi was the sort of person who would fly onto the bandwagon and have me calling senators and organizing boycotts of restaurants before I knew it. As she'd just pointed out, we had very different styles. "But there is actually something bigger going on. Do you and Eliot know what's been going on at Simmer?"

Naomi's boyfriend, or "partner" as she preferred to call him, owned an art gallery right near Simmer. His name was Eliot Davis. Now that Naomi and Eliot were together, she was a frequent visitor to Newbury Street. Naomi was not Newbury Street material, and I was always deathly afraid that some Prada-wearing, size-zero woman would point and scream at the sight of my tree-hugging supervisor and that the fashion police would then scoop Naomi up and haul her off for an extreme makeover. So far, I'd heard no reports of any such happenings, but it was only a matter of time.

"Eliot told me about the tragedy. Everyone must be in incredible pain right now. This is a perfect opportunity for you to hone your skills by making yourself available as a resource to everyone at the restaurant. You may want to organize a few support meetings with the staff until the immediate feelings of anguish pass." Always the social worker! It was vintage Naomi advice.

"Oh, of course. I'm definitely doing that." I nodded my head sincerely. "How is Eliot? How are you and Eliot?"

"Thank you for asking. I appreciate that." Naomi patted my arm and squinted her eyes in thanks. "Our relationship is taking a lovely path. The journey we are sharing together is such a positive experience for us both. We've enrolled in a couples' class in aromatherapy deep-tissue massage. Oh, you and Josh should take this with us! So you can do some massage work together! I have a pamphlet somewhere here." As Naomi rummaged through her massive folder in search of the dreaded pamphlet, I made faces at the thought of the two of them doing "massage work."

I cleared my throat. "Josh is very busy at the restaurant, though, and he's exhausted, so I'm not sure we'd have time right now. Maybe when things ease up." *Or when pigs fly. Whenever.*

"Oh, in that case you should definitely work this into your schedule, because they teach a fabulous black pepper rub to counteract exhaustion."

"That sounds very . . . unusual."

Naomi temporarily abandoned her search. "You know, Eliot eats at Simmer quite often. He adores the food there. In fact, he's taking me there tomorrow for a late lunch. Around two o'clock. You should stop by and see us." She reached out and grabbed my hands enthusiastically.

"I'll see if I can do that," I promised. I wondered what in the world Naomi would eat at Simmer. Her strictly organic, politically correct vegan diet left her consuming almost nothing besides locally grown bean sprouts.

"We're going with his gallery assistant, Penelope, because we are actually trying to do a little matchmaking."

She sang the word *matchmaking* as if the activity were slightly naughty and daring.

"Who are you trying to set her up with?" I asked. "Someone at Simmer?"

Naomi bobbed her head up and down dramatically. "Yes, with that nice bartender there. Kevin. He seems to have developed quite the crush on Penelope. Eliot told me that Kevin has come into the gallery with flowers and other little gifts for her on a few occasions. He is very sweet. I don't have the impression that Penelope is quite as smitten, and, according to Eliot, she has lots of men who find her alluring. But we thought we'd give it a try. Kevin seems *so* interested." I could practically see the lightbulb go on in Naomi's head as she added, "Maybe they might like this massage class. I'll have to give them the information, too. Couples massage could be a profound way for Kevin and Penelope to connect with each other. A little myrrh, a little orange blossom . . . Who knows what might happen!"

Poor Kevin and Penelope had no idea what was about to hit them. I doubted that romance would bloom among smelly oils, but I crossed my fingers for Kevin anyway. He seemed like a good guy, if somewhat of a misfit. And spring was the time for romance! Could I even help to move things along at lunch tomorrow? I wrapped up my meeting with Naomi, got swaddled in another tight hug, and assured her that I'd see her tomorrow. With Eliot and Penelope, too, of course.

I got in my car, flew down Commonwealth Avenue, and dropped off a term paper at school. After all the work I had put into it, I'd probably never see it again unless I flunked the course. In that case, someone would presumably get in touch with me. With a few hours to kill before the memorial service, I headed home to lie down and shake off the remains of my headache.

The nap was a success. I awakened with the conviction that I just might make it through this thing. As I was changing into black clothes, I realized that people might be expected to speak at the event. I hurried to the computer, did a search for "funeral readings," and printed out the ones that seemed most appropriate. I shoved the materials into the memorial book and took off.

I reached the sidewalk outside Simmer at exactly three o'clock. The service would be blessedly short, because everyone present would have to finish preparations for dinner service, which started in a few hours. I took a deep breath and pulled open the front door. Oh, there was food! One could act appropriately mournful and yet enjoy a tasty treat at the same time. I knew what I was smelling, too. The wonderful aroma drifting my way came from Josh's spring rolls. These weren't on Simmer's menu, but I'd tasted them when I'd first met Josh. His spring rolls, which were unlike any others I'd ever had, were made of oversized wonton skins filled with a mixture of fresh vegetables, roasted garlic, coriander, cumin, and other ingredients that he refused to reveal, even to me. But I did know that once filled, the spring rolls were deep-fried. I wondered what kind of sauce he'd serve with them today.

All of Simmer's employees seemed to be here, most of

them seated at tables or leaning against the bar waiting for the big event. I walked toward the bar, where Josh and Snacker were talking together. "How are the hungover boys today?"

"Ah, we're good." Snacker pounded his chest. "You know us chef types. Nothing knocks us down!"

"I see you're feeling fine." I turned to Josh. "How are you, hon? Am I smelling what I think I'm smelling?"

Snacker answered. "His stinky ass, you mean? Yes, you are, and you'd better get used to it!"

Josh laughed and waved him off. "Don't mind him. He's still drunk. And you bet I made those spring rolls just for you. Come here." Josh pulled me in for a kiss. "Food is love, baby."

"Then you must really love me." I kissed him back.

"Do you know they're still making these at one of my old restaurants?"

"What? How can they do that without you there anymore? It's your recipe!" To my mind, Josh's spring rolls were his signature dish. It appalled me to think of anyone else making them and taking credit for Josh's genius.

"There's nothing I can do about it, because, technically, it became the restaurant's recipe. But don't worry, there's no way they're as good as mine because the recipe they have on file is missing a few things." He gave a sneaky smile. "If they want to try to do what I do, let 'em."

Gavin stepped into the dining area, and the room quieted. "Would everyone please take a seat so we can begin." He was dressed in a fashionable black suit and looked ready to walk the red carpet and give E! a stellar interview on his latest film.

I quickly served myself a spring roll and sat down next to Josh at one of the dining room tables. Josh had made my favorite mango sauce to go with the spring rolls, and I greedily inhaled the mix of crunchy shredded vegetables and smoky spices. Blythe took the seat next to me, and Snacker sat next to her. I simply had to tell Josh that Blythe was stealing more than silverware and napkins from Simmer; she was stealing Wüsthof knives from him! I dreaded breaking the news. Josh was obviously under stress right now. Blythe's betrayals would seriously tick him off. The moment that this memorial gathering ended, he'd rush off into the kitchen, and I wouldn't get a chance to talk to him for the rest of the day. Maybe I could catch Josh tomorrow after I had lunch with Naomi, Eliot, and his assistant, Penelope. Another day wouldn't hurt, right?

Gavin stood at the bar while his employees and I sat like expectant diners waiting to give our drink orders. A framed eight-by-ten photograph of Gavin and Leandra in a tight hug rested on the bar, and a garish heart-shaped floral wreath sat on a wooden easel. The heart was made of red roses, and the overall effect was Valentine's Day gone bad. A sash draped across the front of the heart read In Loving Memory. Isabelle approached Gavin and appeared to whisper gentle condolences.

"Thank you, everyone, for coming. As some of you might know, Leandra had no family. At least none that we know of, so in many regards, we were her family. I thought we could all take a few moments today to speak some final words about Leandra." He paused, placing one hand on the bar as if to steady himself. "I guess I'll start."

Gavin coughed a few times and then broke into heavy sobs. It was an uncomfortable moment as we all sat there, unmoving and unsure of how to handle his grief. I hoped that this was a time when the best thing to do was nothing. When the worst of his crying had subsided, Gavin held his head up high. "As you can see, I am having a terrible time dealing with Leandra's death. I cared for her very deeply, and in the short time we were together, we became closer than most of you probably know. She made me happier than I could have imagined, and for once it seemed like my life was perfect. That incredible woman was a force of nature." He chuckled lightly. "She was opinionated, tough, sassy, and driven. But, oh, what a woman she was! After years of waiting, I finally had my dream restaurant, my restaurant that was meant to be, and I had the perfect relationship. Leandra had a special light around her that touched me profoundly."

I swear to God, if he lifted his hands and started signing *You complete me*, I was going to puke. People were shifting in their chairs at Gavin's expression of profound devotion to a person who'd otherwise been universally disliked. There was only one possible explanation for Gavin's infatuation with Leandra: the two had shared an incredible sex life. Needless to say, I did not stand up and voice that conclusion.

"I am shocked and heartbroken at this sudden and totally

unexpected loss." Gavin's voice began to rise. "Whoever murdered my beautiful Leandra deserves to suffer for the crime, and I know that the police will find her killer! It is intolerable that someone would strangle this innocent, loving soul! That someone would do this to us!" Gavin broke down again. He was barely comprehensible as he asked others to come up and speak.

No one volunteered. Four or five employees began eating their spring rolls, a response that was obviously a tribute to Josh rather than to Leandra. Desperate to generate the kind of response that Gavin needed, I pulled out a copy of the Twenty-third Psalm that I'd printed from a Web site, and I shoved it into Josh's hands. "Go read this," I ordered quietly. "With feeling!" However deluded Gavin was about his beloved Leandra, he was undeniably in real pain. We were obliged to make an effort to support him.

"Oh, man," Josh muttered under his breath as he took the paper and moved through the tables. He whispered something to Wade, who was seated near the bar, and then stood next to his tearful boss. Wade rose and helped Gavin to a seat.

" 'The Lord is my shepherd: I shall not want. He maketh me to lie down in green pastures: he leadeth me beside the still waters. He restoreth my soul: he leadeth me in the paths of righteousness for his name's sake.' " Josh managed to deliver what at least sounded like a heartfelt reading. Josh looked at me, and I urged him on with repeated nods, indicating that, yes, he was supposed to read the entire psalm. For Pete's sake, he was halfway through already! " '. . . and I will dwell in the house of the Lord for ever.'" Josh shook Gavin's hand and then returned to his seat next to me.

I sent Kevin up to the front with "The Road Not Taken," followed by Wade with a poem called "The Final Flight."

I leaned past Blythe and passed the rest of the readings to Snacker. "Pick one of these." One more speaker should be enough to round out the memorial service.

Snacker distractedly took the last page of my collection of readings and went up front. "'Disorders in this category include failure or extreme difficulty in controlling impulses despite the negative consequences. This includes the failure to stop gambling even if you realize that losing would result in significant negative consequences. This failure to control impulses also refers to the impulse to engage in violent behavior—for example, road rage—sexual behavior, fire starting, stealing, and self-abusive behaviors.'"

Wait, what? Oh, shit, I must have accidentally mixed in my DSM notes with the readings I'd printed out! I began frantically gesturing and shaking my head at Snacker while simultaneously trying not to draw attention to myself.

Josh leaned in to me. "Chloe, what the hell is he talking about?"

Oblivious to the meaning of the words he was mechanically sounding out, Snacker continued. "'Intermittent Explosive Disorder. This disorder is characterized by frequent and often unpredictable episodes of extreme anger or physical outbursts.'"

Of all the inappropriate things to read aloud at the memorial service of a woman who had been strangled! "Wrong page! Wrong page!" I yelled out. "The Keats poem! Read the Keats poem!"

Snacker looked up at me. "Yeah, I thought this was sort of weird." He shuffled through the papers until he found Keats. " 'Oh, soft embalmer of the still midnight! Shutting with careful fingers and benign . . . ' "

Thank God! Except that I probably should have chosen something that didn't include the word *embalmer*. Too late now.

Snacker's horrendous reading came to an end, and I did my best to salvage the mess I'd created by presenting Gavin with the memory book. I stood next to the grotesque flower heart and spoke to the seated employees. "Thank you, everybody, for all the extremely loving memories you shared with me." While Gavin took the book from me, I quickly shot the room a snotty look, admonishing everyone for the across-the-board failure. "I hope that the words in this book offer you some comfort."

"Thank you so much for this, Chloe. This means everything to me." Gavin leaned in to give me a polite hug, and I returned to my chair. "To end the service today, I would like to have a final toast to Leandra." Blythe and Kevin rose from their seats, retrieved glasses from behind the bar, and began pouring drinks. "Her favorite drink was Oban, a wonderful, smooth, and satisfying single malt scotch."

A glass of whiskey? What kind of favorite drink was that for a young woman? And the last thing I needed today was hard liquor.

Blythe carried a tray full of glasses and placed four on our table. "Enjoy. It's a miracle that there's enough Oban to go around. Wade is forever walking off with it."

In response to my questioning look, she nodded. "Oh, yeah. He kisses Gavin's ass and then helps himself to the top shelf. Prick." She continued serving the other employees. Josh and Snacker were leaning behind me talking and missed what Blythe had said.

While we raised our glasses in a final farewell, I couldn't help focusing on the news that Wade was stealing, too. And stealing expensive bottles of single malt scotch at that! Here was yet another person who could have been found out by Leandra and would consequently have been motivated to silence her. I looked around the room and watched Wade and Kevin lift their glasses of Oban and swallow their drinks in one gulp. I touched my glass to my mouth but didn't let any of the whiskey cross my lips. I was pleased to notice that Isabelle did the same thing; she was underage. There was at least one law-abiding person here. Or was Isabelle refusing to drink a toast to Leandra and secretly celebrating the young woman's demise?

"I have to go, babe." Josh grabbed my hand. "I'll try to call you later."

Within minutes, the entire staff was bustling to get ready for dinner service. Gavin again thanked me for putting together such a lovely book. I brushed off his thanks. "It was no problem. Everyone was happy to contribute."

Happy to have this memorial service over, was more like it.

# Fifteen

BACK at my apartment, I put the finishing touches on my second paper, which was due the next day. I fed Ken the hermit crab some crab food that looked like mouse poop and then distracted myself from thoughts of the thievery at Simmer by researching names for Adrianna and Owen's baby.

They had decided not to be told whether the baby was a boy or a girl, so all possibilities were open. And for a world of possibilities, no place on earth beats the Web. Using a baby-name site that allowed me to save a list of names under consideration, I put together an appealing selection and then looked up the meanings of the names in case I'd misguidedly chosen something that meant "idiot woman" or "son of burglar." While I was on the site, I looked up *Noah*, which turned out to mean "wanderer," "peaceful," or "comforter." Well, the wanderer part rang all too true, and if "comforter" was the bedroom variety, then it fit, too. Peaceful? Well, Noah probably felt peaceful after having sex with one of his random one-night stands. *Chloe*, I discovered, had two meanings, both pleasant: "young green shoot" or "blooming." I typed in my last name and was disappointed to learn that *Carter* meant "cart driver." Dull!

Josh called and interrupted my important research.

"Listen, I can't talk long, but I just had a pretty weird conversation with a friend of mine, Dan, who's a chef at Asiago, one of Owen's restaurant accounts." I heard the usual kitchen noise in the background.

"Uh-huh. What'd he say?" I entered *Joshua*. The word looked funny, since I never called Josh by his full name. "Lord is salvation" or "God rescues."

"Owen told me he was delivering to Asiago, so I asked Dan how Owen was working out and all that. Dan had no idea what I was talking about. He said that Owen had come in but that his prices were too high, so Dan didn't use him."

"So? Maybe Owen just meant he was trying to get the account."

"There's more." Josh spoke loudly to make himself heard over the restaurant din. "Dan is good friends with the chefs at a few of the other places Owen said he delivers to, so I had Dan call over to them and see what they had to say. Turns out, Owen only has one of those accounts, and they only order a few of their products from him and still use their other fish purveryor for most of their orders. I called Porcaro, too, because I'd sent Owen over there when he first started his job, and I forgot to ask Porcaro about it the other night. Owen told me Top of the Hub was one of his biggest accounts, and they were giving him great orders five times a week. When I talked to Porcaro today, he said he only orders scallops from Owen twice a week."

"Owen is lying about his accounts? What's going on with him? Maybe he's been trying to keep Adrianna from worrying."

"I don't know. But Mark also told me that his friend Sam from Danielle's Bistro does use Owen and has gotten to be friendly with him."

"Okay, so that's good. He's building a relationship with his account." I felt desperate to find something positive.

"Owen told Sam that he *bought* the delivery truck. It doesn't belong to the Daily Catch company. It's his. Owen was showing it off to Sam and told him how much he paid for it, which was a lot, by the way, and how he got a brand-new refrigeration unit put in himself. Chloe, Owen must have huge car payments every month for that thing."

"No, no, that can't be right," I insisted. "He's said a hundred times that his delivery truck is a company truck. Adrianna said he doesn't have to pay for the insurance or maintenance on it because his boss takes care of all of that." Josh had to be mistaken; Owen wouldn't lie.

"No. Mark was sure about this because he heard that Owen made a little bit of a spectacle of himself by flashing off his new truck. You know Owen. I don't think he was being a jerk about it, but he definitely made a show of it." That *was* like Owen.

I shut my eyes and sighed. "I don't even know what to say right now. But don't say anything to Owen, and especially not to Adrianna, about this."

"I agree. I don't know what the hell to think. Something weird is going on with Owen. Listen, I have to go, but I wanted to tell you what I knew. I'm coming!" Josh shouted out to someone in the kitchen. "I'll talk to you later tonight or tomorrow."

I hung up, stunned by what Josh had just told me. Owen was lying about something significant to Adrianna, his fiancée and the mother-to-be of his child. How could he possibly afford a new truck? And now, of all times? And the maintenance and the insurance! Especially without the major accounts he had described to us. He was being so uncharacteristically deceptive about the truck and the accounts that I had to wonder whether he was also lying about other things. I already knew that he had asked Adrianna to tell the police that he had been with her the night Leandra died. Why had Owen asked her to lie for him? Convenience? Maybe he'd simply wanted the police to stop pestering him. Or could Owen really have something to hide? Could he possibly have killed Leandra? No. There was no way. I knew Owen.

I thought back to the morning when I'd discovered Leandra's body in the back of his truck. Owen had wanted to show me the truck himself; it had been strictly my idea to explore it on my own. Maybe he'd had no intention of showing me the inside. He could have planned to drive the body away and dispose of it! Still, why would he have murdered Leandra? An unwelcome answer came to me. Months ago, Adrianna had had a minor fling with Snacker. She hadn't outright cheated on Owen, but she had betrayed him. What if Owen had had his revenge with Leandra? Owen had been to Simmer's New Year's Eve opening, and he'd been there many times since then. He now made daily deliveries to Simmer. It would've been easy for him to run into Leandra and flirt with her. Owen was still furious with Snacker, but I thought that he had forgiven Adrianna for her indiscretion. Maybe not. Maybe he had stupidly, foolishly hooked up with Leandra as payback. And then Leandra had threatened to tell Adrianna. If Leandra was as coldhearted as people had been telling me, she wouldn't have thought twice about breaking Gavin's heart. Or Ade's. In fact, Leandra had enjoyed needling people and taunting them.

A much more tolerable alternative was that Owen had been set up. Someone else had killed Leandra and tossed her body into Owen's truck. Almost everyone liked Owen. The only person I could think of who didn't was Snacker. But Snacker didn't hate Owen; he was just sick of having Owen shoot him dirty looks and throw obnoxious comments his way. In response, Snacker stood up for himself. The rest of the time, I thought, Owen never crossed Snacker's mind. It didn't make sense that Snacker would have killed Leandra, placed her body in the fish truck, and waited for Owen to suffer the consequences. Snacker loved women and loved fooling around with them; the notion that he'd killed a woman, especially one he found "hot," was ridiculous. But I couldn't think of anyone else who'd deliberately have framed Owen.

My thoughts returned to the day we'd found the waitress's body. Owen's behavior had been strange: he'd tried to convince me to move Leandra's body out of his truck, and he'd seemed far more worried about himself than about the dead woman, as if his selling fish were more important to him than staying alive had been to her. It was, however, possible that Owen had had some sort of affair with Leandra. The other night at Simmer, Leandra had said something that hadn't sat right with me: *So, when am I going to get a ride in that new truck of yours? I hear the fish business is booming.* Did getting "a ride" have a double meaning? Ick! Or did she know that he had bought his truck and was she taunting him with what she knew? Leandra's words bothered me.

I looked up Owen's name in the online baby-name database. *Owen* meant "warrior." I abruptly shut down the computer and walked away.

# Sixteen

MY sleep that Monday night was dreamless, and I awoke on Tuesday morning feeling healthy and energetic. After a day of hungover grogginess, my system was finally free of beer, and I was back to normal. I showered, dressed, and ran my second term paper over to school. Back at home, I was forcing myself to review my notes on the DSM and pathological behavior in general when Adrianna called.

"Chloe, I need your help!" Worried that my best friend had discovered Owen's lies, I braced myself for an onslaught of screaming and wailing. "The movers left a little while ago, and I can't deal with this disaster! Can you help me get started with unpacking? I think I have that nesting thing going on, and I feel like I have to get everything settled as fast as possible."

The last thing I felt like doing right now was unpacking boxes, but it would be better to help Adrianna move in than it would have been to console her about Owen's deceit. "Sure. Give me your new address again?"

Adrianna and Owen's new apartment was around the corner from mine. Within minutes, I was outside her building. Their place, like mine, was on the top floor of a house that was surrounded by other houses. Ours were two of the rare streets left in Brighton that weren't jammed with large apartment complexes. Ade and Owen, however, had the only apartment in the house; unlike me, they wouldn't have Noah-esque neighbors who sunbathed in skimpy clothing. The owners lived in the main part of the house for half of the year and spent the other half in South Carolina. Consequently, Ade and Owen wouldn't have to worry about irate neighbors when the baby cried. The building was attractive: a yellow house with a lovely front porch and black shutters. The front lawn, with its tall shade trees, would be great for the baby. A separate entrance on the side of the house gave them private access to their top-floor apartment. As I ascended the narrow, twisty staircase, however, I wondered how in the world they'd carry up a stroller or a baby in a car seat. The door to the apartment was open. I had to squeeze past two cardboard boxes to get into the hallway. I nearly cried.

This was a beautiful place, with freshly painted walls, but

God, it was so tiny! The front door opened into a minuscule hallway. To my right was a small living room, ahead of me was the doorless doorway to the galley kitchen, and to my left were three doors. I'd have given anything to be able to buy my friends a big, fat house in the suburbs where they'd have the space they needed to raise their child.

"Ade?" I called.

"In here," she answered.

I took a left and found Adrianna in what was obviously a large closet. Matching up the closet with a description Ade had given me of the apartment, I realized that she was in the nursery. In spite of a small window with an old radiator under it, the closet was a closet. But she could definitely get a crib in here. And almost nothing else. I was heartbroken.

Ade stood up and smiled at me. "Thank you so much for helping. I didn't know where to begin, so I've been trying to push some stuff in here for now."

"You're not supposed to be pushing anything!" I admonished her. "I'll move whatever you want." I did some quick muscle poses to demonstrate my Herculean strength.

She laughed. "Don't worry. I haven't been lifting couches or anything. I just have to get some of this put away, because with my belly sticking out like this, I can hardly move around here."

"Tell me where to start. I'm at your service."

"Well, I found a couple of boxes of sheets and towels. Maybe you could unload those into the bathroom closet? Right there."

I stepped out of the "nursery" and went to the bathroom at the end of the hall. There was barely enough foot room for me to stand, but the bathroom did indeed have a skinny linen closet with plenty of shelving. Boxes with Adrianna's neat labeling were next to the door. I yanked the packing tape off the tops and began refolding and storing the contents.

"How did it go with the movers?" I asked. "And when is Owen going to be here to help?"

Ade stood in the hallway. "The movers were great. I just stayed out of their way, and they had all my stuff out within a half hour. Right after they finished unloading here, Owen's movers showed up, so the timing worked out well." She looked at her watch. "He should be here by midafternoon. He has a meeting scheduled with a new restaurant he's hoping to get, but I don't know how long that will last. I need some water. Want some?"

"Sure." I nodded.

"Hey, can you pull out a set of sheets for me? The movers actually put together the bed for me. I want to get it made up before I collapse later."

Ade went to the kitchen, and I poked through the boxes until I found a matching set. "Gosh, how many sheets and towels does one person need?" I was discovering set after set of white linens.

I traded her the sheets in my hands for the water. "That really nice set of heavy sheets?" she said. "That's from my vacation to Cabo last year. And those superthick towels? Same place." She shrugged.

"You wasted suitcase space on towels you could buy here? Why didn't you just wait until you got home?"

Adrianna laughed. "I didn't buy them, silly. That's what hotels are for!"

"You stole these?" I myself was barely able to use the little hotel soaps and shampoos without feeling pangs of guilt. And that was when I was staying at the hotel. "All of these?"

"No, of course not. Not all of them. I'm not stupid. But probably half the stuff there, yeah, from different trips over the years. For what it costs to stay in a hotel these days . . ." She shrugged again. "It's no big deal, Chloe. Don't look so shocked. Do you think I'm the first person to take shit from places?"

Was everyone on the planet except me so light-fingered? Was everyone else a damn thief? Was I expected to pick up the habit and start leaving the nail salon with files and polish remover? Start grabbing life vests from public pools and popcorn machines from the movie theater? Had the rest of the population gone crazy?

"What other stuff do you take?"

"Just little stuff. Souvenir kinds of things. Cream pitchers, salt and pepper shakers. I'm not leaving restaurants with barstools or anything. I'm sure people take stuff from Simmer all the time. Josh'll tell you that." She looked at me doubtfully. "You've never taken anything in your life?"

"Apparently I've been missing out this whole time."

"Are you mad at me?" Ade looked hurt.

"No, no, not at all," I said honestly. "I just didn't realize . . . I just didn't know that people do it all the time. But I guess you're right about it happening a lot." It was certainly happening at Simmer.

As I continued filling the closet with purloined goods, I couldn't help thinking that Adrianna needed a linen service as much as Simmer did! I smiled to myself but then, at the thought of linens, my mind turned in a serious direction: toward the apron-turned-murder-weapon that had been used on Leandra. Until today, I'd assumed that the murderer was someone with access to Simmer; that is, someone who had been inside the restaurant, grabbed an apron, strangled Leandra, put her body in the truck in the alley, gone back into Simmer, set the alarm, and locked up. But if everyone except me was pilfering everything, then Owen would have had no need to enter or leave Simmer on the night Leandra was murdered. Owen, who was often in Simmer, could have taken an apron anytime he pleased. He could have waited until Leandra left for the night and strangled her with an apron that was already in his truck. It was even possible that the apron thief had been Adrianna and that Owen had used one that she'd stolen!

"Chloe?"

"Ahhh!" I looked at Adrianna's surprised face. "Sorry. You startled me."

"What the hell is wrong with you?"

"Nothing." I shook the growing panic out of my head. "What did you say?"

"I said, I hope Owen gets this account he's meeting with today. This restaurant is actually one of three that the owners have, so he could get three new accounts!"

"I'm sure he'll do great."

"I hope so. You know how charming he can be. I bet he'll be able to schmooze them into going with him."

"Yeah, he is very charming," I agreed.

Charming the way the DSM described certain pathological people as being charming? Charming meaning manipulative? What then popped into my head was the Psychopathy Checklist, a rating scale designed to measure the traits of people with psychopathic personality disorder. The first item was "Glibness/superficial charm." Owen scored a two on that one, meaning "item definitely applies."

"Are you done in there? Do you want to help push some furniture around in the living room?"

"Sure." I started breaking down the boxes to clear some room. "Let's get you guys set up!" I did my best to sound cheery.

The living room was small, but it had a beautiful bay window that overlooked the street and let light into the room. Once everything was unpacked, the visible floor space would make the room feel larger than it did now.

"Shit, what a disaster area this is!" Ade looked exasperated.

"Easy there, Mommy. You better start watching what you say," I scolded her. "Are you gonna kiss your baby with that mouth?"

"Sorry. You're right. But what else am I supposed to say about this chaos?"

My sister, Heather, learned the hard way to clean up her language when her son, Walker, spent six months exclaiming,

"Son of a bitch!" at every mundane event. "Heather did it, and so can you," I encouraged her.

"Great, you think I should be like Heather saying 'Jeepers creepers!' and 'Mercy me!' when the kid throws up on me? Or 'Criminy! What a giant, disgusting poop you made!'"

It was true that Heather had resorted to expressions so old-fashioned that it was embarrassing to be caught in public with her. She said stuff like "Heavens to Betsy, that cab driver almost ran us over!" and "Goodness sake's alive, what a bozo!"

"Just work on it, Ade. Okay, the first thing we should do is get all these boxes into the rooms they're supposed to be in. Why don't you take a breather, and I'll do that." I didn't want pregnant Adrianna moving anything larger than a salad bowl. I made her sit down. "Give me ten minutes, and then we can move some furniture."

I successfully pushed boxes down the hall into the bedroom but ran into problems in the galley kitchen, where the boxes were too wide to fit in at all. Ade started unpacking the kitchen boxes just outside the tiny area. Meanwhile, I shifted boxes from the living room into the hallway so we could arrange furniture in the living room before moving the boxes back.

Ade stood in a corner and directed me. "The couch should go here, in front of the window." I heaved and pushed and prayed I wasn't scratching the wood floors. So much for a security deposit. "And obviously the coffee table in front of it." More pushing. "And this armchair facing the window. Then the TV stand can go here. I'll let Owen hook up the whole sound system later."

"See, this is better already," I said, wiping sweat from my brow.

"I think Owen will like how we've set this up. I can't wait until he gets home! I'm dying to hear about his meeting. It's so nice that he's finally found a regular job. Remember when he worked for that blimp company? But I really think the puppeteer was the worst. I thought I'd spend my life surrounded by freaky marionettes with wooden jaws. And at least this delivery job isn't boring. You know how Owen isn't a desk-job kind of person, and with the Daily Catch, he's always on the move driving, delivering, talking with people. It's really perfect for him."

Another Psychopathy Checklist item: "Need for stimulation/proneness to boredom."

Ade continued talking happily as she cut open a box of books. "Once he's able to buy his own truck, his commission will increase, and all these big accounts will get even bigger!"

Owen already had his own truck! Another checklist item: "Pathological lying. Lack of realistic, long-term goals." Owen was certainly lying about quite a bit these days. The debt he'd gotten himself into suggested that he was being completely unrealistic about the future. The DSM's antisocial personality criteria included the "failure to conform to social norms." Owen was one of the most nonconformist dressers I knew; he drove according to his own idiosyncratic traffic rules; and his odd career path, no matter how amusing, was hardly the steady work that the DSM and the checklist valued.

And what about Adrianna's stealing? Was it as harmless as she thought? Hers was yet another name to add to the list of people Leandra might have witnessed taking Gavin's possessions from Simmer. Leandra sounded like someone who'd have taken nasty delight in reporting even a single incident of thievery to Gavin. If she'd seen Ade making off with restaurant property, she might have threatened Owen with the knowledge.

Even worse, Leandra had worked in restaurants for quite a while and could easily have heard the gossip that Josh had passed along to me: that Owen had bought his truck and that he was lying about the quality and quantity of his seafood accounts. Leandra and Kevin, I remembered, had worked together somewhere. Digger and Lefty had both known her. She could easily have tapped into the restaurant grapevine. I was sure that Leandra would've enjoyed confronting Owen with what she knew and making him squirm. Because Owen was determined to provide for his new family, he would have interpreted her slightest taunts as major threats; and in a person with a psychopathic personality, the result might have been homicide. Owen, in a fit of protective rage, yanked out his stolen apron and choked the life out of Leandra!

Okay, I had my doubts. Still, I simply had to have a frank discussion with Owen about his recent behavior. Adrianna deserved better than lies, and Owen had to let her know what he had been up to. I'd worked hard at Adrianna's, but

I'd worked efficiently. Maybe it was still early enough in the day for me to get to Simmer before Owen made his delivery and to wait for him there.

In a crowded, public place with a host of witnesses.

# SEVENTEEN

"ADE? I'm sorry, but I just looked at the time, and I told Josh I'd meet him over at Simmer," I lied. "Will you be okay now? We got a lot done, I think."

"Absolutely. I'm fine. I feel better having put some of this stuff in place. Thanks for your help."

I hugged Adrianna and left her to store her stolen cream pitchers and salt shakers. Lord knew what else she had hidden in those boxes! I ran home to get my car. On the way to the restaurant, I called Josh to see whether Owen had arrived with Simmer's seafood.

"Nope. He's late with his delivery. He was supposed to be here earlier, but he just called and said he'd be here within the hour."

I contemplated the idea of warning Josh not to be alone with Owen but decided that there was no way Josh would take me seriously. "I want to talk to him," I said. "If he gets there before I do, do you think you can stall him for a few minutes?"

"I guess so, but why don't you just call him yourself and tell him to wait for you?"

"Because . . ." I stammered. "I just don't want to. You might not want to be alone with him."

"Why wouldn't I—"

"I'll be there soon." I hung up.

By the time I got to Newbury Street, every legal parking spot was taken. I gave up trolling side streets and parked in an expensive lot. I scurried through tourists and shoppers to reach Simmer's patio, where I immediately saw Naomi with her boyfriend, Eliot, and a beautiful young woman who was, I assumed, Kevin's crush, Penelope. The three were seated at one of the outdoor tables. I had forgotten my promise to Naomi to stop by for lunch.

Naomi's face lit up when she saw me. "Chloe! I'm so glad you can be with us. We're having a wonderful lunch, and Josh even worked around my dietary needs to create an incredible salad." She leapt from her seat to swaddle me in her usual hug. "Obviously you know Eliot, but I'd like you meet Penelope, his assistant at the gallery."

"Hi, Eliot. Nice to see you." I shook his hand. Eliot had the most bulging eyes I'd ever seen. His striking combination of bug eyes and frizzed-out hair evidently struck Naomi and me in rather different ways. In her gushy, New Age fashion, she was crazy about him. Penelope, on the other hand, had no peculiar features and was very pretty by anyone's standards. Her straight brown hair was parted in the middle and fell softly to her shoulders. "Great to meet you, Penelope." I smiled at her.

"You, too. Your boyfriend is an excellent chef. Eliot has brought me here quite a few times, and it's always been just great."

Naomi slipped something into my hand. I looked down to see that she'd given me a sample-size bottle with a label that read Intimate Oil with Nutmeg and Tangerine. I shuddered and dropped the gift into my purse. "Thanks."

Blythe appeared at the table to clear the plates. "Hi, Chloe. Josh said you were coming by. You can go right into the kitchen if you'd like." She turned to her customers. "Can I get you some dessert and coffee?"

I quickly apologized to Naomi. "I have to go see Josh, but I'll try to come sit down after." I rushed off before anyone could protest. I was just about to push open the door to Simmer's interior when Kevin opened it for me, said hello, and eagerly moved past me to Penelope's table. For his sake, I hoped that she returned his crush.

Simmer's dining room was almost empty. It was nearly three o'clock: the lunch rush was over. When I found Josh in the kitchen, he immediately shot me a quizzical look.

"What was your phone call all about? Why shouldn't I be alone with Owen?" Then his mouth dropped open in disbelief. "Chloe, don't even try to tell me that you think he has something to do with Leandra's murder!"

"Okay, just listen! I know it sounds crazy," I agreed. I pulled Josh into the office, dropped my purse onto a chair, and explained my two theories. Josh dismissed the first one: he thought that it was unlikely that Leandra had known anything about Owen's lying binge. Then I moved on to the second theory. I began by describing the things that Adrianna had taken from hotels and restaurants, and I went on to point out Owen's possible motive for killing Leandra: she could have threatened to report Adrianna to Gavin or, worse, to the police. "Owen or Ade," I said, "could have swiped an apron from Simmer. And then Owen used it to strangle Leandra!"

Josh laughed uncontrollably for a few moments before he pulled me close to him and rubbed my back. "You are so funny. I love that you are innocent enough to think that this stealing business is so alarming. It's totally normal in restaurants and any hospitality industry, really. Blythe and Snacker even said so the other night. Besides, this software that Gavin is making everyone use makes it impossible to keep track of the inventory anyway. It's practically an invitation to people to take whatever they want."

I pulled far enough away from Josh to look up at his face. "Listen to this. Blythe is stealing from the kitchen and selling things on eBay. I know because Adrianna made a bid and won a peacoat, and the seller turned out to be Blythe, who is also listing some of the things that you realized were missing the other day. The mandoline, the stick blender, and the Wüsthof knife. Oh, by the way, you better check your knife collection. She's selling *two*."

"Jesus Christ!" Josh said angrily. "I'll deal with her later. But I bet Leandra was doing the same thing. Call it a gut feeling, but this has her name written all over it. Either way, no one rats on anyone else around here, because everyone is doing it. You think I'm going to tell Gavin that Snacker took a bunch of chicken to make tamales? Actually, the only person around here who isn't stealing shit is probably Isabelle. But that's only because she hasn't been in the industry long enough to know we all do it. So there. You think that makes her a suspect? Because she's the only one not stealing?" He winked at me.

"Well, Isabelle obviously idolizes Gavin and didn't think Leandra was good enough for him, so maybe she told Gavin about Leandra, hoping that he'd feel so betrayed that he'd dump her." I paused. "But instead of just feeling betrayed, he killed her!"

"Are you done with this nonsense? Gavin may have some quirks, but he didn't kill Leandra." Josh leaned out of the office. "Santos! Take the bread out of the oven, will ya?"

"*Sí*, Chef!" Santos called back.

Josh obviously wasn't taking my theories seriously. "Okay, smarty," I said, "who do you think killed Leandra?"

Josh shut the office door and leaned against it. "Here's what I think. Like I was saying, in restaurants no one rats on anyone else because no one can afford to. Except for Wade. He'll throw anyone under the bus if it makes him look good."

"Right, like you guys were telling me the other night at your place."

He nodded. "The night Leandra was killed, Wade and

221

Kevin were closing. Supposedly, they gave each other an alibi, but that means nothing, because Wade is a lowlife. You have no idea how much crap he's said about me and then turned around and told me how much he admires me. Horseshit like that all the time from him. And the truth is, he's a lousy GM at that. Anyhow, Wade is the one with the faulty personality, not Owen or Gavin. If you're looking for a suspect, I'd put my money on him. Look, Chloe, I have to get back to work. Snacker just got here, so I'm going to be really busy."

"All right. I'm going to hang out and wait for Owen, if that's okay with you." I wasn't looking forward to my conversation with him, but it needed to happen.

"Stay as long as you like. You can come watch me prep if you want."

Josh and I left the office, and I sat on a stool a few feet from where Josh began seasoning some rib eye steaks. I loved watching him work, but I was always worried that I'd cause a kitchen calamity by hanging out in the wrong spot, so I sat frozen to my seat.

Kevin entered the kitchen and spotted Josh. "Hey, dude. Any chance I could get three desserts on the house?"

"Depends. Who are they for?" Josh flipped over the steaks and continued generously sprinkling salt, pepper, and sugar across the meat.

At that moment, Blythe entered the kitchen and said exactly what I was thinking. "They must be for Naomi, Eliot, and Penelope, right?"

So, Kevin was trying to impress Penelope with Josh's dessert. Cute! The strategy always worked for me!

"Yes, actually, they are," Kevin said shyly.

"Sure, no problem. Let me see what I have that's ready to go." Josh washed his hands and then went into the walk-in refrigerator, where prepped desserts were kept.

Snacker materialized from behind a counter. "Miss Penelope is out there, huh? Nice going, Kev!"

"Kevin's got a girlfriend," sang Blythe.

Josh came out of the walk-in with three ceramic ramekins that held raspberry crème brûlée. He set them down near Kevin. "Here you go. Can you just finish them off for me? Sprinkle them with sugar and throw them under the broiler for a minute or two." Josh handed over three ramekins. "And there's some more fresh raspberries around here somewhere, too, for garnish."

While Kevin sprinkled sugar, Blythe leaned over to me and whispered in my ear. "You probably don't know this, but Kevin has it bad for that Penelope girl!" She giggled. "He's been making eyes at her for weeks now, and I don't think she's interested in the least. It's pathetic, really. He keeps asking me if I've seen her outside, and he made all of us say that we'd go find him the minute she comes in. Maybe if he got rid of those stupid sideburns!"

I giggled and then noticed Kevin looking over at us. "Mmm," I muttered vaguely, trying to cover up my smile. Seriously, though, Kevin did need to get rid of those things. At a guess, he'd grown the sideburns in an effort to make himself look young and trendy, but their effect was exactly the opposite.

Blythe must have seen Kevin watching us, too, because

she said jokingly, "Yes, we're talking about you, Kevin! And Chloe's going to go tell your new girlfriend everything I'm saying!"

Kevin took the raspberry desserts to the broiler and ignored Blythe's teasing.

The kitchen phone rang. Josh picked it up. "No. Not yet . . . I have no idea . . . Okay. Bye." Josh turned to me. "That was Adrianna calling to see if Owen is here. Where the hell is he, anyway? We're supposed to get our fish in the morning, not just before dinner!" Josh put his hands on his hips. "God, I barely got through lunch with what we have. Owen better get his ass here fast, or I'm gonna drop him!" Josh continued his prep work.

"Dammit!" Kevin yelled as he pulled out three burned brûlées from the broiler.

"I got you!" Josh said, retrieving more raspberry delights for the nervous bartender. "Keep an eye on those. They'll burn in a second."

"Thanks, man." Kevin took a breath and started cleaning up the mess.

Owen stomped into the kitchen in his heavy work boots, a white box in his hands. "I know! I know! I'm sorry!" he hollered out to the entire room. "I'm totally behind schedule today, and I forgot your razor clams at the warehouse, so I had to go back to the waterfront, and there was an accident right at the turnoff to—"

Josh held up his hand to stop Owen. "Just give me my clams, you loser," he said, grinning at the frazzled Owen.

Owen smiled back at him. "Let me grab the rest of your stuff from the truck."

"Hey, Chloe." Blythe nudged me and started whispering again. "You know how I told you that my friend Katie picked Kevin up at a bar? Well, you won't believe what else she told me!" Blythe raised her eyebrows and bit her lip. "Kevin doesn't know that I know that they slept together, and it's a good thing, too, because then he'd *really* be afraid of me making fun of him."

Oh, this sounded good. "What?" I asked, always eager for a little gossip.

She softly cleared her throat. Speaking so softly that I had to strain to hear her, she said, "Apparently . . . How do I say this? Kevin's, you know, *thing*," she said with a knowing look, "is very . . . um, weird."

I choked back a laugh. "What? What do you mean?"

Blythe spoke out of the corner of her mouth, as if twisting her lips would somehow lighten what she was trying to say. "Katie said his penis is bent. Like, not just a little, but, you know . . ." Blythe held up one hand in the shape of the letter *C* and put her other hand over her mouth to stop herself from laughing.

"What are you talking about?"

"Like, seriously bent. Curved. Whatever it is, it's not, well . . . straight!"

"Oh, my God, Blythe, I *so* didn't need to know that!"

"You think *I* want to know that? I had to tell someone, though!"

I turned so that my back was to Kevin. There was no way I could watch him hover over the crème brûlées right after hearing this weirdly intimate detail. "I'm definitely not repeating that! But if Kevin winds up with that Penelope girl, I guess she'll find out for herself."

"Yeah, but by then it'll be too late. Who knows?" Blythe continued whispering. "Maybe Penelope the Beautiful won't care. Anyhow, Kevin gets crazy whenever he talks about her, so that's why we all tease him. It's like being in junior high around here. We love each other, but we have to give each other hell."

"No kidding. I don't want to know what you guys say about Josh and me!"

"Oh, nothing bad," she said at normal volume. "Don't worry. Anyhow, I have to get back to work. Kevin, you want me to help you carry those out?" Blythe made kissy faces at Kevin as they left the kitchen to deliver the desserts to Penelope, Eliot, and Naomi.

"I haven't seen you in ages, Chloe." Owen walked toward me.

Everything about Owen was familiar and comforting. Instead of feeling enraged at him for his stupid lies, I felt happy to see him. There was simply nothing threatening about Owen. My DSM theory was falling apart. Owen was empathic and kind. He was a great friend. No one in Boston obeyed traffic rules; Owen's driving was no more deviant than anyone else's. Yes, he was unconventional but unconventional in a healthy, interesting, lovable way.

"I know," I said. "Not since we found Leandra. How are

you doing? I've missed you." I gave Owen a hug and ignored the fish smells coming from him.

"Good. Well, okay. I guess Ade must've told you the police are still asking me questions. I don't even have my truck back yet, so I'm using another company one right now. I've got to get going, though. My truck is still running outside, and I've got a few more deliveries to make." Owen brushed his black hair off his face to reveal his bright blue eyes. They were not the eyes of a killer! Even though I knew Owen, *really* knew him, I'd still let that silly DSM book brainwash me. Yes, Owen was a dunce but not a killer.

Adrianna burst into Simmer's kitchen looking madder than I'd ever seen her before. She charged over to Owen. "Anything you want to tell me, Owen?"

"Adrianna? What are you doing here?" he asked his furious fiancée.

"I just got a phone call from the bank about truck payments! You lied to me, to the police, to everyone else about that goddamn truck! Are your stupid fish more important than I am?"

Owen blanched. "I'm sorry, Ade. Listen, I'll explain everything later, but I really have to get out of here."

I backed up out of the kitchen and into the dining room. I felt relieved that I wouldn't have to break the bad news to Adrianna, but I was still in danger of getting sucked into her fight with Owen. Consequently, I had no desire to stick around. Just as I backed into the main dining area, I almost bumped into Kevin. He had a bar towel over his arm, but he didn't appear to be doing any work. Rather, he'd apparently been listening in on the beginning of Adrianna and Owen's fight. I couldn't blame him for his prurient curiosity. If they hadn't been my friends, I'd have been dying to hear what was going on, too.

"Kevin." I took a step back. "Did they like the desserts?"

"I think so. But, Chloe, listen. I need to talk to you about Josh and Simmer. It's something big. Can we find somewhere private?" Kevin suddenly looked deeply worried. My bet was that he wanted to tell me about Wade and his obnoxious habit of bad-mouthing Josh to Gavin. I hoped that the two-faced GM hadn't done anything to get Josh in real trouble.

"Yeah, sure. Where do you want to go?"

Blythe was out on the patio with Naomi, Eliot, and Kevin's inamorata, Penelope; other servers were arriving for their shifts; and Wade was probably around somewhere. I could hear Adrianna's voice as she continued to chew out Owen, who was going to be stuck in the kitchen for a while. That was for sure!

"Um . . ." Kevin looked around the room. "Why don't we go talk in the back hallway? Or outside?"

I began to feel increasingly alarmed that Kevin was about to deliver terrible news. I followed him down the hallway. When we reached the end, he held the back door open for me. Owen's truck was still out there in the alley, its engine running, its rear door open. If Owen had known that Ade was going to interrupt his deliveries, he'd certainly have lowered and locked that sliding door. He might even have turned off the engine. I remember that as Kevin and I walked down the back steps, I was trying to see into the back of Owen's truck and wondering whether any seafood that might be in there would spoil if the engine were off. Then it occurred to me that if Kevin was on the verge of making a horrible revelation, I should probably sit down. It was just as I was about to take a seat on the grimy back steps and tell Kevin to break the news that he wrapped his massive arms around me and engulfed me in what I at first mistook for a bear hug. Why was Kevin embracing me? The delusion lasted for no more than a second. The pressure of his muscular hands on my upper arms was ferocious. Lifting me almost off my feet, he began dragging me toward the open rear of Owen's truck.

Terror and confusion shot through me. "Kevin! What are you doing?" Of all the foolish questions! Why didn't I scream? I probably couldn't have. As it was, my voice cracked, and I was breathing rapidly. His arms gripped mine so tightly that I couldn't break free, and my toes barely touched the ground as he hauled me across the pavement.

"Just shut up!" Kevin snarled. With no apparent effort, he lifted me up and threw me into the truck. I landed hard. The only thing that broke my fall was a plastic tub filled with ice and bags of clams. With the wind knocked out of me, I was helpless. I lay there in a near stupor as Kevin pulled down the sliding door. The inside of the truck was now completely dark. I heard the sound of a lock. Within seconds, the truck was moving. I had, of course, been caught completely off guard. I'd been expecting to hear that Gavin was firing Josh, maybe, or that Simmer was closing. I'd been entirely unprepared for this . . . What the hell was it? A kidnaping? An assault? Finding words for what was happening, I found my voice and started screaming.

Kevin maneuvered the truck around a corner, and Owen's heavy metal dolly slid into me so painfully that in my mind's eye, I could see the bruise that would appear on my leg. I tried to stand up, but my timing was bad: my mad chauffeur slammed on the brakes, and I was immediately thrown against the front wall. I crawled to the back door and started pounding my fists against the metal so fiercely that my hands hurt. I switched to kicking the door over and over with my feet. "Help me! Help! Get me out!"

I started crying in panicked gasps as a terrifying thought raced through my head. Somewhere on the Web or maybe in a magazine, I'd read advice about what to do if you ever become the victim of an attack. A major point was to do everything possible to avoid being taken to a second location. If you are being moved to a second location, you are being moved there to be killed.

I was heading to that second location.

# EIGHTEEN

IT was Kevin who had killed Leandra. That was the only conclusion to draw from this attack. But never mind what he had done in the past! Where was Kevin taking me now? And how could I have let this happen? I was disgusted with myself for not having screamed loudly enough when the truck was still in the alley behind Simmer. I should have tried to fight Kevin off before he locked me in this truck. Well, it wasn't too late to estimate where the truck was now and to figure out where it might be heading. We'd taken a few turns since Kevin had driven us out of Simmer's alley. After that, there had been a few short spurts of movement followed by stops, presumably at traffic lights. I'd continued to hammer at the door with my sore fists and feet, and

I'd shouted for help, but the truck kept moving. Now we were beginning to pick up speed; there were no more stops. I felt sure that we were on the Mass Pike.

I felt around on the floor of the truck in search of my purse, which held my cell phone. Dammit! I'd left my purse in Josh's office! I continued exploring the floor. Somewhere in this truck there had to be something I could use in my own defense. My hands encountered what I easily identified as four tubs of ice and seafood: clams and fish. Ice and seafood were the last things I needed; even without the ice, the refrigerated truck would've been freezing cold, and the air reeked of fish. The metal dolly was heavy. It had already bruised me. I also found a long piece of metal, a rod of some sort with a curve at the end. I knew what it was! A long hook that Owen used to reach into the truck, hook the sides of the tubs, and pull them close to the edge of the back opening. The hook meant that Owen didn't have to climb into the truck and push all the tubs around; he could hook and drag them instead. This seafood hook helped Owen. Maybe it could help me.

Shit, it smelled in here. I did my best to breathe through my mouth. On top of being abducted, I didn't need to be sickened by the stench of pounds and pounds of fish. How long could I tolerate the foul air without doubling over? How long had we been on the highway? Five minutes? Ten? At least I had a weapon now. Two weapons: the hook and the dolly. Being armed gave me the beginnings of a sense of confidence. Kevin, I realized, had acted impulsively when he'd tossed me into the truck; he couldn't have planned ahead, and whatever plan he had now wasn't one he'd thought out. Someone was bound to look for me. And for Kevin, too. We'd abruptly vanished. We were going to be missed, right? And if Adrianna ever quit screaming at Owen, he was going to see that his truck had been stolen.

I was moving on from straight fear to fury. How dare Kevin do this to me! What was he, after all? A vain, aging bartender with weird facial hair and an embarrassing anatomical oddity, that's what he was. I felt ashamed of my doubts about Owen's character. I should never have suspected him of any romantic, not to mention murderous, involvement with Leandra. The dangerous one was Kevin. But my rage made me even more dangerous than he was, I told myself. I was not going to let Kevin hurt me!

Kevin would have to stop this truck sometime. When he did, I would act. I searched for the heavy metal dolly, found the handle, and rolled the dolly so that it faced the door. When Kevin opened the back, I was going slam this metal hunk on wheels into him and knock him to the ground, bash him over the head with the metal rod, and run like crazy. I sat with my hands on the dolly and waited.

The truck began to slow down. It took a curve. We must be exiting the Mass Pike. After only a few minutes of slow driving and turning, the truck came to a halt. When I heard the driver's door slam, I readied myself to smash Kevin onto the ground. The fear that had transformed itself into fury had now become an ardent desire for revenge: *Come on, you bastard! Come on! Open the door!* Enraged, I was more than ready to kick some serious ass, but I forced myself to keep focused. With luck, Kevin envisioned me cowering in terror in a corner of the icy, stinky truck.

Minute after minute ticked by, and the door didn't open. Eventually, I loosened my grip on the dolly. Kevin, I realized, had left me here. Damn! What an anticlimax! How long was he going to be gone? And where had he gone? What if he had gone to get a gun? If so, I wouldn't stand much chance of overpowering him with the dolly and the metal hook. Listening hard, I waited a few more minutes but heard nothing. Once I felt sure that Kevin had left the area, wherever the area was, I started kicking the door and yelling again. To maximize the noise, I banged the door with the metal hook. I screamed until my throat hurt. No one came to my rescue.

Slowly, my adrenaline rush decreased as I accepted that I was alone. Except for the dead fish, of course. At least I wouldn't die of starvation; I could always eat some raw haddock or smash open clam shells with the metal rod. And I could suck on fishy ice cubes to prevent dehydration, if I didn't freeze to death first. A slight, almost imperceptible, gap along the edge of the sliding door was letting in air; I wouldn't suffocate. Starvation, dehydration, suffocation: three ways in which I *wasn't* going to die. I was not reassured.

Kevin must have returned to Simmer with some excuse for his absence. He would have to come back for me. But why hadn't he tied me up before leaving? Or killed me? More importantly, why had he kidnapped *me* at all? Why me? What did I know that could implicate him in Leandra's murder? I reviewed the knowledge I had about Kevin. His only alibi for the night of Leandra's death was based on Wade's word that the two had been together and had closed up the restaurant. According to Josh, however, Wade was untrustworthy. So there went that alibi. I knew that Kevin had Simmer's keys and alarm code. I'd made the disillusioning discovery that everyone at Simmer was stealing. Therefore, Kevin was stealing. But my theory that Leandra had been on the verge of ratting someone out for stealing didn't hold. If everyone was light-fingered, then Leandra was, too. Besides, Josh had said that stealing was par for the course. Josh had also insisted that restaurant people just didn't report their coworkers for thievery. And Josh knew everything about restaurants.

I pulled my legs in close to me to fight the cold, but the shivering didn't stop. The refrigeration unit ran only when the truck was turned on, but it was still very cold in here. *Think! Think! Why would Kevin kill Leandra?* I knew so little about Kevin! What else did I know? He had slept with a friend of Blythe's. He was infatuated with Penelope. Then there was the unsolicited information that Blythe had passed along about his unusual body feature. Yes! What if Leandra had known about that, too? She liked digging at people and hurting their feelings. Look at how she'd treated Blythe and Isabelle! She'd ridiculed Blythe about being flatchested. Had she teased Kevin? Or threatened to tell Penelope? Something must have happened between Kevin and Leandra last Tuesday night. But what did that unknown something have to do with my present predicament? Why had Kevin suddenly decided to abduct me? Why today?

Shortly before he'd lured me to the alley, he'd seen Blythe and me talking in the kitchen. We'd been giggling. The expressions on our faces had probably made him guess what Blythe was telling me. He had also seen me with Naomi, Eliot, and Penelope. He'd even seen Naomi hug me. Penelope had been at the same table. He could easily have assumed that I was friendly with her, too. One conversation with Penelope, and I might blow any chance he had with her. If that was the case, Blythe was in terrible danger, too.

I yanked on the door, but the lock held. The narrow gaps on either side of the door were too small for the metal hook; I couldn't even try to use the rod as a lever. I grabbed the dolly again, mainly to remind myself that I had a weapon and a plan. Yes, I was increasingly chilled, in fact, shaking, but I was not actually going to freeze to death. Was I? I could be here for hours, I realized. I absolutely could not panic! I just had to wait to put my plan into action.

I tried to distract myself with thoughts unrelated to fish, dead people, or funny-shaped body parts. I thought about my DSM test and ran through symptoms in my head. How stupid I had been to stick Owen with a demeaning and wildly incorrect diagnosis! I made lists of baby names for Ade and Owen, thought about Josh's new menu, and reminded myself to tell him to add another cold summer soup. I made mental notes on ways to eradicate sexism in the culinary industry and then quizzed myself on *24* trivia. *What was the name of Jack's covert operation in Belgrade? Operation Nightfall!* I couldn't honestly give myself credit for my answers, since I was the one formulating the questions. I ran through song lyrics until I had Paul Simon's "You Can Call Me Al" stuck in my head. That wouldn't do! It was no kind of attack song. So, to boost my fighting spirit, I made myself hum the theme for *The Sopranos*. Not that I expected music to blare when the time came to defend myself against Kevin—and I wasn't going to burst into song—but better to think about waking up and getting myself a gun than to ponder the possibility of ending up a cartoon in a cartoon graveyard.

I did such a fine job of distracting myself that I was violently startled when the truck door suddenly began to rise. Fortunately, I managed to maintain my grip on the dolly. Rising to my feet, I kept my knees bent and stayed low. Filtered sunlight burst into the back of the truck and temporarily blinded me. I blinked my eyes rapidly and waited until the door was two-thirds of the way up. When I could see Kevin's waist and torso, I lunged forward and smashed the dolly straight into my kidnapper. Kevin stumbled back but quickly regained his footing and then, to my horror, grabbed the dolly with one hand. Terror-stricken, I yanked back. I wasn't strong enough to shake his hand off the dolly, but his continued grip worked to my advantage: to maintain his hold on the dolly, Kevin had to bend at the waist and lean forward. I put all my strength into one mighty thrust and slammed the heavy dolly right into his head.

"You bitch!" He fell to the ground and moaned.

*Bitch.* For once, I loved the sound of the word. But I had no time to savor it. In using one weapon, the dolly, I had lost track of the other. After fumbling around, I found Owen's metal hook and then leapt out of the back of the truck. For no good reason, I had assumed that the truck was outdoors. In fact, I found myself inside a small garage. Light filtered through its dirty windows. Kevin lay on his back on the oily cement floor. I raised the metal rod. My plan was to hit him where I'd do the most damage. As it turned out, however, I just didn't have it in me to play it safe by delivering a blow to his head. In spite of everything, I did not want to risk killing him. But I did need to hurt him. I absolutely had to disable him. I smashed the rod down onto his legs. I did it three times.

Pain made Kevin roll onto his side and curl up. When he did, I spotted his cell phone, which was sticking out of his pocket. He lay between the truck's back tires and the garage door. With no room to maneuver, I was reluctant to get close to him, but I wanted that phone so desperately that I forced myself to reach down to grab it with my left hand. As I did, Kevin snatched my wrist. He had left me no choice. The metal hook was still in my right hand. I drove the curved end of the rod hard into his gut.

With Kevin immobilized, I made my escape through a side door of the garage. With the phone in my left hand, the heavy metal hook in my right, I started running and didn't stop. To my surprise, I was in a residential neighborhood. Once again, my assumption had been wrong; I'd senselessly imagined a rural spot. The truck hadn't covered enough miles to reach one; there were no rural areas within easy driving distance of Newbury Street. In any case, the neighborhood was one I didn't recognize. Somewhere in

Brighton, maybe? Not in my own area. Possibly near Oak Square?

I flipped open Kevin's cell phone, paused to dial 911, and picked up speed again. As I jogged down a steep hill lined with almost identical three-decker houses, I sobbed information to the 911 operator. I stayed on the phone and read off street signs as I passed them. I kept looking behind me to see whether Kevin was in pursuit, but the streets were empty. Out of breath, I slowed my pace to a fast walk and kept moving until a siren sounded, lights flashed, and a police cruiser pulled up beside me. I climbed into the car. I was safe.

After I'd assured the officer that I was uninjured, he wanted me to show him where I'd left Kevin. Somehow, I was able to help him retrace the path I'd taken. "There! That's the door I came out of!" The officer radioed in the address. Within what felt like seconds, three more police cars appeared and screeched to a halt in front of the garage.

"Wait here!" My savior jumped out of the vehicle and joined his fellow officers while I waited to see Kevin appear in handcuffs.

An ambulance arrived. The officer who had picked me up returned to the cruiser. I rolled down the window. "He's not there? He got away?" I cried in frustration.

The officer smiled. "No. He's there. But he can't walk. You got him pretty good. We had to call an ambulance for him."

The police eventually drove me to Simmer. All I wanted was to be with Josh, the only person who could make me feel truly safe. On the way, I detailed what Kevin had done to me and explained that he was the person who had murdered Leandra. Explaining his motive was awkward, of course. I used the phrase *disfigured manhood*.

Two cruisers were outside Simmer, and Josh stood out front with a policewoman. He had both hands on his head and was talking quickly. When he saw me step out of the car, he dropped his hands, rushed to me, and engulfed me a tight, protective hug. "Oh, baby! Thank God you're okay! That bastard!"

I sobbed in Josh's arms and looked up only when I began to stop shaking. "I'm fine, Josh. I'm going to be fine."

# NINETEEN

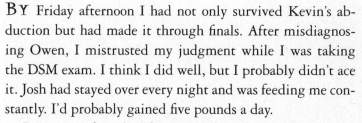

BY Friday afternoon I had not only survived Kevin's abduction but had made it through finals. After misdiagnosing Owen, I mistrusted my judgment while I was taking the DSM exam. I think I did well, but I probably didn't ace it. Josh had stayed over every night and was feeding me constantly. I'd probably gained five pounds a day.

I was seated with Adrianna and Owen inside Simmer. The weather was cool this afternoon, so we'd forgone the patio in favor of a table in the dining room. Officially, the restaurant was between lunch and dinner service, but Josh had filled our table with plates of food. His latest creation was running as a special: a phenomenal spaghetti and lobster with a fantastic green and red tomato sauce, flavored with saffron, ginger, and fennel, and then topped with fresh basil. Nothing made for more perfect comfort food than a steaming bowl of pasta, and this one was outstanding. I breathed in the aroma and sighed before twirling my fork in the spaghetti and scooping up a generous bite of lobster meat.

"Let me see your ring again," I said to Adrianna. She proudly held out her hand to show a beautifully simple silver ring with a pale olive stone.

"It's the baby's birthstone," she said with a grin. "It's called peridot."

"I know." I smiled at her. She had told me the same thing about forty times in the past twenty-four hours. "It's just beautiful."

Adrianna was happier with the inexpensive ring than she'd have been with the one that Owen had had in mind. One of the reasons that my dear deluded friend had bought a truck for his new fish-delivery job had been to increase his commission: he'd wanted to be able to make payments on a pricey diamond solitaire engagement ring. Adrianna had now convinced him to sell his truck when the police returned it and to use one of the company's instead. But I'd also learned that Leandra had, in fact, known about Owen's four-wheel purchase, and she had been taunting him her last night at Simmer simply because she was, as Belita and others had put it, a bitch.

"I wish I could give you the ring you deserve, but I guess this will do for now," Owen said sadly. "I'm sorry about everything. I really apologize to both of you for acting like such a jackass. I just want to be able to take care of you and the baby, Ade, and I thought you'd feel better if you thought I had a lot of big restaurant accounts. It's just taking longer than I thought it would to build up business. Do you know how much this baby is going to cost? When Ade stays home next year, I'll be the only person supporting us, and I guess the stress got to me."

I hadn't told either of my good friends that I'd suspected Owen of being involved with Leandra. The notion was so stupendously dumb! And I'd sworn Josh to secrecy. I took Owen's hand. "Wipe that sheepish look off your face. We understand why you lied. And Adrianna let you have it pretty good. So, you probably learned a lesson, right?"

Owen's eyes widened. "Our child is going to learn quickly not to mess with Mommy, that's for sure!"

Adrianna took his other hand. "Honey, we'll work it out. Plenty of people have babies when only one parent is work-ing. Besides, do you know day care would be over a thou-sand dollars a month? That is crazy. And it would eat up my income anyhow. Plus, I want to be home for a while with the little guy. He's going to need me." She gave me a know-ing look.

Little guy? I nearly jumped out of my seat. "It's a boy?"

They both flashed huge smiles, and Ade said, "I couldn't wait any longer, so I called up my ob-gyn and told her we'd changed our minds, and she told us we are having a healthy baby boy."

"Actually," Owen spoke proudly, "what the doctor said was that there was *no question* that it was a boy because his manhood was quite visible! That's my boy!"

Ade and I rolled our eyes.

Josh and Snacker came to the table, and Josh placed yet another dish on the table. This one was a deep bowl piled high with clams and mussels. Aromatic steam rose from the top. The chefs sat down, and I was happy to see no overt displays of malice from either Owen or Snacker.

"Chloe, are you getting enough to eat?" Josh asked with concern.

I looked at my boyfriend with disbelief. "More food? Josh, seriously, you have to stop hovering over me! I promise you that I am fine. I've eaten enough for me, Ade, and her baby. But thank you. Everything is as good as ever."

Josh scooted his chair close to me and draped his arm over my shoulder. "Just making sure. Here, try this. It's clams and mussels cooked with a spicy orange bouillon. A chef I went to school with stole my idea for this and put it on his menu, but this is the original dish. And a better one." He spoon-fed me some of the broth. "I brought enough for all of you, obviously."

"Josh isn't going to stop feeding you until you puke," Snacker added indelicately.

The bouillon was liquid heaven. I pulled some clams and mussels from their shells and dunked them into the broth. Perfect!

Wade sauntered through the front door. I was convinced that his hair had grown an inch higher in the past few days. Blythe saw him come in, too, and hurried over to our table. "He just came from seeing Kevin."

I bristled at the sound of that man's name. Having

confessed to Leandra's murder, he was safely locked in jail, but none of us knew exactly what had transpired on the night of the crime.

"Come here, Wade! What did that asshole have to say for himself?" growled Josh.

Wade stood next to our group. "That night, Kevin and I were closing together, remember? We were drinking a little while we were cleaning up and cashing out the registers. Leandra was with us for a while, but then she left. Kevin and I finished closing not long after that and locked up together and went our separate ways. It turns out Leandra came back because she wanted to get some stuff that wouldn't fit in her purse." Josh raised his eyebrows at Blythe, who looked down in her lap.

Wade continued. "She ran into Kevin on the street, and they went back in the restaurant together. I guess she figured that Kevin was stealing, too, so he wouldn't care. Apparently, he'd had a lot more to drink than I thought, and he came on to her. For whatever drunk, horny reason, he cornered her and unzipped his pants. Kevin said that Leandra ridiculed him beyond reason, and it was completely humiliating. Then she told him exactly what Penelope from the gallery would think of him."

"And he snapped," I finished for Wade. "Right?"

Wade nodded and sighed. "Yeah."

Blythe and I understood, of course. Everyone else looked confused. "What could she have said that was so humiliating?" Adrianna wondered aloud.

I let Blythe reveal Kevin's secret embarrassment. The

sound of *ohhh* echoed through the room. The amazing thing, I thought, was that if Kevin had just waited to be in a relationship with someone caring and understanding, he wouldn't have had a problem. Now that I was safely out of the confines of the fish truck, a small part of me actually felt sad for Kevin. I wondered whether the intense pressure of Newbury Street, with its emphasis on physical perfection, had made his secret all the more mortifying. How unposh to have a problem like his!

Wade continued. "Ahem, yes. I don't know specifically what Leandra said, but it was apparently pretty vicious. Kevin said he just went apeshit and, without thinking, pulled his apron off and strangled her behind the bar. He didn't even realize what he was doing. He said he was as surprised as anybody that he killed Leandra. He carried her body out to the alley, thinking he'd throw her in the Dumpster, but Owen's truck was there, so he put her in. He wasn't thinking very clearly because he was so drunk, but he did realize that putting her there might make it look like somebody else killed her. Then he just locked up the restaurant and left. When he woke up the next morning, he thought maybe he should move her out of the truck, but by then, it was too late. Chloe and Owen had already found Leandra's body."

I'd been right that Kevin had been afraid that I'd ruin any chance he had with Penelope. He threw me into the truck and drove me to what I learned was his home. He parked the truck in his own garage. Kevin always took the bus to work. Consequently, his car had been at his house. He sped back to Simmer, where he told people that he'd been taking his break and had no idea where I was. Because Kevin wanted to get back to me before somebody heard me, he intentionally burned himself on the espresso machine and left work, supposedly to go to the emergency room. But he went back home for me.

Owen and Adrianna's fight had gone on for so long that Josh eventually told them to take it outside. When they did, they realized that Owen's company truck was gone. It soon became obvious that I was missing as well. Josh called my cell to find out where I'd gone and heard my phone ring in his office. By that time, Kevin had left, supposedly to attend to his burn, but Josh realized that something was dreadfully wrong. My boyfriend called the police, who had him pull Kevin's home address from the office. My 911 call came moments before Josh's call, but it eased my mind a bit to know there would have been backup if I'd needed it.

"How's Gavin doing with all of this?" I asked of the Simmer employees. "Has it helped him at all to know that Leandra's killer is in jail?"

"Yes and no," said Wade. "He's hardly been in here since Kevin was arrested. Of course, he's glad that Kevin was caught, but he also feels responsible. Like he should have been able to predict that Kevin was going to flip out. He might be down one bartender, but at least he has you two holding down the fort," Wade said to Josh and Snacker. "You guys are the best."

Josh opened his mouth. I kicked his foot under the table.

"Oh, and Gavin is working on a new girlfriend already. Did you guys know he asked Penelope out?"

"Oh, God, that's so tacky," said Snacker.

"I have to work on finding a replacement for Kevin, so I'll catch you all later." Wade started to walk away. I was glad to be done talking about Kevin. "Oh, Chloe? Did you know you fractured Kevin's left leg? Not bad." He winked and left us.

Josh and Snacker stayed while Ade, Owen, and I finished eating. Snacker and Owen had apparently called a truce: neither of them threw forks at the other. Blythe leaned in to me. I hoped that she didn't have another piece of unwelcome anatomical information to convey about another of Simmer's employees. "Can I talk to you for a second?"

I followed Blythe to the bar. She took a deep breath. "I talked to Josh earlier today, and I wanted to talk to you, too. You know that I've been stealing from the restaurant and selling the things on eBay."

"Did Josh ask you about that?"

"Yes, he did." Blythe had the decency not to pretend that she was confessing on her own. "I have no excuse. I know I said that everyone steals, but I really took it too far. I needed money for school and for bills. I've been getting crappy shifts here, and I got desperate. Obviously, I knew what I was doing was wrong and stupid, but I didn't realize that the knives I took were Josh's. I thought they were the restaurant's and the loss would come out of Gavin's too-deep pockets. Not that it's a good excuse, but call me Robin Hood. I'm broke, and it seemed like a basically harmless way to get some cash. Just so you know, I gave Josh back everything I took. Nothing sold on eBay yet, so it's all been returned." She shook her head at her own behavior. "I don't know what else to say. I'm sincerely sorry for being so thoughtless and awful!"

Blythe did look sorry, and I appreciated it that she was speaking to me directly about what she had done. "You still have a job, though?"

"Josh made me swear up and down that it wouldn't happen again and threatened to make me eat cayenne cookies if I even glanced at his cooking equipment!" She smiled. "So I promised."

"What about Snacker? Have you talked to him?"

"He's next. I know he's a little wild, but I do like him. I think he likes me, but I don't know what will happen after I tell him. He and Josh seem pretty tight."

"They are. But if Josh hasn't booted you out of here, you might have a chance." I started back to the table but then turned around to Blythe. "And that peacoat better arrive soon, or Adrianna and I are going to give you negative feedback on eBay."

I heard a gasp. "That was you two?"

I slid back into the crook of Josh's arm. "Everything okay, babe?" he asked with concern.

I sent Snacker off to talk to Blythe and popped another bite of lobster into my mouth. "A little stuffed, but I'm good. Hey, have you two picked a wedding date yet?"

Adrianna shook her head. "No. I don't think we want to do a big wedding, anyway. Maybe something simple this summer before the baby is born."

I turned to my boyfriend. "Josh, you can cater it!"

"Absolutely. I'll do whatever the beautiful bride wants."

And then my gorgeous, wonderful chef looked at me. "You know, *you'd* make a beautiful bride, too."

# RECIPES

In this book, Chloe and the gang feast on many culinary delights. Here are the recipes for some of the dishes they enjoy. Many thanks to the chefs, professional and amateur, who contributed their talents to this section! Be sure to read through each recipe before cooking because some of these dishes require preparation the day before or hours before serving.

# Roasted Pork Quesadillas with Apple Salsa

Courtesy of Michael Ricco, Executive Chef and Owner,
Café Teresa, Londonderry, New Hampshire

The apple salsa here is delicious. If you have any left over, you can serve it with grilled or roasted chicken.

Makes 6–8 quesadillas

### Roasted Pork

*1 tbsp. kosher salt*
*1 tbsp. cracked black pepper*
*1 tbsp. fennel seeds*
*1 boneless pork loin, about 1½ lbs.*
*1 tbsp. extra virgin olive oil*

Preheat oven to 350°.

Mix the salt, pepper, and fennel seeds together. Rub the pork loin with the olive oil and then rub the spice mixture onto the pork, covering the entire loin. Place the pork on a cooking sheet and cook in the oven until the internal temperature of the meat reaches 150°, about 45 minutes to 1 hour. Remove and let rest until cool enough to handle. Cut the pork into thin slices and then cut those slices into ¼" strips. Set aside until ready to assemble the quesadillas.

## Fuji Apple Salsa

2   *Fuji apples, cored and finely chopped*
½   *small red onion, finely chopped*
1   *small bunch cilantro, finely chopped*
1   *yellow pepper, seeded and finely chopped*
1   *jalapeño pepper, seeded and finely chopped*
1   *tbsp. honey*
2   *tbsp. rice wine vinegar or cider vinegar*
1   *tsp. kosher salt*

Combine all ingredients and mix well. Set aside.

## Quesadillas Assembly

½   *cup good quality shredded Cheddar cheese*
1½   *cups good quality shredded Monterey Jack cheese*
1   *package of 12-inch flour tortillas*
1   *thinly sliced red onion*
1   *jalapeño pepper, finely chopped*
   *Sliced roasted pork*
4   *tbsp. melted butter*
   *Fresh cilantro for garnish*

Spread equal amounts of Cheddar and Jack cheese, thinly and evenly, over one half of a tortilla. Lay a few sliced onion rings on the cheese and then sprinkle with jalapeños. Place a few of the pork strips on top and then fold the tortilla in half. Brush with a bit of the melted butter, and cook in batches. Lay the quesadillas on a preheated griddle or large pan over medium heat, and cook until the cheese has started to melt. Turn the quesadillas over and finish cooking until golden brown. Remove from the pan and cut into quarters. Place a scoop of apple salsa in the center of the plate and arrange the quesadilla quarters on top. Garnish with sprigs of fresh cilantro.

## Coriander Seared Sea Scallops with Grilled Pancetta, Honey Parsnip Puree, and Warm Pear Chutney

Justin Lyonnais, Executive Chef, Commercial Street Fisheries, Manchester, New Hampshire

One of the things that makes eating out at a fine-dining restaurant so enjoyable and delicious is that chefs often make three or more components separately, then bring them together to create one dish. Each separate element here is simple to whip up, but the combination makes a restaurant-worthy plate. Taking a few extra minutes when arranging the scallops, pancetta, parsnip puree, and pear chutney will give a beautiful presentation.

Makes 4–6 servings

## Pear Ginger Chutney

¼  *cup sliced almonds*
4  *Bartlett pears, peeled and cut into roughly 1" pieces*
1  *cup golden raisins*
½  *cup rice wine vinegar*
½  *cup sugar*
1  *tbsp. fresh ginger, minced*

Preheat oven to 350°.

Spread the almonds onto a baking sheet and toast in the oven for 5 to 6 minutes until just browned. Keep an eye on them, since they will burn easily. This can be done a day ahead if you like.

In a small saucepan, add the rest of ingredients. Cover the pot and cook over medium heat for fifteen minutes, or until the pears are tender. Cool the chutney and mix in the toasted almonds.

## Parsnip Puree

1  *lb. of parsnips, peeled and sliced into ½-inch-thick slices*
½  *cup honey*
½  *cup water*
   *Salt and pepper to taste*

Place parsnips in a large pot with just enough water to cover them. Bring to a boil, cook until very tender, and then drain. While still hot, puree the parsnips in a blender with the honey and ½ cup water until smooth. The puree should be the consistency of mayonnaise, so add more water if needed. Season to taste with salt and pepper.

## Pancetta

*12 slices of pancetta, about ¼ inch thick (sliced like bacon)*

Simply cook the pancetta slices over a grill or on a stove top skillet until nicely browned on each side. Remove from pan and pat off any grease with paper towels. Set aside.

## Scallops

*4   tbsp. whole coriander seeds*
*1   tbsp. salt*
*1½  lbs. of fresh sea scallops, patted dry with a towel*
*1   oz. canola oil*

Preheat oven to 350°.

Spread the coriander seeds on a baking sheet and toast in the oven until golden brown. Grind the toasted seeds in a clean coffee grinder and mix with the salt. Generously season both sides of the scallops with the coriander and salt mixture. Heat a sauté pan over medium high heat. Add the canola oil and sear the scallops for two minutes on each side.

## To Plate

Arrange three slices of the grilled pancetta in the center of a plate. Top with some pear chutney, and place the scallops around the plate in a circle. Drizzle with the parsnip puree.

# Fish Fillets with Vegetables and Herbs
Jessica Park, Manchester, New Hampshire

This is a very easy way to cook fish fillets. It is nearly impossible to mess up unless you absolutely forget about the fish and let it completely overcook! Feel free to substitute or add whatever seasonal vegetables you like. Fresh herbs will really make a difference here. You may want to stick with one variety if it is particularly pungent, like thyme. (Basil and parsley will match up well with other herbs, but you wouldn't want thyme competing with cilantro.) If you've got a grill fired up, these fillets will cook up beautifully for an outdoor supper.

Serves 4 people

4 6–8-oz. pieces of white fish (cod, haddock, red snapper,
  halibut), preferably fresh
Salt and pepper
2 plum tomatoes, halved and then sliced, or a handful of
  yellow or red cherry or pear tomatoes, sliced in half

1 *red pepper, thinly sliced*
1 *small zucchini, thinly sliced*
1 *small yellow summer squash, thinly sliced*
2 *scallions, finely sliced*
1–2 *cloves garlic, minced or finely sliced*
1 *cup white wine*
4 *tbsp. butter*
4 *tbsp. olive oil*
  *Handful of fresh herbs (thyme, basil, cilantro, oregano, parsley), roughly chopped*

Preheat oven to 350°.

Spread out four good-sized pieces of tinfoil (roughly 15" to 18" long) on two baking sheets. Place each fish fillet on one half of the foil piece. Season well with salt and pepper. Lift up the sides of the foil so your toppings won't leak out and then top each fillet with equal amounts of tomatoes, peppers, zucchini, squash, scallions, garlic, wine, butter, olive oil, more salt and pepper, and the herbs. Fold the foil over the top and seal the edges. Place the trays in the oven and check after 12 minutes. When the fish is fully cooked and the meat is flaky, remove from the oven. Top with more fresh herbs if you like and then serve with plain couscous, rice, or French bread (to soak up all the delicious juices), and a salad.

# Crispy Calamari with an Asian Slaw and Roasted Pineapple Dressing

Mark Porcaro, Executive Chef, Top of the Hub, Boston, Massachusetts

The roasted pineapple dressing in this recipe is outstanding and very simple to make. You will need to let the slaw marinate in the dressing for a bit so that the vegetables will soften and all the delicious flavors will come together. Topped with the hot fried calamari, this slaw creates a fantastic summer entrée!

Makes 6 servings

## Roasted Pineapple Dressing

1   tsp. canola oil
½   pineapple, skin and crown removed, quartered
1   cup orange juice
½   tbsp. red Thai curry paste
½   cup honey
2   cups canola oil
    Optional: 1–2 tbsp. scallions, cilantro, chives, or lemongrass

Preheat oven to 350°.

Rub 1 tsp. of canola oil onto pineapple quarters and roast on a baking sheet for about 15 minutes or until nicely browned.

Puree the roasted pineapple in an electric blender with the orange juice, curry paste, and honey. Add canola oil in a steady stream until the dressing has emulsified and thickened. Add any of the fresh herbs listed above and pulse the blender a few times to incorporate.

### Slaw

1½ cups cooked cappellini, cooled under running water
1 tsp. canola oil
1½ lbs. Chinese cabbage, shredded
1 cup shiitake mushrooms, thickly sliced
½ cup carrots, shredded or julienned
1 bunch scallions, thinly sliced
½ bunch cilantro
½ cup water chestnuts, sliced
1 Vidalia onion, thinly sliced
1 tsp. black sesame seeds

Preheat oven to 350°.

Toss cooled cappellini with oil, spread on a baking sheet, and bake for 15 to 20 minutes or until crispy. Remove and set aside.

Mix the rest of the slaw ingredients together and then toss with as much Roasted Pineapple Dressing as you like, reserving any extra dressing for another time. Refrigerate the slaw for 3 to 6 hours before serving so the slaw can marinate and the vegetables can soften.

## Calamari

*Peanut oil for frying*
*1 lb. calamari (frozen is fine), cut into ⅛" rings*
*Kosher salt for seasoning*
*Cornstarch for dredging*

Add enough peanut oil to a deep skillet to reach halfway up the pan and heat to 350° (or you may use a deep fryer if you have one). Season the calamari rings as you like with the kosher salt and then dredge in cornstarch. Fry the calamari in batches until golden brown, being sure not to overcrowd the pan. Drain the rings on paper towels.

## To Serve

*Fresh mint*

Toss the baked cappellini and hot calamari rings into the slaw and top each serving with a sprig of fresh mint.

## Guatemalan Tamales
Julio and Anjos Veliz, Boston, Massachusetts

Don't panic when you see the list of ingredients and the huge amounts for these tamales! This recipe will make 100 tamales but can easily be cut in half or quartered. As Snacker pointed out in the story, if you are going to take all the steps necessary to make these delicious creations, you might as well make a very large batch and freeze a portion or give some away as gifts. Get together with a friend or two and spend an afternoon in the kitchen rolling these phenomenal treats!

*Note: Maseca corn flour is readily available in Hispanic markets and even in some large grocery stores. The frozen banana leaves are also found in Hispanic markets and in some Asian stores. The dried chiles and pumpkin seeds can be found in most good markets or natural foods stores.*

### Prepare the Night Before

> *50 chicken thighs, skin removed, bone in*
> *Salt for seasoning*
> *10 cups of uncooked white rice*

Using a good, heavy knife, cut the chicken pieces in half, chopping through the bone. Season the chicken well with salt, and refrigerate until following day.

Set the uncooked rice in a bowl or pot and cover with cold water. Let the rice soak in the water overnight. The rice will absorb most of the water, but do not drain any excess the next day.

## Sauce

40  *plum tomatoes*
15  *red peppers, cut in half, stems and seeds removed*
7  *onions, cut in half*
1  *head of garlic, skin removed, cloves left whole or slightly crushed*
2  *quarts water*
⅓  *cup salt*
4  *guajillo chiles*
4  *ancho chiles*
2  *whole sticks cinnamon*
3  *cups pumpkin seeds*
⅓  *cup extra virgin olive oil*

Place tomatoes, red peppers, onions, garlic, water, and salt in a large pot and bring to a boil. Let cook over medium-high to high heat while you prepare the chiles, cinnamon sticks, and pumpkin seeds. Stir the sauce occasionally so it doesn't burn.

Cut all the chiles in half and remove the seeds and stems. Place chiles and cinnamon sticks in a nonstick pan and toast over high heat for about 2 minutes until they release their aroma. Do not burn these or your sauce will be bitter! Add to sauce.

Toss pumpkin seeds into a nonstick skillet and stir over high heat until they begin popping and are gently browned.

When the vegetables in the sauce have softened, stir in the pumpkin seeds, and then remove the pan from the heat. Ladle the sauce in batches into an electric blender and puree each batch until smooth. When all the sauce has been blended, strain through a mesh colander or sieve to remove any excess chunks and seeds. Return to the pot and add the olive oil. Bring to a boil once, and then set aside.

## Dough

> *Rice that has been presoaked, with any remaining liquid*
> 1 *bag (4.4 lbs.) Maseca corn flour*
> ⅓ *cup salt*
> 1 *gallon whole or skim milk*
> 4 *cups chicken broth*
> 1 *bottle of extra virgin olive oil (25.4 ounces)*

Puree the soaked rice and any liquid that remains in a blender. Add water as needed to avoid clumping.

In a large bowl, combine the rice puree, the Maseca, salt, milk, and chicken broth. Use your hands to mix these ingredients until they are well combined and the salt has dissolved. At this point, the mixture should be watery, but you may add some cold water if the dough is too clumpy. Add the entire bottle of olive oil and mix with a wooden spoon. Scrape the dough into a large pot and place over high heat. Cook the dough 5 to 10 minutes while stirring constantly. The dough will stick easily if you leave it unattended! The dough is done when it becomes spongy and difficult to stir.

# RECIPES

## Banana Leaves

*100 (2 pkgs.) frozen banana leaves*

Boil a large pot of water and add banana leaves in batches. Cook for roughly 30 minutes until pliable. Drain and rinse with cold water. Cut the leaves into roughly 5" × 6" pieces.

## Tamale Assembly

Per tamale:

- *1   sheet of 12" × 12" aluminum foil*
- *1   sheet of softened banana leaf*
- *¾ cup dough*
- *1   piece of raw chicken*
- *2   strips of red pepper*
- *1   Spanish green olive, pitted*
- *2   capers*
- *⅔ cup red sauce*

Lay the aluminum foil sheet on a flat surface and then lay the banana leaf on the foil. Place the dough, centered, ⅓ of the way up from the short edge of the banana leaf. Top with the chicken piece, red pepper, olive, capers, and then the sauce. Roll the short edge of the banana leaf over the top and then fold in the sides. Now roll all the way down, keeping the banana leaf package nice and tight. Repeat with the aluminum foil wrapper. You may repeat with a second sheet of foil if necessary to make sure that the tamale is sealed and waterproof.

Repeat the process until you have all of your tamale bundles wrapped. Pack as many tamales as you can fit into a deep Dutch oven, Le Creuset, or other heavy pot so the tamales fit together snugly. If you have extra banana leaves, you may use those to line the pot. Fill the pot ¼ high with water, cover tightly, and place over high heat. Cook for 2 hours, but check periodically to make sure that the water has not evaporated. Add more water if needed.

When done, tamales may be eaten immediately. Remove the foil wrapper, or fold back neatly, and enjoy the tamales right from the banana leaf. These also freeze very well for 3 to 4 months, so you may simply place the foil packets as they are in the freezer. To reheat, place in a pot as you did to cook them, and boil for 30 minutes.

## Basic Vinaigrette
Jessica Park, Manchester, New Hampshire

This spicy dressing really has a bite to it and works with almost any salad. There is no vinegar in this since the lemon provides enough acidity, but there is certainly no lack of flavor. I like this best tossed with beautiful fresh red leaf or Bibb lettuce, feta cheese, and Greek olives. Josh and Chloe don't mind garlic-laced kisses, but if you do, you may not want to serve this before a romantic evening.

1½  cups good quality olive oil
3   large garlic cloves, minced
1   tbsp. lemon juice
1   tbsp. Dijon mustard
¼   tsp. salt
¼   tsp. pepper

Whisk all ingredients together with a fork and let sit for at least an hour before serving. This will keep perfectly in the refrigerator for up to three weeks.

## Spaghetti and Lobster
Jody Adams, Executive Chef, Rialto, Cambridge, Massachusetts

This is the most delicious pasta recipe! After discarding the shells from the lobster tails, claws, and arms, you save the lobster bodies and use them to add incredible flavor to the wonderful green and red tomato sauce. This aromatic dish is perfect any time of the year, whether you are dining on your deck in the summer or huddled up by the fire during a winter snowstorm.

Makes 4 main course servings

Kosher salt
4   1-lb. lobsters
½   cup extra virgin olive oil

# RECIPES

1   *medium onion, chopped into ¼" dice*
    *Freshly ground black pepper*
4   *tbsp. chopped garlic*
1   *tbsp. minced ginger*
½   *tsp. fennel seeds*
¼   *tsp. hot red pepper flakes*
1   *pinch saffron*
2   *lbs. green, unripe tomatoes, cut in half and charred
    under the broiler, skin removed and meat chopped into
    ½" dice*
1   *cup canned strained tomatoes*
2   *lbs. ripe plum tomatoes, cut in half and charred under
    the broiler, skin removed and meat chopped into ½" dice*
16 *oz. spaghetti*
4   *tbsp. freshly chopped basil*

Fill a large pot with 1" of salted water. Invert a colander in the pot. Bring the water to a boil. Put the lobsters in the pot and cover tightly. Steam for 5 minutes, then open the pot carefully (steam is *hot*) and, using a pair of tongs, change the lobsters' position. Quickly replace the lid and steam for 5 more minutes. Remove the cooked lobsters from the pot and allow to cool. Separate the tails, claws, and arms from the body of each lobster. Chop the bodies into 4 pieces and set aside. Remove the lobster meat from the tails, claws, and arms, and discard the shells. Cut the tail meat in half lengthwise and remove the digestive tract, the dark veinlike structure. Cut the tail into 1½-inch chunks. Cover and refrigerate the meat.

Heat 4 tablespoons olive oil in a sauté pan over medium heat. Add onion and lobster bodies, season with salt and pepper, and cook 6 minutes, or until the onions are tender. Reduce the heat to low, add the garlic, ginger, fennel seeds, hot pepper flakes, and saffron, and cook until aromatic, about 1 minute. Add the green tomatoes, strained tomatoes, and 1 cup water, and cook 15 minutes. Add the charred red tomatoes and cook 10 minutes more. Remove from the heat. The sauce should be fairly thick.

Bring a large pot of salted water to a boil. Add the pasta and cook 7 to 10 minutes, or until al dente.

While the pasta is cooking, heat the remaining oil in a large sauté pan over medium heat. Add the lobster meat and cook 3 minutes. Remove the lobster body pieces from the onion mixture and discard. Add the tomato sauce to the lobster pan and keep warm.

Scoop the cooked pasta out of the boiling water and transfer the pasta to the pan with the sauce. Add the basil and toss well. Serve immediately.

## Clams and Mussels in an Orange Bouillon

Bill Park, Manchester, New Hampshire

The sweet and salty broth from this dish is perfect for soaking up with bread. Ideally you should make the bouillon part of this dish the day ahead so the broth will have time to reach its full flavor potential, but you can certainly make it on the day you will serve it. If so, prepare the orange bouillon first and then cook the shellfish just before serving. You can find frozen fish stock in most fish markets or in the seafood section of your local supermarket, but you may use clam juice or chicken stock if needed.

Serves 4 people

3  cloves garlic, minced
1  onion, thinly sliced
1  tbsp. oil
1  cup white wine
2  cups fish stock or chicken broth, or 1 cup clam juice
½  gallon orange juice
1  tsp. crushed red pepper
1  tsp. cornstarch mixed with ⅓ cup water
   More white wine or fish/chicken stock for cooking
   shellfish, roughly 3 cups
24 clams (countneck or mahogany), well cleaned
48 mussels, well cleaned

In a large pot, sauté the garlic and onion in the oil for 5 minutes, until the onions have softened. Add the wine, and over medium-high heat, simmer steadily for about 20 minutes until you have reduced the liquid by half. Then add the fish stock (or chicken broth or clam juice), orange juice, and crushed red pepper, and reduce by a third. Stir in the cornstarch and water mixture to thicken the bouillon, and cook for 2 to 3 more minutes. Remove from the heat. If you are making this bouillon the day ahead or a few hours before serving, cool and then refrigerate. Otherwise, just let the broth rest while you prepare the shellfish.

In a separate large pot, pour in enough wine or stock so that you have about ½" of liquid in the bottom of the pot. Heat over medium-high heat and add the clams. Cover and cook until the clams open. Add the cold bouillon and the mussels, and cook until the shells open. To serve, place equal amounts of clams and mussels in each serving bowl and top generously with broth.

## Raspberry Crème Brûlée
### Bill Park, Manchester, New Hampshire

All bias aside, my husband makes the best crème brûlée I've ever tasted. The little ramekins of creamy custard are topped with a crispy crust of sugar and fresh berries. Don't worry if you don't have a special torch for browning the sugar, because you can certainly do that under the broiler. This is an easy dessert to make, but, as Bill says, "It has to be babied!" He also says that when browning the sugar top, under no circumstances should you thoughtlessly stick the ramekins into the oven and leave them unattended, since the difference between *perfectly done* and *burned* is a matter of seconds. So stick by your ramekins unless you want to tick off a chef!

# RECIPES

Makes 6–8 servings

     1    *quart heavy cream*
     ½   *pint fresh raspberries*
   12  *egg yolks*
     1    *cup powdered sugar*
         *Sugar for browning*
         *Optional: extra raspberries for garnish*

Preheat oven to 300°.

Bring the cream and raspberries to a boil over medium-high heat, stirring occasionally so the cream does not burn, and remove from heat. Strain through a mesh colander or sieve to remove seeds, mashing the raspberry pulp down with a spoon.

In a mixing bowl, beat the yolks and powdered sugar with an electric mixer until the mixture becomes pale yellow and thick. Using a wooden spoon, temper the eggs with the hot cream and raspberries by slowly adding in a small amount to the yolks and mixing thoroughly. (It is important to mix with a spoon here, since you do not want to add air to the custard.) When fully incorporated, add the rest of the cream and raspberries and stir well.

Fill individual ceramic ramekins with custard and place them in a large baking dish with enough water to reach ½ to ¼ the depth of the ramekins, about 1" of custard. If you do not have individual dishes, you may use one larger ceramic baking dish, and again, fill the dish with only 1" of custard. Cover the entire dish with foil and bake for 30 to 40 minutes until the centers of the custards are almost firm but still have a slight jiggle to them. Remove from the oven, uncover from the foil, and let rest in the water bath for 30 minutes. Remove the ramekins from the water bath and refrigerate until thoroughly chilled.

Just before you are ready to serve, turn on the broiler. Sprinkle each ramekin with sugar so that you have a thin, even covering and place them on a baking sheet. Set the custards under the broiler and keep a close eye on them. Cook until the sugar bubbles and browns (3 to 5 minutes, depending on your oven) and then quickly remove them. You may need to rotate the baking sheet during this process to achieve uniform browning. Serve with a few fresh raspberries on top, if you like, or eat as they are!